THE WORTHY THE WISE AND THE WICKED

JACK B. RIEDEL

This book is dedicated to Pete. He united people like no one else and through his friendship many other friendships were forged. His storytelling always entertained. I am blessed to have had a best friend in Pete. He was a gift from God.

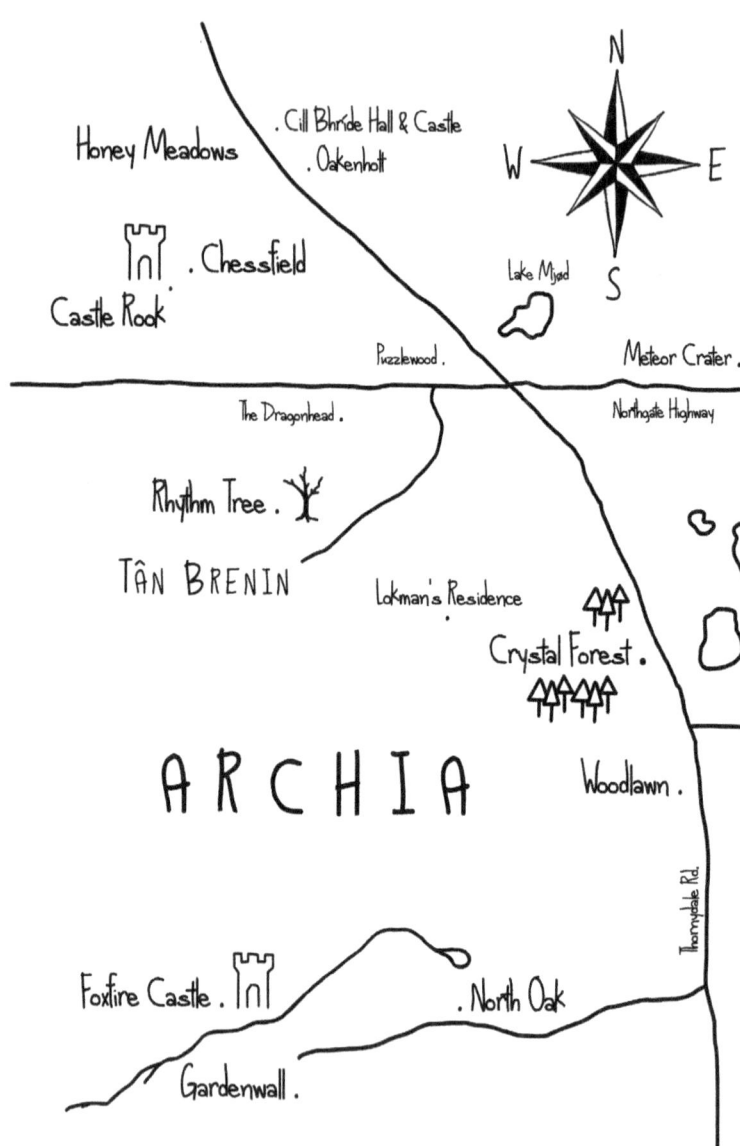

THE WORTHY THE WISE AND THE WICKED

JACK B. RIEDEL

Gardenwall

In the land of Archia, where the trees grew tall and wide, where Foxfire Castle overlooked the rolling hills, stood the village of Gardenwall. Its rooftops burst from the bottom of a promontory over the plains like trillium in radiant bloom. The community of farmers, merchants, and artists that called it home enjoyed a hospitable atmosphere filled with natural splendor. Doors were left unlocked and concerns were kicked away like stones.

High Street, the major thoroughfare, offered all the necessities: a music store, bakery, public house, blacksmith shop, horseshoe and trimming pavilion, antique store, post office, church, several eating establishments, rare book shop, stream, central square, town park, and even a falconry school. It was well-known for farmers markets, variety shows, and open invitation musical performances where people donned wild, vibrant clothing.

During the high season, days were warm and comfortable with occasional showers; during the low season, days were crisp and windswept. Some remembered the year powerful gusts sent hay mattresses cart-wheeling through the square and left window washers clinging to lofty eaves.

Mason Ross, one of the few hundred residents, stood out for his good cheer and eccentricity. His dry stone dwelling, marked by conical roofs and pure white walls, lined up shoulder-to-shoulder with others that were nearly mirror images. Some hung pennants with family crests, some kept flower boxes, and some had outdoor spaces where their owners pottered around or entertained guests.

Residents of Gardenwall were often multi-talented. An agronomist by trade, Mason was also an artist, writer, stargazer, birdwatcher, capable athlete, traveler, puzzle solver, dreamer, and lover of all things poetic, scientific, and mystifying. He dabbled in woodworking, cooking, falconry, and was not one to shy away from a forge and hammer. His handmade implements were modestly priced, aesthetically pleasing, and garnered much praise. "As someone who has no use for an axe, I'd like one," quipped one customer. "I was not expecting an actual forge," declared another. "Are you spoken for?" inquired one timorously.

Mason venerated the night sky and spent hours under shifting constellations. The star system in which he lived teemed with exotic debris, magical moons, and arcane phenomena.

He was an accomplished singer, a writer of ballads, and a guitarist whose talent was celebrated throughout the countryside. He was enthralled by architecture, captivated by the work of luthiers, and had a strange fascination with antique books.

This is a story of Mason's travels across fantastic and dreamy landscapes, who he encountered along the way, his confrontation with fear, and how his particular gifts were instrumental in a much larger campaign.

One morning, Mason awoke to the faint sound of shovels striking dirt. Sunbeams cut through the silver birch and flooded his room. He rolled onto his side and, while shifting his pillow, upended a cup of water. A tiny current swept a piece of parchment with a scribbled map to the edge of the nightstand and onto the floor. Mason let out a yawn.

Waking ahead of schedule meant he could avoid rushing to the neighboring town of North Oak. This afforded him ample time to eat breakfast, read, and have coffee. Mason threw back his bedding and planted his feet on the cold floor. He rubbed his eyes, shook off the last vestiges of sleep, and headed to the kitchen.

Shovels struck dirt again and through the window Mason observed a property wall taking shape.

Eggs and smoked bacon sizzled in a hot pan. When perfect daisy heart yokes formed, he added seasoning and spice. Fresh citrus from his trees was prepared. It would all culminate with that delicious morning elixir—brewed hot coffee! He preferred it strong, dark, and sweetened with clover honey. From the periphery he procured pastries with lemon buttercream icing. Nothing, not even chocolate, compared to fresh lemons. Cane sugar was dangerous. He had learned it was possible to add too much; overly sweet frosting was an insult to the pasty. Mason opened the door to let in pleasant scents from an early morning rain. He turned toward two farmers whose voices rose above the strains of commerce and animal noises.

"Sure is heavenly on the hill this morning," said the one decked in green and black tartan. "That light downhill breeze was a pleasant surprise," he continued as he chewed a stalk of wheat.

"Guessing we'll see more of the same through the weekend. Hard to get out of bed under these conditions," summarized the one sporting overalls and a flat cap. He held a pickaxe in one hand and led a handsome white and brown horse with the other.

Half way through preparing the meal, Mason peered through the window at the two farmers who had found their way to the square. Then, something alarming happened. Desperate shouts poured from deep within his subconscious. The words were chaotic and washed out. He wondered if he had heard them before. In his mind's eye he saw something opaque and hazy: a man in shabby clothes wildly waving his hands over his head and stumbling in the dark shallows of a river. The man was injured, exhausted, and looking to Mason for help. Dread and confusion rushed in. Then, just as quickly as it appeared, the vision whirled down a tunnel and Mason was dragged back into the moment. His pulse soared and he felt defenseless. *Where did that come from?* , he thought.

The troubling vision would be hard to explain to anyone, let alone an alienist. When his adrenaline subsided, questions crowded his mind. Was it something he already experienced, or something yet to come? Was it fact or fiction? Was he seeing through someone else's eyes?

It triggered an inner analysis. When Mason encountered others in need, he wanted to do the right thing but became engrossed in wondering how to assist, reasoning he couldn't do enough, or even reckoning the individual didn't truly need help—not his anyway. At times, he under-valued pleas and gave his own needs priority. He ignored the opportunity and continued along his path, relieved to avoid the inconvenience. He left assistance to those with greater compassion. He felt guilty about these tendencies since he was indisputably capable of helping; but the best he could do was promise to one day change his inclination to walk on by. He would expect more from himself.

The self-assessment abruptly ended when the odorous smell of burned eggs wafted through the kitchen. Spatula in hand, he rushed to the stovetop, tipped the pan, and salvaged the creation. Deep in thought, he grabbed a muffin and an orange and sat down to eat. Eventually, he zeroed in on the day's meeting with the Archia Antiquarian Society near North Oak. He thought it strange they were not meeting at the society library in town.

He finished his meal, poured a cup of coffee, and sat down with one of his prized volumes: The unabridged history of the Ross family, written by Mason's mother Locke Ross. Several passages were marked.

Mason's great grandfather, Catcher, was a land surveyor who owned a farm. He was warm-hearted, quick-tempered, musically inclined, and well-read. The farmhouse he built was made of stone and featured a deep well. One of the barns became a social venue where local families could unwind after a hard week's work. Some danced and some played instruments. It was at one of these gatherings that great grandfather met Mason's great grandmother. She could carry on a conversation with almost anyone, but she made sure others knew their social manners. She was an outstanding cook (breaded halibut and lemon cake were specialties), a good seamstress, and quick-witted. The children enjoyed roaming the forests picking wild asparagus, fireweed, and clover.

Grandpa Tadhg kept an orderly cottage and made a living manufacturing and repairing parts for horse-drawn vehicles. An array of cabs came through his gates: wagonettes, chariots, arabas, spiders, droshkies, ekkas, phaetons, roadsters, tongas, and even the occasional rockaway. In his free time, he crafted fine rhymes rife with old world charm which described his disdain for wolves and lightning storms. Grandma Úna was shy, had a great sense of humor, and loved her family so much she found little need to make new friends. She was afraid of underground places, cancelled bad luck with a pinch of salt over the shoulder, and frequently visited soothsayers.

Thanks to the new omnibus route, Mason would reach North Oak in a little over two hours. Eager to get to the depot, he picked up the pace as he prepared to leave. His provisions included essential clothing, dried fruit, nuts, and barley bread from the grinding stone, expedition grade hunting knife, fishing gear, and a water skin. The final item, a leather bound journal, was roughly the size of a man's hand. It was part map, part sketchbook, part sacred text, part traveler's guide, and the remainder blank pages. As he laced a stout pair of jackboots, he murmured verses from a song he penned over a decade ago. The lyrics kept him grounded in the moment and singing was indeed a favorite meditation. He found his pitch and began.

Ever since my angels found me walking alone downtown
I've seen faces in the trees
Well I know my devils will be watching my every move
They've planned my life to end in ease

Under Heaven where the season's dry
Beyond the garden catching dragonflies

Some say the buildings cast a
dreary cloud over run down homes
Hey, I never get down there
All I know is one day past the hustling of a small circus town
I'll find my lost electric crown

Under Heaven where the season's dry
Beyond the garden catching dragonflies

It had been ages since he sang that number in its entirety. It seemed to have a certain power and effectiveness when he performed it for a captive audience. He suited up, closed the curtains, and locked the door all with a strange feeling he was forgetting something.

Mason stepped out into the beautiful morning, hands on the straps of his traveler's pack. He surveyed the boulevard's procession of field stone walls and sugar-bushes, again savoring the placid setting. The rising sun, a glorious pale circlet, shot rays into a cloudless cerulean vault.

He paused as a noble edifice came into view. Fox-fire Castle, a popular cultural destination, stood on the bank of a stream. Outside its curtain walls, signs read PRESERVATION IN PROGRESS, though supervised tours were still offered. The royal fortress was one of a series of significant Foxfire properties, which included Cill Bhríde Hall & Castle near Oakenholt (where metals were made), Utley Castle in Woodlawn, and Castle Rook near Chess-field, further north in County Moorland.

In front of the post office, a popular locus for pub-lic per-formances, a guitarist tuned his instrument. The musician, who traveled through Gardenwall with some regularity, dressed in all black, save for a brown leath-er vest adorned with branches and curious symbols. He wore bracelets of silver, carnelian, and lava. Handmade by luthier Kytara, his guitar was a combination of sapele, acacia, and the finest rosewood. Jewelry designer Cama-el created its pearl inlay. It was an instrument made for pattern picking. Pairing perfectly with the deep gold of the body, carved angel's wings wrapped around the up-per bout, and just below that rested four large gold rings. The ornate spiraling bridge ended in dual triangles and the sound hole was wrapped in blazing jasper. A thin stick of incense smoldered between the nut and the capstans on the finely crafted headstock and hanging from this was an ornament resembling a smudge feather fan. He played with ardor as smoke mingled in his long hair and contemplative visage. A small cheery dog with a turquoise scarf accompanied him. Years earlier, as Mason recalled, this same guitarist played in a North Oak variety show and earned a standing ovation in ten minutes. He possessed raw talent, focus, and a charitable nature. Mason listened as though it were millennium's end. The playing was inspired and mood brightening—a perfect fusion of technical precision and artistry.

Laughter and wails of joy drew him eastward where a sign on High Street read: GARDENWALL TOWN PARK, FOXFIRE COUNTY COUNCIL. REGULATIONS: DOGS ALLOWED ONLY ON LEADS; FOWLING FINE: 3 OBLS; FLOWERS, TREES, OR SHRUBS MUST NOT BE DAMAGED; FIELD GAMES PROHIBITED. Hours were listed. A ball sailed over his head owing to playing children. An adult, firm but kind-hearted in her reprimand, reminded them of the regulations and all was well and good. Within the town limits, exuberant children were perhaps the height of drama and disorder. Playtime aside, the town park was ideal for leisurely walks, daydreaming, and engaging conversation. Winding walkways, a rich arboreal canopy, and flowers bursting in varied hues blanketed the acreage. Wild plants and bushes intertwined as they ran toward distant farmlands and vanished into pale blue infinity. A harpist and a flautist, both offensively talented, performed under a wooden gazebo. A small attentive audience sat on benches and ate grilled sandwiches.

Further on, toward the edge of town, Mason passed the falconry school and was drawn in by birdsong. The name was somewhat misleading, however, as there could be any number of species at the school on a given day. A man in a black vest and baggy red tunic stood nose to beak with a great horned owl. Grasping the ankle lead in his right hand he extended an oversized leather glove where the great bird held sway. Mason recalled how an owl could detect subharmonics with hearing ten times more sensitive than his own. A cloaked woman spoke to a giant red-tailed hawk. A king vulture, in the throes of some aberrant fit, gave a young trainee all she could handle. The final winged warrior, exhibiting tranquil intelligence, was impossible to miss. Falco peregrinus—the peregrine falcon—was gray and white with radiant yellow adorning its claws and beak. Its obsidian eyes had an aspect both innocent and worldly. In static balance, like a marble statuette, it sat atop the leather gauntlet of its master. It deceived in its sedentary stance, as this conqueror of crosswinds could fly faster than the spin of a cyclone. This particular peregrine was named Mica, and though the people of Gardenwall were enraptured with birds in general, it was this creature they adored most. Leaving town, Mason pondered falcons, guitars, music, and the road trip ahead.

The eastern sky cradled thin clouds resembling frayed rigging and a delicate wind stirred the crowns of the fir trees. In dusty boots, Mason approached the over-crowded omnibus station. A stray dog barked half-heartedly at him. Queuing up with other restless passengers, Mason scribbled the time and place in his journal.

"Passengers in rows one through ten, service to North Oak, may begin boarding," said a pleasant female voice. After presenting his boarding pass, Mason stepped up into the horse-drawn omnibus and found his seat. He sat down next to a hooded woman preoccupied with unknown tasks. He pulled out a chronicle, skimmed the page, and paused at a headline which read, "Baron Skyr Pushes for Ban in Oakenholt." Mason, always well-informed, contemplated running for office and hoped to one day campaign. Ever-observant, he shifted his gaze toward two passengers who appeared somehow out of place. Locals had a particular style and demeanor and these men most certainly were wide of the mark. Glances were exchanged as both parties attempted to staunch suspicions.

Wheat fields, familiar hamlets, and sleepy farmsteads rolled past the windows. After a trip as long as a four-course meal, the omnibus pulled up to a station. Disembarking brought with it a sense of relief. Just then, in that wary mindset, Mason realized that he had indeed forgotten one thing: a map to the meeting place. He wrote it on a piece of parchment. To pack without erring seemed impossible no matter how early he started or how many times he checked his list. *Finding people and places in the wild countryside is hard enough as it is,* he thought.

Mason stepped out into the aisle and disembarked with road-weary passengers. Inside North Oak Station, he claimed a table and opened his journal's map pages. The two suspicious passengers, dealing in subterfuge, dealing in subterfuge, lingered like vultures awaiting carrion. Maintaining composure, Mason studied routes and estimated distances attempting to pinpoint his destination. Thankfully, He'd attended concerts in the area and even had a client or two nearby.

"Helloooo Mister Mason!!" bellowed a baritone voice.

Turning briskly, Mason spotted the familiar round face of a man named Winter. "Crazy timing! How the blue blazes are ya?"

Winter was Mason's distant cousin. He wore a moustache and beard, thick sideburns, and parted his black shoulder length hair straight down the center. A cotton tunic, secured with a broad silver-buckled belt, reached below his waist. His sleeves were narrow at the wrist and jeweled rings wrapped his thick fingers. Standing a full head taller than Mason, he had a large barrel chest and solid arms. Sunlight gleamed off the crossguard, pommel, and blade of his oversized falchion. But all was not as it seemed; Winter's high-pitched laugh belied a playful and jovial personality. The wittiest soul Mason knew, he was a good man to have on your side whether it be a battlefield or a public house.

"I'm alright but I'll get over it," joked Winter. "It's great to see you cousin." He squeezed Mason's shoulder.

"You'll love this," explained Mason. "I'm having

some trouble remembering the location of our meeting place, ha! Forgot the address at home, and the people at the counter looked too busy to help. Great start eh?"

"I figured it's been close to five years since our last off-site meeting. "I wonder what news we can expect to hear?" inquired Winter.

"Same question I had. FIVE years? Murder, robbery, and fire! It seems like another lifetime."

"I don't know fella. Hey, I bet you're hungry. Whatta ya say we grab a meal at Finn's Table, down by the piers? I'll take us to the meeting place. I am not as forgetful as you are."

"Yes sir, I'll endorse that great idea," replied Mason.

"Great! Get settled and I'll meet you down there just past midday," said Winter.

The cousins shook hands and parted ways in the swift stream of pedestrians that flowed through the station. Mason took a circuitous route ensuring no one trailed him. Eventually, he found his way to the lobby of the Treehouse Inn and checked in. A doorman escorted him to clean affordable lodgings, perfect for a two-night stay. Mason unpacked and headed for the piers.

Two things drew the community down to the square that afternoon: the warm mellow air, and a grand art and wine festival. Festive sunshades stood as welcome beacons along the main parkway.

A troupe of jugglers, wands aflame and wheeling, entertained a wide-eyed audience. "Now kids, make sure to try this at home," shouted one sarcastically. They wore matching tights, breeches and tunics of motley colors, and spoke in silly rhymes while they set up their next maneuver. A brawny anchor man leaned forward tightening a length of rope that ran from his waist to the rear wall. Three-pronged fire wands were lit and leveled on the rope. An acrobatic young woman climbed from his knees to his folded arms and eventually took her post on his shoulders. She lit her three torches. The third entertainer stepped from a small platform onto the rope. He grunted as he walked the tightrope amid anxious applause and whistling. "It's not over yet," he cried out and then dropped to a horizontal crane pose. He balanced on the taut rope as the young woman juggled the torches, in an undeniable display of strength, hand-eye coordination, and balance—not to mention bravery. They received a raucous applause as they dismounted and flowers were thrown on the stage.

A jewelry designer fitted clientele with copper and agate bracelets. Her fair haired dog, donning a red and black bandana, passed a curious eye about the visiting party: supervising, approving, and finally losing interest, she darting her head toward some resonance only dogs are aware of. A vintner showcased wine making equipment, a meat cutter chopped and packaged jerky, a pastry chef doled out blackberry pie, an artisan sliced chunks from a giant block of soap, and a teacher showed children the finer points of drawing. People ate at picnic tables. The aroma of open fire cooking churned about, keeping the mob blissfully entranced.

Buyers and sellers intermingled in age-old commerce. Mason purchased jerky and a block of soap then continued through the heart of the festival. A psychic palmist spoke to a young couple and made grand gestures with her hands. Sign-boards with pictograms and bold lettering lined the parkway: "Fine Blended Oils", "Stoneware & Pottery", and "Apothecary". A man called out "FINE PEWTER" as Mason passed by, and a woman enticingly announced "SHIIIINY THINGS." The funnel cake queue was at least fifty people long, begging the question: what exactly are they made of? A street performer, appearing first as an old and bent peasant woman, transformed into a tall regally dressed count before everyone's eyes, drawing astonished applause.

Mason stopped to watch a nameless three-piece musical ensemble reach deep into their repertoire. The frontman, not a day over fifteen, leaned back on one boot heel and adjusted tuning pegs with adept swiftness. He wore a light lace-up tunic with embroidered suns and moons and a rough leather vest. His hair, a rumpled curly mass, flew about his face as he strummed his instrument—a twelve-string harp guitar with painted rose branches all about its bindings. To his left, a younger woman wrapped her arms around a primitive hurdy gurdy adorned with a carving of waves and a swimming fish. Carefree and relaxed, it looked as if she could be holding a sleeping lamb. Her gypsy ensemble, a mishmash of styles, included a thick fancy roundlet, a black mesh top with sewn-in gold ribbon, a bodice with an array of geometric shapes, a blue and gold pleated skirt, and knee-high boots with oversized buckles. Her hoop earrings, with regalia reminiscent of lavish coins, reflected sunlight unpredictably. She sported necklaces of varied lengths and thicknesses; one with parallelograms dangling all askance; one holding a mandala disc. The drummer sat on a small throne amid makeshift scaffolding which held bodhrán, tabla, tom, and tambourine alike. He popped a muffin hat on his head and began to beat his menagerie. Low sounds emitted from the girl's hurdy gurdy and the front man began his ode to willow trees.

As he strolled past the docks, Mason gazed up at the derelict North Oak Castle and considered the vast army that kept its gatehouses and curtain walls secure an age ago.

Extinguishing his half bent taper pipe and returning it to its wooden case, he approached Finn's Table. He eyed its dual portico entryway and freshly painted signage. Positioned foremost was a metallic sculpture of a mermaid entitled 'Roisin'. Her welcoming arms curled backward, took the shape of waves, and connected to her tail. A thatched roof, stone water well, and bright yellow doorway provided quaint inviting appeal. The outdoor seating area, enclosed by a short pony wall with capped pillars, featured small trees and flowers in half whiskey barrel planters. Mason leaned into the wooden door and entered the establishment. A roaring turf fire projected light onto the uneven walls and stone floor. Famous for its "storytelling nights" and musical puppet shows, Finn's Table was known to many a wandering poet, minstrel, and hooded stranger. It was the noted portal to the wild and enchanted east. He sat down at a table and perused an anchor-shaped menu. Scanning the offerings, he felt a hand grip his shoulder.

"No map for the music man this time?" joked Winter.

"Ha! Who needs 'em? I followed my nose," returned Mason. "Hey, it's good to be here again. Busy as ever I see."

The cousins sat down and, as they call it in the old country, peeled the onion. There was some discussion of recent travel, work related projects, a relationship update, some light-hearted harassment, and plenty of discourse on music, theater, and the top venues to watch premier musicians. Winter's latest life goal was to adopt and raise a child with Nova, his significant other. His storyline constantly evolved.

"Hey, take yourself back with this one," said Winter. "Wheels spin around, lost in flight my feet don't touch the ground."

"All is fine since you've been around," Mason joined in. "We're taking turns down through the fields as the sun it burns." They ended in a near shout, "IT BEATS DOWN ON A FARMING TOWN."

A server took their order.

"You do the honors, Winter. I haven't sampled enough North Oak cuisine to make a confident choice."

"Suit yourself music man. We'll take two seagull sandwiches with everything on em...and two ales." The server disappeared through a pair of swinging doors carved with cat's eyes.

"Still sailing around the world with your show?" inquired Mason. A mariner and carpenter by trade, Winter was a street performer known throughout the south for his escapes, feats of strength, and illusions.

"You know me, soon as I round up resources, I'll fix up the *Archangel* and make my way to Baranik Bay. I guess it really doesn't matter where we wind up. I just want to take Nova on a second honeymoon."

"I knew there was a little romance left in you."

After a brief discussion of North Oak history, the food arrived. A pitcher of bitter ale was placed on the table.

"I can't make it very far without one of these gems," expressed Winter with the sandwich in his hands. The two men indulged. Mason chewed the sandwich and gave Winter a look of concern. His features locked.

"I had another one," explained Mason.

"A premonition? Clairvoyance? You called them visions?" inquired Winter.

"Yes, but this one was more intense. Like I'd been there. I feel a bit mental trying to explain. And you're my cousin!"

"Aye, pretty serious the last ones you were talking about. Don't worry, I'm not here to judge. I'll help as best as I can. At least listen, no matter how mad I think you are," he winked.

"And one more thing," said Mason, "no sudden moves. It seems two men followed me here and they just took a seat at the bar."

Winter eased back.

"Don't look! We must lose them at once. I'd hate to lead them to our off-site meeting. This calls for one of your phantom illusions. Unless, you have a better idea?"

"Meet me on Thornydale Road in one hour," said Winter. "Standard rally point." Today's lunch patrons were in for a spectacle. With a nod, the stage was set.

Winter turned himself ghostly white and winced. His eyes bulged, he choked, and his dishes fell in a ruckus. Mason remained stock-still, affixed to the floor like a potbelly stove. Winter seized his throat, knocked over his chair, and darted out of the establishment. Onlookers stood paralyzed while Mason burst through the door in pursuit.

Winter's suicidal leap off the pier was followed by a deafening shriek and a dull thud. Shock and panic ripped through the crowd. Mason grabbed the dock rail and leaned over to see Winter's body soaked in a crimson pool fifty feet below. His body floated motionless beside the wooden deck of a balinger. Winter was dead, or so it appeared. Mason sank against the rail, dropped his head into his palms, and shivered in the breeze that swept through the bay. Shortly afterward, authorities, medics, and mobs transformed Finn's Table into a place where anyone with a suspect agenda would not want to be seen. The two men who had been following Mason slipped away without a trace.

After a swift and stealthy detour back through the Treehouse Inn to retrieve his belongings, Mason sought the eastern gates of North Oak. Instinct took over. With cool caution, one heartbeat at a time, he carved a route behind buildings, hedges, and fences.

Before long, he cut the distance to the rally point in half. As the tension slipped away, he was able to enjoy the scenery. He slowed for a moment in the late afternoon's austere beauty. A bleached pumpkin sun peeked through the trees on its way down to meet the ground. A stand of silver birch reached skyward like alabaster fingers. The shrill songs of bramblings, the aria of the backcountry, cascaded from nearby branches. Mason remained alert, stepped lightly with his head low, and kept clear of approaching riders. He traversed a lowland plain overrun with red valerian, ragged robin, and scores of yellow flags. Further ahead, the amethyst cloaks of wild thyme and spotted orchids congregated like spectators in an amphitheater before vanishing into a powder blue perimeter. The day's travels yielded a bounty of useful plants: chamomile and mint for tea; borage and gentian in case of fever or cough; fennel for digestive ills; saxifrage for wounds; and primula for body discomfort. He arranged them in his pack with care.

He sang a canticle, melancholy in verse and melody.

Sparrows climb on ascending wings
So aligned in battalions sing
And they stay aloft impossibly
Waiting for some confidence from me

Daylight moon on a canvas blue
Highway soon changing hues

In your dreams return to castles you've seen
Pushing pins in places that you've been

Choose a way to create the year
Fill the page, make directions clear
Curtains close on an empty room
Into dreams in the afternoon

And its round and round the wheel it goes
Riding out the waves of highs and lows

All of his senses awake, Mason took inventory of his surroundings. He noted the calming smell of lavender, the spectral form of a white deer, and the long even breath of a lofty breeze. With singleness of heart and action, he remained on the lookout for any suspicious man or beast.

The deep tone of a gjallarhorn swelled from some remote stronghold.

The weathered mossy walls of a saintly abbey and cemetery appeared. Mason paused at the open gate, panned the yard, and stepped inside. A field mouse scurried away and there was a strange stillness normally reserved for the small hours. A bough groaned and the wind carried the sweet hazy tones of hawthorn. He knew he was not alone. He crept over the long grass and wild daisies, hand on his hunting knife. His pulse accelerated. A low even whistle broke the stillness and Mason calmly exhaled and advanced to a hidden corner of the churchyard where Winter extended his hand. They broke bread behind the remains of a crumbling mausoleum.

Chapter 2

Black River

**Black River - Calon Du - History - Philosophy - Rise
Painting - Scout's report - Silver mines
The Chamber of the Wolf**

In the mountains, far to the northeast of Gardenwall along a secluded watercourse, stood the fortified city of Black River. Troubled, timeworn, and frequented by cold winds, it was the center for silver refining, the regional seat of power, and home to many a poor and downtrodden soul. From frigid headwaters, goods were shipped downriver, transferred to pack animals, and delivered to the markets of the south. For centuries, local leaders controlled the entire network.

The highway to and from the city held the sobriquet "The Road of Bones" and very few gambled with its lonely and savage miles. The highway terminated at a gate of monstrous proportions which featured ominous architecture and writing from a lost language. Watchmen kept pitiless eyes on the surrounding landscape as they patrolled lofty ramparts in high-collared coats. Inside the walls, ramshackle houses lined dreary lanes in a grim dialogue with the natural elements. Built on a foundation of a more ancient settlement, legend said it was once the setting for ancient festivals, idol worship, and other acts of devotion both dark and dubious.

For Black River's sorry lot life was cheerless. Each morning they awoke with heavy hearts and slipped into uninspired routines. Like prisoners, they worked long shifts in boathouses, offices, and factories, and performed repetitive tasks as the days dragged on. Sorrow filled their souls and optimism was a concept both foreign and difficult to grasp. They grumbled and moped as their shabby city fell apart. One thing after another went wrong. Hope foundered and a sense of inevitable doom reigned supreme. Often enough, unrest led to protest and rioting. Empathy and trust lacked and rebellious masses became desperate.

Crime, corruption, and peace disturbances led to suspicion, frustration, and fear. Little respect was given to person, place, or thing. People often went missing and assassinations of high officials were not uncommon. Selfish individualism pushed the limits of the law and tested nerves. Aggressive confrontation became the accepted means of problem solving. Neighborly interaction diminished to a bare existence and many preferred to stay indoors or stick to their own small tribes. Anger was vocalized without restraint. There were cavalier invitations to street fights. Crowds gathered and fueled tense encounters. Misfits lurked in the shadows. Due to strings of burglary barred windows and guard dogs were essential. Weary and jaded authorities restored peace though disciplinary action was rarely taken and dissonance remained.

Of all the inhabitants, the most prominent was

the Chief Moderator, a firebrand called Calon Du. His sprawling fortress, financed through silver trade, stood on a crannog in the river. Often referred to as "the most wicked man in the land", some claimed his heart was the color of ash. He presided over the city's mysterious council, which in turn governed lawmakers and local authorities. Misguided and wrought with grim philosophies, he was a boiling concoction of hatred and calamity. A quick history lesson will shed light on his motives and reveal how the denizens of Black River came to embrace such a fiend.

As a boy in his first decade, Calon was exposed to a life of uncertainty and violence. As a runaway orphan, the places he called home were no better than scrap piles. Those he came in contact with cared little for his health or safety and soon he became as cold and hard as the mountains around him. Through hardscrabble days he felt the burden of guilt, hopelessness, and shame.

As a youth in his second decade, Calon lived as a restless wanderer. One of the few scattered among bleak foothills, he was isolated in the worst way without the security of friends or family. Hunger and poverty were his constant companions. He spoke little but developed exceptional observational and analytical skills. He was prone to bursts of madness and rage that he was powerless to control. The young Calon became obsessed with politics and surrounded himself with books on varied topics: history, art, science, and mythology. He picked up on the practices of the region's great leaders making astute observations as to how they achieved success. Along the way, he vowed to stay in touch with the common people. In all his pursuits there was a hint of genius.

Advisors counseled him on power and position. Capitalist instructed him to align his efforts with a financial gain. Mediums said he would make a great name for himself. Decision makers took note of his talents. Education, creativity, and free thinking were repudiated. Tension built.

Disregarding much of this advice, he explored the fascinating world of art. Creating from scratch was exciting. It required exceptional observational and analytical skills. The sheer challenge of a project propelled him.

Meanwhile, naysayers bombarded him with negativity. Like nimble pickpockets, they robbed him of enjoyment. Few shared his viewpoints which made for a slow uphill battle. More tension. One thing led to another and soon he entertained the notion of ignoring societal thought altogether. These thoughts haunted him and drove him to strange and morbid places. He began to live in confusion and fear, applying his deviant logic to all things. He became faithless and fiercely independent.

Even though he was never taught the ways of truth and light, he still had the freedom to choose a positive upright path. But he did not. He chose to stay on this damning path. Knowing where it could lead, he dabbled in a life of excess, not yielding to any vice. He developed runaway desires and harmful addictions, like one who fell from a great height. Though his foolish actions gave him a sense of control, their powerful influence enslaved him. His addictions were not only to wealth, lust, and mind-altering substances, they included power, magic, and sadism. A mind, once able to determine right from wrong, was hijacked. He craved intensely, often lost control, and developed a profound chasm in the core of his existence. Paranoia ensnared him. On the other hand, he was crafty. Those who interacted with him found out quickly he had intelligence and ambition far beyond his years.

As a man in his third decade, times were turbulent and he became a swindler. Beguiling as a serpent, he made political relationships which could be leveraged. People noticed he was strange, serious, and utterly alone; they never saw him in the presence of friends or family. Though all wagers seemed to be against him, he was not easily discouraged. He studied the speeches of luminaries, developed a deep passion for the magic of spoken words, and began to excel as an orator. A wayward star, he pulled away from the accepted thoughts of the day, forming his own ideology. Mentors and chance meetings, as they often do, influenced future events.

Upward the spellbinder climbed, from post to post and office to office, giving fiery speeches and making a name for himself. His teachings spread like gangrene. Knowing he must win support of long-established institutions, he included select individuals in his plans to gain control of the bankrupt and transitional region of Black River. At one point, he attempted to seize power over a local tribe in a failed coup near Silverbridge and was imprisoned. His sentence was short and painless but he discovered he could operate from a distance with a long arm.

Subsequent to his release, he and his hard-boiled advocates, who began to call themselves The Chamber of the Wolf, developed a plan to seize complete and total power over the region. Master deceivers, they ran roughshod, lambasting the old written law, and oppressing the weak. They used manipulation, bribery, and carefully planned provocation. They burned a government building and passed blame onto a rival party.

As the upheaval continued and stability unraveled, he sensed the masses were eager for a wholesale shift. More and more they sought a strong voice that could lead them to prosperity and a position of power. Like a hypnotist, he began to alter perceptions. His disciples reinforced his position. The timing was perfect and the stage was set for a critical phase. Amid unsavory political circumstances, Calon was appointed to the top political position of the region: Chief Moderator. He had wormed his way in.

As a man in his fourth decade he was well-established and feared; the reach of a one-time runaway orphan extended far into the region. "I found the keys to Black River in the gutter," he declared "and I picked them up." His primary initiatives were to expand his empire, control goods transportation, forge silver weapons, and crush all resistance through a united Black River. "Well marked roads lead to solidarity," he would say.

His organization needed a symbol. While poring over ancient texts he began to experiment with different shapes and colors. He decided upon an array of three arrows on a red shield: the number three symbolizing change, the arrows representing silver, the shield epitomizing martial glory, and red for sacrifice. These symbols, with occult auras of their own, had been around since men first took up arms. These symbols, as Calon would say, were "found among ruins and would endure into the new age".

Uniforms were designed, a high-security administrative compound was erected, and modernistic laws were drafted and enforced. An anthem was penned, and though its melody was buoyant and cheery, its lyrical content was of the darkest order.

Mountain echelons awake! New divisions from the quake.
Marching steady, marching tall, trident shields for one and all.

As his influence over the region expanded, so too did an intricate network with myriad subgroups. There were factions for fighters, artists, women, youngsters, and merchants alike, all arranged with meticulous detail by this master organizer. Funding poured in from the production of silver and from the wealth of private individuals who supported his cause and wanted immunity. Fanatics appeared on the scene, some bearing gifts and making bizarre requests.

The cacogen accelerated, inciting change through radical measures. Rake offs and skims prompted finger pointing. There were exhortations, public threats, and blackmail, but most prevalent of all, there were cold fabricated lies; lies of every conceivable type; printed on signs; spoken at rallies; spread through streets and marketplaces. Grotesque fact twisting knew no boundary.

One late evening, fatigued and discontented, Calon Du sat fireside, evaluated his initiatives, and pondered his place in the universe. Beside a blazing bonfire under starlight, he pondered a life to come: one filled with goals of power and triumph. Slaves to a primordial determination, he consulted dusty volumes, studied arcane terminology, and manically scribbled in journals. Corrupt, byzantine plots ricocheted in his skull. The moon passed in front of a distant planet, occluding it. The forsaken call of a demon dog shattered the silence. As the night grew on, patterns began to form. In suspended animation, Calon peered deep into burning branches and glowing cinders. A streak of emerald fire raced overhead, splitting the sky like a giant sabre. The falling star vanished into the maw of a mythical beast. Dawn drew near while he contemplated his place in the universe.

As a gray-haired man in his fifth decade, he taught himself myriad creative expressions: drawing, stained glass, sculpture, tapestry, smelting, pottery, and bookmaking. But it was painting that gripped him like an addiction. It was the missing piece. Consistent with his ideology, he felt it necessary to control what people saw. He planned to use art exhibits and public areas to extol the virtues of his beliefs ensuring others would follow him. "I will ascend above the heights of the clouds!" he proclaimed.

He became obsessed with color. He experimented on canvas, walnut board, and even slate. He wanted his subjects to shock people. As he created, he placed utmost attention on subtlety, nuance, and the tiniest detail. Soldiers, war, and animals of the wild were top subjects. Excitement mounted after each completed work. Like a rising wall, each work was built upon the one before it. So propelled, he created work that was personal, profound, and penetrating. Rows of his creations lined the halls of his castle. Themes and interests evolved. All things were considered. He refined his talent and continually progressing. Destiny called.

Many years later, Calon found himself peering into the clear night from the window of his painting studio. It smelled of amber and smoke. The moon's brilliant white arc, like a caravel's sail, navigated the astral menagerie. Cleaning his hands with damp linen, he searched his mind for a subject: dark mountain landscapes or stark snowy trees; basilisks or barghests. He scanned his tools: brushes; charcoal and chalks; burnishers and gravers; saws and lengths of wood; templates for geometric shapes; dried flowers and eggshells; flasks of varnish and beeswax; oils and mineral pigment. A sectioned container for chunks of locally-mined metals.

Black candles lit the room. Calon took his position at an easel which held a poplar board. His resident musician played somber scales on a violin. He poured wine into a goblet decorated with crescent moons and bezel set with brilliant-cut sapphires. He dipped a wide brush into white pigment and began the underlayers. Adhesive and fragile gold-leaf were applied. Using white and ultramarine, a cloudless sky emerged through long indiscriminate strokes. With dark pigment and a fan brush he crafted treetops. Ruins took shape; its tones of copper, brown, and gray reacting nicely against the gold-leaf. Blending edges and testing transparency, he created realism and depth. He added highlights and angled his head for a fresh perspective. Figures occupied the foreground, two travelers with shrouded faces. He detailed their clothing and took a step back. He typically worked from a physical model or landscape, but not this time. The creation flowed easily, from brush to board, as if he'd created it before.

Heavy eyelids and back strain broke his reverie. He realized he had lost his sense of time, utterly absorbed in the creative endeavor. Many hours had passed, the musician retired, and only a small bead of wine remained in the well of the goblet. The sky to the east was clear as a cold sun broke above the peaks. To the south, diamond dust touched the ground. He stepped away from the easel and set his brushes in a tin of water. Observing the vivid imagery, he found no answer for its origin. It seemed to paint itself. Awestruck, Calon contemplated the scene: the weathered mossy walls of a saintly abbey and cemetery. He wondered if, like some ancient seer, he had painted a current event. He stood baffled. The two men in the foreground, made familiar through his spy network, were his prime targets—Mason and Winter of Archia.

An incessant fist pounded on the studio door and Calon beckoned the visitor to enter. The head watchman crossed the threshold and formally announced he'd received intelligence from the field. He turned to a second visitor—the Greyguard's premier sprinter spy, Trusis. The sprinter entered, bowed, and stood with hands crossed over his chest, a sign of respect for Calon.

He spoke in a rigid and impassive tenor. "Your Excellency, the musician and his companion have evaded our scouts in North Oak. They created a diversion which attracted too many potential witnesses. Our scouts were forced to abandon the assignment. May it be known: they attempted to track the targets after the commotion settled, but found no trace of them. They extend their sincerest apologies."

Calon took a deep breath then added a few soft fluid brushstrokes to the painting, not once looking at Trusis. His eyes went from one lancet window to the other, then back to the painting. The scouts' directive was uncomplicated, yet it somehow failed. A disingenuous grin washed over Calon's face. The sprinter was dismissed. The head watchman was then given a simple nod which carried much information. The Chamber of the Wolf would convene immediately.

With haste, Calon adjourned to his sanctuary, a three story baroque philosophical hall and laboratory. This center for learning was replete with marble columns, ceiling frescoes, gothic paintings, and ornamental iron. Esoteric shapes and patterns decked the tiger wood floors. Velvet curtains with metallic trim covered the windows. Thousands of volumes filled curios and shelves, several open on plinths. An impressive collection of terrestrial and celestial globes divided in the hall. Carved busts, bronze figures, and marble statuary sat atop elegant pedestals.

One entire transept was dedicated to the practice of alchemy. Standing near its entrance was the complete skeletal specimen of a neanderthal man labeled: homo neanderthalensis. Chalk-written formulas covered a wall; theorems, coplanar vectors, motion calculations, and pi written out to over one hundred numbers. A console was littered with beakers, distilling apparatus, subliming pots, and the coiled tubing which connected them. Glass retorts in silver tripods bubbled and emitted fine vapors. Here and there rested metal blocks, prisms, and other accoutrement of scientific significance destined for utility in the transformation of matter.

A deep apse with wall to wall cabinetry was dedicated to the healing arts. The apothecary housed elixirs, magisteria, and arcana in a multitude of labeled flasks. Ampoules of galenicals were neatly arranged behind smoked glass doors. Bronze scales, bowls, and tools for crushing and grinding each had their own appropriate storage place. It was the ambition of Calon's practitioners to prevent bodily decay altogether, thereby perpetuating life without end.

The centerpiece of the entire philosophical hall, running the full length of the back wall, was an enormous built-in organ. It was an unmistakable musical treasure and true feat of engineering, its brobdingnagian pipes like a forest of iron trees. The tiered keyboard needed leveling and the instrument was missing keys and pedals. Stops the size of wagon wheel spokes were faded and missing their ivory end caps.

Elymas, the old mystic, was summoned. Bent with age and wearing a blue ritual robe, his long gray hair was pulled back revealing a fanatical expression. He joined Calon in his quest for knowledge. A fire was lit and the two locked themselves away engaged crystal scrying, stereomancy, and the consultation on metaphysical texts. These were preparations. Calon would soon deliver his diabolical address to the Chamber of the Wolf deep within the Black Mountains.

In the late afternoon, red kites caught the wind, circling the castle in search of prey. Snow fell from a cloudy sky and the sun failed to rise over the jagged peaks. Calon followed a tunnel from the philosophical hall to a hidden exit in the outer curtain wall where a horse-drawn chariot waited. Its driver, resolute in selfless service, drove them to a cave entrance.

The silver mining operations, which ran all day and all night, unearthed a continual bounty of white, lustrous metal. A surveyor used a crane to lower a weight into a shaft. Ladders were used to gain access to the higher and lower work areas, and oil lamps were the only sources of light. Ramps zigzagged to access ways which disappeared into cliff tunnels. Steadily up an incline, two stocky laborers heaved a wooden pillar which would support a section of a roof. As they climbed, they sang in a deep vocal register:

Half the moon and half the sun
They came out to play their tricks
Dancing on the river all the cattails
I'm singing songs for ten clicks

Drifting with my hands in the water
For nine days I've been out a flatboat
Come along now there's a place I got to show you
'Cause every time I'm on the river it's true

Have you ever walked along the Black River?
Have you ever seen the sun so red?
Have you ever walked along the Black River?
Or would you like a drink instead?

Water deep and dark I'm on a stormwatch
And the smoke is a silver wall
Voices in my ear and I'm back on the front
Back where I had to crawl

Dive in where the rainbow opens
And someday I'll be rich like you

Geologists wandered the subterranean lair examining points in the rockface. The entries to bell shafts and drift mines could be seen all along the black ridge where the miners inside broke through rock with picks, shovels, and hammers. Silver ore was hacked out of the stone, placed in buckets, and raised to the surface by hand-cranked windlasses. Machines composed of beams, drums, and axles dissected the earth like dingy skeletal surgeons. Carts of raw ore were pushed and dragged to the surface where a conveyor transported the crushed pieces to a ball mill.

Giant waterwheels, submerged in the river, supplied hydropower to the bellows feeding smelting furnaces. A man used tongs to retrieve a glowing clay crucible from a kiln. He recycled the slag and poured the remaining blazing syrup into casting dishes for bricks, plates, and coins. Purity was judged. Markings on a touchstone were compared to markings from a standardized spectrum of needles. Refined silver in various shapes was counted and itemized for inventory then transported to hidden vaults.

The driver stopped in a pine-needled clearing and awaited Calon's escort. The cave entrance stood at the base of an escarpment. It was reinforced by great stone pillars adorned with faces of deities, alchemical symbols, and other esoteric depictions. A guide met Calon and led him by torchlight down into the mountain.

They unlocked an iron gate, followed a rift, and descended a flight of stairs. Here, the route opened wide enough for four or five men to walk side by side. They passed through vast chambers with limestone columns, rooms bursting with quartz clusters, shallow cave-pools, a bat or two, and now and then the fossil remains of a prehistoric animal. Warm and cool air moved through the tunnel system as if the mountain itself was drawing breath and the sound of falling water perpetually reverberated. In one stretch, abstract formations of gypsum grew down from above resembling chandeliers in a ballroom.

The rumble of a small rockslide relayed through the passage and the guide turned nervously, then proceeded. It was said that the mines were haunted by goblins and indeed some laborers had reported ghostly sounds, phantasms, and whispers in strange languages. No forest or sea can compete with the mountain mine in terms of lending credence to the supernatural. The absolute blackness, the weak light sources that animate shadow and warp shape, the magnified groan of massive slabs, the howl of air and gas, the distorted crumbling, and the endless echoes of sliding rock all create a haunting symphony where sound speeds exponentially.

Descending, they followed the gloomy route along a subterranean lake, past a dim grotto inhabited by troglobites, through a cool damp cavern with karsts shaped like hulking beasts, and over a suspension bridge traversing an obsidian chasm. Inscriptions lined the walls in several places and in one cavity phosphorescent glow worms had completely taken over, making their home on the ceiling amid anthodites. Down they went, toward the heart of the mountain.

In time, they came to an open area with stone benches and a tapestry. Gypsum crystals and the frostwork of selenite needles sparkled on the walls. Spear-topped fence work occupied a portion of the circumference where a shallow stream disappeared into a fissure. An arched entrance door with sprawling silver hinges and astrological symbols rested in the face of the rock. Calon nodded to his guide, opened the door to the throne room, and entered.

The hall inside was a vaulted expanse with a flat, polished floor, inlaid with pagan monograms and symbology. Translucent stone in various shades and colors extended down from the ceiling like drapery. The centerpiece was a broad high reaching throne which had been carved from one immense block of labradorite— the treasures of the mountain on full display. Its cresting rail was elaborately chiseled and studded with chunks of silver and its arms featured wolf heads with radiant cut diamonds.

Calon greeted the members of the Chamber. An attendant in a black robe was managing the room's light—filling oil lamps, positioning floor candelabras, and placing fresh torches in wall sconces. Raw brimstone and corundum deposits in the sheer jet walls caught the light and gave participants the illusion they were floating among the stars.

The Chamber of the Wolf consisted of five members, four of whom awaited Calon's arrival as directed. Forming a five-pointed star in the center of the room, they stood stern and deliberate like the ravening wolves of the wood. They whispered in unison then performed a cronane chant, deep and monotonous. Siol Dona, Calon's right hand man and fellow agitator, wore a mantle of vermilion and a wolf mask. Myrkrið (MEER-ka-vid), a key organizer, donned a robe the color of midnight festooned with silver stars and moons. She held two opalescent cylinders. Viximar, spiritual leader, and Rhyfel, economics mastermind, both in hooded capes of deep green, stood with downcast eyes.

Calon Du made a ceremonial gesture then began his address as he slowly circled the four, hands behind his back. "Deputies, members of the Chamber, I have always been an enemy of half measures and weak decisions," he said with a sneer. "A revision of borders has been imposed on us by the Shadow Masters who dwell in these ancient mountains. Dark clouds have begun to gather overhead and they have called on us to lead. Now is the time to win the day and secure a homeland for us and our distant generations. As for those who refuse our offering: misfortune to them and their associates!"

He continued with ardour. "First, we will strike the towns of Heddwich and Ft. Kerr to the west of Black River. We will maintain that insurrections within those towns spiraled out of control, and force was our only option. Currently assembled in an offensive position, our infantry will soon be unleashed to burn the gates and crush any opposition wielding weapons forged from these very veins. There will be no hesitation. No remorse. Would there be someone so incredulous to doubt that everything in this vast universe is subject to the empire of destiny?"

"Second, we must fix our eyes on a menacing enemy to the southwest. We must eliminate the two men who have tactlessly chosen to plan secret sessions, sing their songs of triumph and faith, kneel in prayer, and stand in direct opposition to the goals of the Council of the

Wolf. Let it be known, they will neither find refuge in this world nor any other. Yours will be the greatest chapter in the book of strength and power, and you shall wear silver crowns—eternal memorials of your valour and honour. There can be no misunderstanding our intentions if we are to be rulers of this land and we will continue along our path even if thousands of Masons and Winters conspire against us!" He paused and let out a mad cackle. "Et figura mea manu mundum." My hand will shape the world.

Calon carried on like this for some time, occasionally thrusting his fist into the air or increasing the volume of his voice. Every so often he fell silent as if drawing energy. From the four at the center of the hall, there were ritualistic gestures, unison responses, and other cryptic practices, the details of which are better left unwritten.

At the conclusion of the assembly, the men filed out of the hall and Calon gave final direction to the attendant to extinguish the flames in a specific sequence. When the footsteps ceased, the attendant emerged from a darkened recess and stepped toward the middle of the hall. As the hood was drawn back, red-orange curls fell to the shoulders of a young woman with a soft symmetrical face. Perhaps in her late twenties, she had high cheekbones, a small nose, and wide set eyes now under a lowered brow.

"I'm not sure how much more of that I could have listened to!" she mumbled, hands sweating and heart racing. On the back of her small cave map, she jotted down the details and locations she overheard. She calmed her nerves with deep even breaths. Though it was too late to aid the poor souls in Heddwich and Ft. Kerr, there was a greater war at hand and the lives of many were balancing on the tip of a cutlass. She recalled a melody and began to sing in no more than a whisper. It quieted her mind.

These old stairs that carried my feet one time
Now they're worn away from the rain and the gold sunshine
The fool on the hill must reach the shore some other way
Like the hitcher's thumb or the changing face of the bay

In a summer's dream it almost seems like we found the farm
Where I was kicking stones and kicking away my days

She found her way back to the surface, picked the lock at the entry gate, and proceeded cautiously to the small pine-needled clearing. She saw no one, but looking back toward the entrance to the caves, she locked eyes with a lone white lynx standing atop an escarpment. Staring intensely, its head was low to the ground, trying to get a scent. Its body was stiff, and with a low growl, it bared its teeth and drew back its ears. In a strong gust of wind, the lynx crept away out of sight. The young woman swiftly entered the woods hoping to cover plenty of ground before daylight.

Chapter 3

Dark Times

Camp - Conversation with Winter - The factory
Woodlawn - The Archia Antiquarian Society
The hard road

Mason and Winter departed from the churchyard, northbound on Thornydale Road, en route to the meeting place. The rest and meal brightened their moods, though the chance of hostility kept them in a state of heightened awareness. Their plan to stay the night in North Oak went up in smoke so they decided to camp near the main road. They plotted a course through the town of Woodland, to Edgewild Trail, and northeast to their destination: a small lakeside shelter.

"Your illusion was a brilliant bit of deception. Flawless execution," praised Mason.

"Most appreciated," stated Winter. "It's a staple in the repertoire, only a minor bruise or two. I managed to keep a stern face when I popped up, dusted myself off, and thanked the medics. So, what do we know about the two men that caused us to take such drastic action? Doubtless, there was something malevolent about their intentions."

"Seeing them twice in one day, yeah. I couldn't shake the feeling. Their presence did not align with any standard business. No theories yet, I'm afraid," surmised Mason.

"A good bet the gathering crowd altered their plan, whatever it was. And now that I have a fresh perspective; there seems to be something savage in the air. I didn't spot anything suspicious during that first leg to the abbey and I had eyes in all directions," put in Winter.

"At any rate, as I was saying before we were so rudely interrupted: I had a vision before I left. I know it sounds strange but I saw more detail than I have in the past. Someone was in bad shape and needed help. An incredibly intense moment," explained Mason. "Not related to what just happened by the way."

"I've heard and seen much stranger," consoled Winter. "All things are connected."

"Between premonitions, track downs, and a secluded meeting, I'm reeling. There'll be better days than this one," insisted Mason.

"Hold that thought; let's not over-think on an empty stomach. Yeah? Fresh fish tonight. You catch and I'll cook?" Winter remained positive.

They passed placid green pastures and natural archways of thick foliage. On a bucolic farmstead, apple trees grew in rows true as zither strings. A cool breeze moved with them as they touched on music, travel, and rumors. The occasional excursionist took little notice of the pair. Pleasant exchanges dwindled, trusting faces grew scarce, and the sound of wildlife became ever more strange and exotic. Ahead they could see the tranquil ruins of a once-imposing castle and its surrounding forts, their builders long forgotten. Once some bygone monarch's bustling center for commerce, it was now home to only starlings and squirrels.

Kicking up dust, they pressed on through lonely heather moorlands, parcels with modest estates, and gloomy glens with rickety covered bridges. The ground angled upward. The sun sat on the western hills and cast wondrous lines of green-gold brilliance all about the wild country. It was as far northeast as either man had ever ventured. They knew the territory ahead only by way of travelers' stories and atlases.

"We're in the middle of nowhere!" exclaimed Winter. "I guess search and rescue is pretty much out of the question!"

In the old tradition, they sang as they rambled steadily toward unknown obstacles.

Time can heal as time it flows
Time has answers only Heaven knows, it goes
Time can pass you, time can stall
If your heart was broken like a billiard ball, recall

Open light still shining through your shady road
Tell you time is just like a bomb waiting to explode

Time in capsules, time in hand
Time can slip away when you're in demand, quicksand
While you're sleeping in the bed you made
Time can cut through like a shiny blade
Open light still shining through your shady road

Tell you time is just like a bomb waiting to explode

I've heard of heroes, some they fall,
The heroes I know stand ten stories tall, install
It's time to borrow if it's time you need
Time alone will tell you, guaranteed. Proceed...

They approached the stone symmetry of a high cross where a priest was seated. His garments, woven from blue, purple, and scarlet yarn, were covered by a dark cloak secured by a pin with animal head terminals. In his lap rested a small pear-shaped lute made from ivory, pearl, and rosewood. Elaborate gold crocus flowers and peacocks drank in the last rays of the sun. The cousins would have exercised more caution but for such captivating imagery and a peace that passed understanding. The parties exchanged looks and appraised the moment without words. As priest huddled around the instrument, the swept the strings with eloquent dexterity. Quiet arpeggios rang in natural purity while Mason and Winter traversed the woodland cathedral, measuring it against all that was holy and chaste. Their schedules restricted lengthy discourse, but kind words were exchanged. Almost out of earshot, Mason heard a soft, glorious refrain, "Cast all your fears on Him".

The cousins emptied stones from their boots, adjusted their gear, and pressed on. They gathered edible items, sampling some here and there. There was much commentary about the local wildlife and, to pass the time, analysis of a book had both read. An earth-toned skylark accompanied them for a stretch, singing with exaltation. Its sable eye beamed a transient benevolence, then it took wing and flew out of sight. Winter collected a sturdy limb, subtracted the twigs, and fashioned a crude walking stick. His wood-crafting abilities were noteworthy and, as he worked with a chisel and sweep gouge, he carved the likeness of a hound's head into one end. He stripped back the bark and added small paw prints. Toward the end of the undertaking he asked Mason when he started playing guitar.

"Around twelve. It was either guitar or field games, glad I chose the former. I found a guitar in our attic and showed it to my father. He told me it was made from buried thousand-year-old timber. Why I sold that guitar is a mystery. Those instruments are rare today and good luck finding one with a rounded top and back. And the detail! The fret designs and sound hole were spiral shaped, symbolizing new life. Let me know if you ever find one!"

"Of course. And you live in an area that puts high value on cultivating musical ability. More top-notch talent than anyplace I can think of and some ensembles known far and wide. Any favorite songs?"

"No end to them. "Border" by Brass Tacks was an early favorite and perhaps THE catalyst; the bass line was like a white-hot beam, straight into my impressionable mind. The quiet cool sounds from tuned rattles followed by sharp contrasting horns, all within the first few seconds. Distinguished, elegant, impossible to ignore. I learned any and all songs I heard. I gained interest in other bands essentially on my own. Less hand-me-down, and more methodical in selection. My tastes veered toward the brash and hypnotic. Did I inherit musical genes? Do we inherit interests in certain things? I often wondered and still do. I filled a journal with notations of fingering positions. Music quickly became my passion. Area musicians inspired me, sound captivated me."

An embankment obscured the land beyond. They climbed to a higher vantage point and beheld a sight of wonder: a grand stone circle from some lost age. Its crooked wedges were tinged with gray and white, often dressed in mossy coats, and occasionally adorned with symbolic carvings. A red fox eyed them from a distant lookout, motionless as if stone itself. It lost interest and bounced away through dense overgrowth with black and white ears pointing the way.

On the dim edge of twilight, they found a campsite in a wooded hollow where a stream ran. Well out of sight from the main road, it offered comfortable high grass, wind shelter, and dry fallen trees for firewood. Winter built a fire from applewood logs and embedded two Y shaped branches on either side—a primitive rotisserie.

Mason roamed the stream's edge, throwing his line about the surface and experimenting with retrieval speeds. After a bit of patience, the stream surrendered two brown trout. The fish were de-scaled, gutted, and skewered on spits. Bread, wild mushrooms, and bilberries were doled out and they consumed a savory and filling meal. After washing up, Winter produced a flask of malted barley whisky which was passed back and forth for the better part of an hour. Carrying orange-cinnamon aromatics, it was vibrant and complex on the palate and it ended with a hint of peat smoke, dry oak, and caramel. For some time after, Winter enjoyed the aroma of the cork.

Trees whispered all along the hollow's edge and the tones of burning applewood lingered sweet and delicious. The night's indigo facade, studded with grains of ancient fire, held them entranced like an audience awaiting the opening of a curtain. Leaning against a great fallen log they lit pipes and faced east through a break in the trees. From this vantage point, they watched an immense thunder moon rise over the shore of a lake handsomely nestled between hills. A nightjar sang from somewhere in the firelit canopy, its ghostly staccato cascading like a high speed guiro.

"I once heard of an enchanted lake in this area," stated Winter. "It was under the spell of Magnús Galdur, also known by the name Baron de Galdur. He was a magician who practiced black magic. It was said he could shape-shift into creatures of all kinds. As the legend goes, one day he turned himself into a bullmastiff, but the spell went wrong and he couldn't change himself back. He was doomed to spend his remaining days as a dog, it seemed, until his mentor, a sorceress, offered help. She agreed to reverse the conjuration but, as punishment, she banished him to the bed of the lake where evidently he remains to this day. One night every ten years, under the beams of a full moon, he emerges from his aqueous dungeon and rides a mare, white as untrodden snow, around the lake until dawn. His sublime stallion is fitted with silver horseshoes and, as the fable states, only when those horseshoes are worn out, will the curse be lifted from the Baron. Locals claim if you row a boat to the center of the lake and look deep into the void, you can see a drowned castle, its ramparts broken-down by the weight of time. And if you look on Bealtaine, you will see the windows alight from an ancient feast and festival and even hear the dull blasts of the carnyx and dord!" Winter stopped to ponder his narrative, carved another detail into his walking stick, looked over to his cousin, and expressed mild disapproval. Mason had fallen asleep with his pipe in his mouth.

First light revealed an overcast sky; to the north, puffy white clouds against azure; to the west, blankets of iron and pewter where little sunlight penetrated. It looked to be a fine day for the next leg of their journey through rolling country and the town of Woodlawn.

Mason felt it important to begin the day with healthy mental posture. He gave himself a pep talk, read inspirational phrases, summoned powers against anything cruel or merciless, logged what he was grateful for, and prayed. This procedure was armor in an unpredictable, indifferent world.

They snacked on bread and jerky as they navigated a peaceful green quarter. The road grew narrow and rocky, complicated by tree roots. It was a favored environment for giant ferns whose feathery fronds burst past waist-height in shades of hunter, harlequin, and burgundy. Winter, whose involvement with religion and spiritual worship was fairly modest, inquired about Mason's morning ritual of prayer, writing, and reflection.

With an understanding nod and a deep breath, Mason began a discussion on the topic. "There certainly are many aspects to explore. Consider this: deity worship has existed for thousands of years. Look to the past and you'll find cultures, clans, and tribes with a common characteristic of belief and worship. That's important because some feel evangelism is a fad, or has strings attached. Here we are, modern day, discussing a subject that's been contemplated since the dawn of time. It's not new thinking; it's part of us. There's a question of method and strategy, too. If not from God, where does strength and guidance come from? The town crier? Your supervisor? An astrologer? An adjustment to diet or exercise? The tarot or numerology? Let me put it another way. You've spent lots of time on the open sea, Winter. A ship's tools help you navigate: the telescope, sextant, astrolabe, map, and compass. But it's quite different navigating the turbulent seas of life. Heartbreak, disappointment, and knowing whom to listen to are great challenges. Maps and tools are no good here. Consider that scripture is a spiritual roadmap and a moral compass. If not to God, where do you turn for answers, direction, strength, and support? We all experience pain, confusion, sickness, or worry to some degree. Those pushed to the edge often lack method and strategy. Applying logic to all things will leave you short of answers and often far from the truth. Some are helpless when it comes to improving their situation. From those stuck in a career, to those unhappy in a relationship, to those who want to fight the whole world. The truth is we all need help at some point. We can't do this alone and it's too taxing for one person's mind. Through your early years, you needed parents for food, shelter, and love—right? Things change as we grow older, but we have needs just the same. God offers a free gift to anyone who believes. So many tears and so much heartbreak stem from loss, but you won't lose Him." He pointed skyward.

"That's valuable insight. I've explored similar topics and, quite honestly, I struggle with some concepts. Here's one I get stuck on: If God knows what I want, why do I have to ask him," inquired Winter.

"To show our dependence on Him. There are certain situations where you can do nothing but trust. Surrender. Empty yourself," put in Mason.

"Ok. Here's another one: Let's say I'm an atheist. If I'm a good person, my intentions are positive, I follow the law, and I act forthright, why don't I get rewarded? I face challenges and struggles just like anybody. Why must Heaven be forfeited if I don't accept or believe in God?" challenged Winter.

"Well that's another wonderful question; indeed something many struggle with." Mason said, and then enlarged on the theme. "Man wants answers for everything. The best strategy is not to try to understand God's master plan and not make his decisions for Him. Faith lives where there is doubt. So often we don't know, and that's the point. We don't know what's best for us, just

51

like children. Some prefer to wish away religion when really they want to wish away negative consequences. We shouldn't try to make sense of a plan that we're not meant to grasp. It's too big to comprehend! We see and understand only a tiny fraction of any given person or problem. That person, in turn, doesn't understand who they are. The point is to place your trust in God and not lean on your own understanding. I can't tell you how many times that doctrine has reset my thought process and halted over-analysis. It's crucial! Lean not on your own understanding. It's silly to think we're going to have correct answers for every situation. And if you think that way you are attempting to control it. Another concept is that the battle is God's. Let Him fight your battles for you. Talk to Him like you would a friend or a family member. Share with Him your doubts and struggles. Even if parents have a general idea of what issues their children face, it's still important that there is a dialogue. Communication strengthens the relationship. Talking eases the tension and lessens the load."

To this, Winter added, "Yes, that's familiar territory. Sometimes I feel it's just all so hard to believe. Patience is difficult. I pray and pray and nothing happens. I watch others receive blessings, but not me. It seems like God is silent. And why do so many bad things happen anyway, I'm just trying to live right!"

"Yes, that's a common concern. People get stuck in the fruitless search for reasons. I think it has to do with trusting God's timing and his plan. Just like your parents didn't give you everything you wanted growing up. They gave steady guidance, love, and care, yet placed restrictions and rules on certain things. These things will become clear if you adopt a child. Think of God that way; trust Him most in the midst of struggle. We're circling right back to leaning not on your own understanding. Try not to figure out why He hasn't answered a prayer. We don't know where all the rest of the chess pieces are on this vast board. We don't need to know. Put him in control, he loves you and he wants to make a way for you."

"Good words, cousin, and helpful. It's given me a new frame of reference. I guess I didn't really think about trusting. I always feel I need to do things on my own. I'll digest it over the next couple of days. It opened my eyes and I can tell there's a whole lot more to this from the way that you're talking," concluded Winter.

The wayfarers came upon a forest clearing where they detected a faint pulse, low and repetitive, like the gears of a giant clock. Past a declivity of fallen trees, the sounds reverberated with metallic qualities, like the peals of church bells. Over and over with regularity they rang, and it became evident the clamor stemmed from some industrial pursuit. An oversized shelter came into view. Immense wooden timbers with knee brace joinery supported a roof of dry leaves and moss. The imposing structure was a gong factory on a grand scale. The smell of burning metal greeted them. Barefooted workers in leather aprons roamed the dimly lit area with tongs, chisels, and hammers—their deep voices in steady dictation of production details and machinery adjustments. A raw block of bronze, refined from mountain ore, was set into place. A barrage of citrine and amber sparks erupted from the forge. Flipped like a giant flatbread, then extracted with tongs, the slab was placed on a hard surface and subjected to hammer blows. Its shape and thickness were carefully considered for tonality. The random pattern of clangs and clanks reminded Mason of an enormous wind chime. The disk was then inspected, marked with chalk, and the process was repeated.

This main workshop was ringed by dingy tents where bellows the size of pub tables delivered air to the furnace. The workers, hot and dusty from the business of manufacturing, took little notice of the passing backpackers. The slabs of bronze, transformed by hard labor and elemental forces, slowly took the shape of majestic gongs of great strength and beauty. Each included the signature of the artist.

Winter sliced off a thin cross section from the bottom of his walking stick.

The gongmaster moved in close to study a newborn gong which hung from a rafter in dazzling, prismatic glory. Crouched in a distinctive position with his weight distributed like a fighter facing an opponent, he struck the gong's center with an oversized mallet. An exotic shimmering echo, seemingly endless, filled the workshop with a range of tones. He dragged a rubber baton across its face and it sang again.

Winter flipped the wooden chip to one of the men and finally he and Mason received a look of approval, even a slight nod. The worker held in his hand a small replica of a gong. He turned it over, gazed upon it with wonder, and showed his collaborators. Gifts were rarely given in this transitional region.

As the men quit the district they pooled their knowledge on gong lore: gongs were said to control wind, water, and fire; their creation was a spiritual endeavor requiring meditation and exercise; practitioner's rituals secured workshops from paranormal interference; gongs were status symbols; gongs were used in ceremonies to communicate with beings from other dimensions; the healing powers of gongs; touching one was said to bring fortune and strength.

As they marched north, the road improved. The occasional inn indicated they were near the town of Woodlawn. Sheep roamed the outlying hillside. It was high noon and their first order of business was to find food and water.

They passed a general store and a sprawling complex of stables and barns fit for any number of horses. A light breeze cooled their skin and the sounds of yapping dogs and chirping finches filled the air. Carts and wagons belonging to travelers lined one side of the avenue and a stream under bridges along the other.

They heard a thin skirl, at first strange and haunting, then unmistakably the magic lingering call of bagpipes. Like a tartan's woven pattern, the attack from drone pipes interlaced with the soaring melodies from chanters in a wondrous pibroch. A banner at the town's front gate advertised: ANNUAL HIGHLAND GAMES, ATHLETES AND SPECTATORS WELCOME. A circle of men wearing kilts and sporrans engaged in lively conversation outside an ivy-decked manor house. Past teahouses and a wool market, a sea of tents and tables encircled the market square. They continued to a central field where the games were set to commence. When the bagpipe fanfare ceased a man sang a traditional ballad. All about the square, patrons poured into pubs. The Hobgoblin, The White Rider, and The Tower House all had lengthy queues.

Down an alley, away from this vibrant setting, the men eyed a pub called Royal Banners. Ducking inside, they claimed oak settles, ordered from the bill of fare, and took in the atmosphere. A brown labrador reclined plaintively on flagstone. Rows of mugs and flagons hung from rafters like ornaments. Sporting equipment, reflecting the heritage of the games, decorated the fireplace mantel. There were no suspicious characters; only gossip, friendly conversation, and an occasional drunken outburst. A young woman played a fast, snappy reel on a fiddle while the two men feasted on hardy plates of roast guinea fowl and vegetables from local farms.

Winter packed half an apple pie in his backpack, turned to Mason, and effused, "That was a feel good meal. I've got energy and calm nerves. On our way back from the meeting, how about we stop to enjoy the games and tent show? We can investigate pubs as we go."

In agreement, Mason added, "I'd like to visit the blacksmith and music shops. Watch a performance or two. There's plenty happening here."

The crowd's roar hurried their pace back to the

square where the games were now in full swing. Names hung on a leader board: MacGregor, Bauer, Lothbrok, Charbonneau. Towering vertical posts for a height event known as the sheaf toss were installed at either end of the athletic field. After a crossbar was set into position, a stocky young man used a pitchfork to hurl a burlap bag of straw. It cleared the bar to the delight and wild approval of onlookers. The bar would be raised until only one person could successfully make the height. Until the sun set, men, women, and children would be entertained by a variety of events: the shot put, hammer throw, and tug-o-war, as well as musical presentations, historical reenactments, and dancing.

On the move again, Mason lit his pipe and unfolded his journal. He scribbled down place names and a potential lyric. Winter, close behind, rolled a coin across his knuckles eyeing the periphery with vigilance. The hypnotic vibrations of sanxians, sitars, and tamburas drifted throughout the festival, their melodies accompanied by doiras, tsams, and piercing reed pipes. A young woman in a dyed cotton dress danced inside a gong chime, her mallets striking bronze disks with steady precise rhythm. A wandering aşık performed a love song and sold bunches of freshly picked lavender as he stole hearts. Along the northbound road, vendors displayed and sold jewelry, blended oils, clothing, whiskey, weaponry, and offerings from local vineyards and farms. A booth dedicated to musical instrument restoration sheltered an old craftsman who studied a bowed lute with a headstock shaped like an antelope's head. With a brass ocular wedged between his cheek and brow, he performed some task few would appreciate. Eventually, the commotion faded and transitioned smoothly into sounds of cicadas, robins, and the open country. Here, the wind had many voices—a crying harpy, an wailing siren, a whispering child. A dog's excited bark relayed through the wood. Mason and Winter appeared as any two pilgrims on any lowly errand.

Before long they found themselves at an intersection near the meeting place. An unconventional marker stood in one corner of the crossroads. A towering goblet drum, the height of three men, bore signs pointing in multiple directions. The names of towns, lakes, and strongholds were painted alongside their associated distances.

Winter consulted his notes with a resolute expression. "The lake is just past these hills, under a certain ring of trees including one unusually tall peppermint tree, The White Knight." He pointed up and away. "Why don't I have a nickname as grand?!"

"Well, perhaps if you were three hundred years old and twenty-five stories tall you would." Mason released a smoke puff, stowed his pipe, and hiked toward the tree.

The Archia Antiquarian Society was a leadership council responsible for a rich archival collection of regional history and culture. The council formed when the first roads of Gardenwall were plotted out. They had other roles as well, which was why they were meeting that day, clandestinely. Mason Ross, the member-at-large, served as a liaison to the general membership. The duties of the position, well-defined in the organization's bylaws, were intended to fulfill board requirements and overall organizational goals.

Winter and Mason reached the meeting site, joining individuals from all corners of Archia. Some had traveled one to two days on foot, some less than a day by horse or omnibus. Food and drink had been set out and a cart and dais rested in the center of the clearing. In small groups, dialogue canvassed news, weather, and speculations about to the meeting's agenda. The cousins did more listening than talking. Burak from Ardenbridge handed out corked vials of honey from his bee farm, detailing production and bottling. Vanora from Braidwood discussed her tulip farm and shared insights on harvesting and handling. Eventually, attention shifted to the business at hand.

The three presiding officers, known formally as Overseers, took positions near the shore and called the meeting to order. In the center, Point Preceptor, Kennari Balt, wore purple. To his right stood Treasurer, Colina Gaspar, in gold. To his left stood Officer of Light, Eadrom Altin, also in gold. The others formed a semicircle—customary at these proceedings—and the presentation began. Typically, there would be a short choral and musical performance with bell trees, panpipes, and guitars; this time, however, Kennari began in a more formal and solemn fashion. He was in a ready posture with both fists at his waistline. His purple high-collar cloak, secured with an aspis-shaped pin, fluttered like a pennon in the wind and in that moment, in front of the lake, he appeared some great explorer on the forecastle of a carrack.

Kennari began, "I'd like to express my gratitude to all who trekked for this special session. It is critical that you are here and on behalf of our entire leadership committee, I do thank you. We found it imperative to take precautions ensuring secrecy. This has been a time of concern for the Overseers."

Winter scanned the attending body. The three leaders stood dignified, eyes wise and ageless, and synchronized with the all-consuming sun. "As foretold in the Great Book, one day there will be a challenge to our peace and way of life. Though we wish that day was far in the future, even past our time here, we believe it is upon us now," lamented Kennari.

Two assistants unloaded the Great Book from the cart and set it upon the dais where its bronze spine and cover threw off light. To Mason, it appeared the size of a cathedral window. The cover featured trumpets and harps of gold, a carved wooden cross, and rows of chrysolyte, onyx, and jasper. It was unlocked and opened. The elegant writing within required years of study to translate and few knew how. The manuscript, timeworn and age faded, was embellished with extravagant ornamentation and illustrations. Colina took her place in front of the book while the two men turned the giant vellum pages. She wore a hooded gold rowan over a skirt and tunic. A pendant with a chi and rho monogram swung from the carcanet around her neck. She placed her hands together near her heart, fingertips and thumbs touching, in a diamond shape. Forthwith she read the passage. "Beware the black heart guided by ancient evil, who shall rise from the hills of slaughter. Beware the one with a broken wing who will fool the world. Beware the combatant who is the product of neglect and violence. Like a wolf at dusk, he shall turn the whole country into a desolation."

The book was closed and locked. Colina spoke slowly so all could understand. "We believe this text is representative of recent events in the region of Black River. We now have a common enemy who has come to steal, kill, and destroy. It is imperative we join together and stand firm in our faith. We will put on the full armor of God so that when the day of evil comes, we can hold our ground. For it is written, we will have much trouble in this world, but God is our safe place and our strength."

It was Eadrom Altin's turn to speak. He wore a gold ephod, a ceremonial hat, and a necklace with a golden triangular pendant. He placed his hands behind his back and paced methodically. "You have all, by now, heard of the man known as Calon Du, Chief Moderator of the Council of the Wolf and Commander of the Greyguard Army. Through our network of spies, ally clans, and others careful of our safety, the Overseers have obtained intelligence pertaining to his recent acts of evil. Days of doom are approaching. Make no mistake, he is a rapacious barbarian and as deceitful as a demon. His lust for power and domination has no bounds and he will stop at nothing to gain total control of the northwest and eventually the whole of the land. Two villages, Heddwich and

61

Ft. Kerr west of Black River, were laid to waste. His divisions devastated the countryside and left carnage in their wake. They wear grey uniforms and march under a silver banner with an insignia: a red shield with three silver arrows."

There were groans, gasps, and sounds of anger from the crowd. Some stood in shock, eyes revealing brewing terrors within.

Eadrom continued. "Fear runs rampant throughout the north and people have hidden themselves away, refusing to leave even for food and water. They are terrified, outnumbered, have few weapons, and their resources are swiftly being depleted. To make matters worse, we know Calon Du intends to further his aggressive campaign to the west and south. Archia stands directly in the path of war. Know this, he will not yield."

Eadrom paused and angled his head upward as if recalling a memory. His expression revealed a trace of hope. "If we can defeat him, all of Archia and the surrounding lands will be free, and life as we know it will move forward toward days of light. But if we fail, the whole world and everything that we know and care for will sink into an abyss of wizardry and woe. Let us therefore prepare ourselves for duty, and know that if Archia and its neighbors last for perpetual generations, men and women will proudly say: This was our immaculate moment."

The Overseers again took their positions near the shore and Kennari made a final statement before an intermission. "Our proposal is to send a small tactical force to Black River to cut off the head of the snake. The elimination of Calon Du should leave his Greyguard in disarray and vulnerable to our smaller attacks. It is our best chance of putting a stop to his campaign. We will pick up from here at sunset."

The announcements stunned the majority, though some who watched Calon's activity from afar were in the know. It was quiet at the site. Trepidation, sadness, and uncertainty were in every heart. There were tear-stained faces. Some wandered the water's edge in search of comfort. A dire wind stripped them of spirit and left only dried shells.

The world had been turned upside down and inside out. Priorities shifted. Things that once brought joy now seemed lackluster. Mason felt as though a massive stone rolled over his chest. He was fatigued and restless simultaneously and what appetite he had ceased to exist. He was concerned for families awash in uncertainty and loss. As the trees reeled around and around, he thought of his home in Gardenwall, his collection of instruments, and his comfortable kitchen and bedroom. Even though he wished he were there, he knew it was no longer safe. He sat down overtaxed, adrift, and disgusted. His whole body was under the pressure of a bearhug. Then it happened again.

The next thing Mason saw was Winter's round whiskered face peering down at him and he realized he was lying on his back in the grass. His head spun while he slowly pulled himself together. Others were standing close, awaiting a sign from either of the two. Someone offered water.

"It's ok. I think he's just had a little too much sun. Steady now." Winter helped Mason to his feet and they walked. "Another vision? What did you see this time?"

"I think I remember a circle of hands, a circle of friends, pictures in a gallery, and an open road. I recall a tall gate with strange writing and cold eyes peering from a house of ash. Then all went dark; a patchwork this time; difficult to understand; a piece of a larger puzzle I suppose." Mason looked more pale than usual. He felt frail.

"Listen," began Winter, "this is all happening quickly, and we had a good trip here, but time isn't a luxury at this point. People need us: the people near us now; the people of Gardenwall; the people far to the north by the sea; everyone in the Black River area; the entire land! That speech moved me and strengthened my spirit. I think this is our time. You and me and whoever else will join us."

On the horns of a dilemma, Mason spoke. "Wait a moment." Mason wobbled. "Who am I to face Calon Du? He has an entire army! What if they destroy us? Torture us? I'm no warrior." He put two fingers to his neck, "My pulse is racing. My head is foggy and I feel like I might...." He leaned over to empty his stomach.

Winter witnessed it before and knew his cousin only needed time to get back on track. He left food, gave him space, and rejoined the group. He explained there was no need for alarm. "We all have our weaknesses," he joked to those around him.

Just then, Mason's face became like iron. He retrieved his journal and read passages he had prepared for this very type of scenario. He read with focus, prudence, and the deepest faith he could muster. He whispered partly in prayer and partly in a self-motivating declamation. Though he addressed no one in particular, it may just as well have been addressed to every man, woman, and child in Archia.

It gives me peaceful rest at night. It makes me strong and light. It's everything I hoped it would be. Concise, well-tuned, and bright. Inspiration. A flowing well, a revelation, an answered prayer, a sacred space, a sighted goal, a balanced scale, a guarantee. My immaculate moment, my joy, my quiet reflection. Inspiration. Complete and lacking nothing. The truth revealed. All targets accounted for. All movements synchronized. All debts paid. No detours.

Mason stood up, seamed together by a needle and thread, and approached the Overseers. He took a deep breath, lowered his brow, and in a voice barely audible said, "I will go."

Chapter 4

The Good Things

Encouragement - The Crystal Forest
Lokman's Residence - Intelligence - A surprise

As the sun was sunk in the west, the attending body awaited the words of the Overseers. What cruel fate was in store for a region so unfamiliar with war? Were these truly the final days of peace? Mason and Winter pondered such questions as they stood alongside the Overseers.

Kennari spoke in a slow and passionate tone. "We've found our heralds of hope. Two familiar faces have accepted our proposal and volunteered. Here they stand, our desired bucklers—bone, sinew, and soul—to be put to work against the day of reckoning. They risk everything to abolish the abuses, usurpations, and insidious purposes of a despot, and will lay down new defenses for our future security. Some may call them enlightened, some may call them purpose driven, but let no one claim they lack conviction. These uncertain times call for strength and composure of mind. Mason and Winter leave at dawn with our latest intelligence and best-devised strategy. May God walk every mile with them."

Most Society members planned to spend the night and journey homeward in the morning, others preferred to travel under the cover of darkness. Security was a thing that could no longer be counted on. Mason and Winter set up camp among pines. They had little appetite and even their flask of whisky was left untouched. They gazed endlessly into the beechwood fire making occasional comments but not altogether present for extended conversation. The logs scraped and grunted as they settled. Winter snatched up a sycamore branch and cut off a small piece. Eyes aflame, he bored a thin chamber through its center with a palm auger. He shaved off the bark, carved a voicing hole through the top, and fashioned a dowel with a flat side for a plug. He held up his creation—an emergency whistle. Mason Mason recorded his logic in the journal. He drew up attack plans that might thwart the enemy's wanton devastation. He made reproductions of blue-white constellations. How brilliantly they sparkled in the gloomy depths.

Horned owls with large swiveling heads observed from sequestered perches. Their hoots relayed through the camp, shot across the lake, then returned as eerie relics. Mason and Winter fell asleep under the pale wandering moon, wanderers themselves, but steadily following a fixed path.

They were awoken by the Overseers just as the last night star evanesced. It was early and time to move. They were given council over a cold breakfast. Their first goal was to reach a mystic, artist, and scientist named Lokman, who lived at the edge of the Crystal Forest. They were instructed not to write out directions to his residence. Instead, they committed a list of landmarks to memory. There were looks of encouragement, hearty pats on the back, many looks of wild wonder, and even a tear or two. Society members provided provisions and bundles of food. Winter and Mason both eyed the salted meats and barmbrack.

The two shouldered their packs and set out northbound. The cotton quilt sky rolled out to the horizon, covering islands of trees. There must have been a chamomile farm or field nearby; sugary, fresh herbal tones floated on the wind. They passed through untouched wetlands, grassy hills, and vast forests. At one bend stood an inviting cottage where an octogenarian sold clothing, boot repair services, and gear.

At an old sign they broke from Thornydale Road and banked west toward the Crystal Forest. The path narrowed and provided copious shade. Corridors of spruce, pine, and beech dipped and curled up into ever-denser wilderness. Throughout the sleepy wood they heard the beeps, rolls, and flourishes of goldcrests. A solitary specimen dropped to a nearby branch and, flicking its tail, sang in cryptic codes. It bounded beside them for a spell then darted off into unfathomable green. Both men lingered deep in morose thoughts that occasionally plateaued to neutrality. They weren't exactly overjoyed by the task ahead but with each heartbeat they adapted to uncertainty. Needs of others were placed above their own.

Mason broke the silence. "Never underestimate the power of adaptation. I think it's our greatest ability. I once knew a man who could have been a successful merchant, but he was afraid to try. He made excuses and claimed commissionable income was too unstable. His unwillingness to adapt was a fear-based negative mindset. I once knew a woman who became a successful merchant. She embraced the challenge and jumped right in. She abandoned her comfort zone and adapted. She developed a plan, followed up with customers, offered free samples, and most importantly, tracked her results. In short, she made it fun. She is the star of Merchant Square!"

Winter realized it applied to their endeavor and put a twist on it. "Take the prisoner who adapts to his cell. The ultimate horror becomes a safe secure home over time. Upon release, it's said a prisoner often struggles to integrate back into society because they've adapted to prison. Reportedly, it takes a minimum of two to six weeks to adapt to a change."

They went on like this, providing example after example of adaptation and perhaps in some way it kept their minds limber and relieved of unreasoning distress. For its physiological benefits, they would return to the practice over and over. Soon, they found their spirits were high enough to sing:

Just for now
Let's pretend that the stakes are higher
And every little move we make
Will determine how the ashes fall
You got to stop, think twice, listen to the wind blow

Every night I got to speak with

The old man down the highway
And every time lets me know, ha
There's good things coming my way
You got to stop, think twice, listen to the wind blow

So even when your dreams are dark
And your road runs up the mountain
Sugar sugar let that be
And row merrily down the stream
You got to stop, think twice, listen to the wind blow

They worked out stylized harmonies within the refrain. Winter kept rhythm with two sticks. After trekking for half a day, they stopped in a clearing to rest. Quill in hand, Mason scribbled fresh thoughts in his journal.

Jump right in! Whether it's gardening, singing, writing, learning an instrument, or starting a business, inspiration and follow through are integral to the outcome. There will be challenges and detours. The comfort zone must be left behind. Fear will always make its voice known. You may want to stop, but let perseverance do its work. It's exactly this that you will be most proud of. Eventually the hard work will transform into the wisdom of experience. One by one, the fruits of labour will burst forth.

What can we do to become inspired? Where does it come from and how does it grow? Here are some simple home remedies: read poetry, listen to music (art inspires art), walk through an art show, observe others, stroll through a glen, learn something new, teach others, volunteer, eliminate clutter, feed the poor, pay it forward, make a map, offer help to someone, make a plan, set a goal. Everyone has access to inspiration. There are no entry fees! It's one way we are all created equal.

Churches and cathedrals inspire me. St. Brendan Cathedral and St. Columba Cathedral in Roundfort, and Hannock Cathedral in Knight's Town are some of my favorites. Cathedral of the Sacred Heart in Valleyview, Stonehaven Cathedral in Westhill, and Mt. Zion Church Silverbridge were also places where I was in awe, at peace, and felt amazed.

I appreciate old houses with finely carved base and crown molding. You see these details throughout the hotels and restaurants of Whitecourt. There is an architectural style in that city that roots it in the past, yet keeps it fresh and moving forward. The old houses in the Garden District have that same quality. The neighborhoods have a personality and they want to show off.

After a conference about distances and landmarks, it was time to crack on. They roved floors of bluebells, stretches of statuesque titan arum plants, and habitats of fauna unheard of in Archia. The pathway opened up delta-like at the rim of a deep, narrow gorge. Here, large cairns were erected to either side. They made note of a rock where wanderers left coins and other items of meager value. This was the gateway to the famed Crystal Forest, subject of superstitious tales, hearsay, and folklore.

The Crystal Forest was once home to an ancient race of fairies called The Hexing. It was said these beings had special powers of healing, mind reading, and intangibility. Crystals found throughout the forest were said to be their source of power. Seeing it all first-hand gave Mason and Winter considerable pause.

The simple suspension bridge before them was the longest they'd ever seen and swung high above a rocky gorge below. They were even with the tops of superlative fir trees, homes to eagles and ravens. In the higher ground on either side of the bridge were immense wooden pillars carved with strange symbols and figures. It was Mason who took the first tentative steps onto the weathered rungs which accepted his weight with bending and creaking. Winter bore a look of wide-eyed distress. Mason continued until he reached the nadir then gazed down at the small stream in the gorge as he held fast to the support ropes. He thought of home, how far they had come, and how each moment was a gift. He looked back and watched Winter inch his way toward him.

"Need a hand?" called Mason.

Winter shook his head and waved him off. Their stances switched: Winter now the anxious one, Mason waxing courageous. Gust after gust pushed in and the bridge rebounded and rocked, threatening to throw him and his wobbly knees off into space.

"Guillotines and gallows!" exclaimed Winter as every muscle locked.

He told himself not to look down, but he did, half expecting to see dead animals, gear, and bodies at the bottom of the gorge. His mind concocted a worst case scenario: *If the bridge fails and I hold on to this support rope, I could possibly swing toward the side of that cliff. And if my injury wasn't too great, I could climb up the rope to the top.* He passed a hand over his brow, wiping away cold sweat. He nervously laughed, shook off the vision, and progressed onward while the bridge lurched underneath him once again. Escapes and illusions were the farthest thing from his mind and the only way he progressed was by looking straight ahead. He felt the dreadful thing had been designed to deter not deliver. He pocketed his fears and crept forward rung by rung. When they reached the relative safely of the other side, they fell down in hearty appreciation of solid ground.

This was an ancient wilderness and many of its trees were thousands of years old. They walked among towering conifers, petrified logs in magnificent hues, spindly trees vibrant with lime-green moss, and trickling waterfalls. Exotic wildflowers with petals larger than frying pans filled the air with perfume and the sylvan floor was a patchwork of deep greens and browns. The forest was named for its enormous crystals—most taller than a man and as big around—which grew in rows like cheval de frise. In the day, their brilliance was almost blinding as they sent glowing trapezoids of sunlight into the flora; under the moon, they radiated a soft purple-blue light like bedside candles. Mason, awestruck by one specimen, created its likeness with charcoal. Studying its proportions, he drafted a shape then added strong contrasts between light and dark. Winter showed his appreciation a different way. He walked slowly along one row observing reflections in the complex geometry.

As shadows grew long, the men discussed the area's legends and superstitions: portals, time warps, shadow people, out-of-body experiences, doppelgangers, hallucinations, false awakenings, and sleep paralysis.

Arrival at Lokman's residence required they follow verbal in-structions turn by turn, step by step. Mason shaped certain sequences into measures of poetry which he could more easily remember: *follow the steeple to the oak tree, follow the water to the darkest stone.* The Overseers advised them NOT to stray from the path. It was easy to get lost in the awesome alchemy of the forest. As the sun fell behind the western tree line, they found a suitable plot surrounded in skeogs.

The travelers lit a fire for warmth only as the crystals emitted considerable light. They feasted on rations and passed the rapidly dwindling flask of whisky. They surmised they would reach their destination by late-morning the following day. Winter wondered if Lokman was expecting them; hopefully he would be at home. Under a red-brown moon, they lit pipes and edged toward sleep.

It was well before dawn when Mason awoke. Winter was propped up against a tree trunk with his mouth wide open, snoring. The forest beckoned Mason and, overwhelmed by curiosity, he set out into its depths. Before long, he noticed a strange metallic object and was hit with numbness and euphoria. His hands felt unusually heavy as he opened and closed them. Dark water flowed among the twisted roots of thick trees. Mason approached it, removed his boots, and sunk his feet into the bed, allowing the water to lick his toes. Without warning, his home-sickness vanished as if the currents drew it out of him. Absurdities jammed his mind and he attempted to stabilize himself. Looking back, the far away camp-fire burst with aquamarine, blue, and purple flames. He wondered how its colors had changed. One reality struck him: a diminutive bearded man, half-hidden by a crystal, regarded him. A minstrel's song rang out like the sound of falling coins. Mason wondered if it was only in his mind. He took out his journal and wrote, "our campfire has strange colors". He held a quill but could not feel it.

A memory from his youth rushed forth: a fell from a fence, a rough landing, and a struggle for breath. His legs were sacks of grain, his hands were pumpkins, and his lips were drooping down below his chin. His movements were sluggish as if he were moving through syrup. His brain locked and he lost all sense of time and place.

The diminutive bearded man approached and moved his mouth to speak but there was no sound. He took Mason further from the fire and showed him the entire the entire Crystal Forest as if from a mountain top. The forest floor glowed like a lava field.

Mason and Winter sat near the bar at Finn's Table in North Oak and recanted their journey through the Crystal Forest. An energetic duo created melodies with a lyre guitar and a plucked zither.

Mason turned to face Winter and asked, "Does this ale taste metallic to you?"

Winter grabbed the mug and dumped its contents onto the floor. "We're not...this isn't happening right now. I mean, we are not at Finn's. We fell asleep in the forest." insisted Winter. "Did you leave the path? We were instructed not to leave the path!"

Mason felt his lips droop down below his chin and he could not speak. Through the window of the pub, he saw a campfire with aquamarine, blue, and purple flames. A diminutive bearded man, half-hidden by a crystal, regarded them. A minstrel's song rang out like the sound of falling coins. Mason looked about the room now empty, save for a woman sweeping the floor. The musicians had gone and the bar was unattended. Luminous memories flooded Mason's mind: a cathedral in the pines, a tarnished doll, and a shaded glen near a river. Suddenly, the numbness dissipated and the campfire rushed toward him. All senses alert, Mason scanned the camp and pulled himself together.

"They told us not to wander off the path." Winter ex-claimed. "Do I have to tie a rope to your leg?" he persisted in a voice devoid of its usual humor.

A morning mist limited visibility; it had rained nearby. The deep earthy smell of petrichor lingered and the ground was sodden. A falcon, riding high in the clouds, was the only trace of wildlife. They initiated a foot-friendly ascent through stands of stately beech trees and out-cropped masses of slate. The glorious faces of violets tilted toward a muted sun. Mushrooms burst forth from dark empty spaces. Destroying Angels, dressed in brilliant white, stood in stark contrast to the deep verdant backcloth as if cut out for a sewing project. Witch's butter, earthstars, and smoky brackets made for an herbalist's apothecary. Each individual component of the landscape linked to the entire cosmos. Dreamily, they discussed how all things drew energy from one definitive source. Yellow-green leaves arched over the path in all possible directions and the reverie continued for hours. Their footfalls kept a quiet rhythm as they approached the next land-mark en route to Lokman's residence.

The sky was a gray blanket pulled over a sleepy landscape. The trees and flowers were wet and shiny. They paused at the bank of a small lake and scanned the waterline. Black and white winged dragonflies on cabalistic errands executed ethereal dances. A lone ash tree overpowered the peninsula it sprouted from, covering a small inlet where a giant bullfrog ruled. The creature's croak was a low droning burst like the bottom note from a barrel organ. It rumbled, rolled, and had its way with the wind. Here time stood still.

They encountered a young woman who played a merry jig on a concertina. She swayed back and forth and bounced her leg bounced up and down. Her eyes remained closed behind long brown curls. They attempted to engage her in conversation but whether she could not hear or chose to ignore them was anyone's guess. Winter commented on the bole of a tree which had been carved into a giant wooden mushroom. The grounds featured cycads and agathis trees and they could not dismiss its prehistoric aspect. Under a canopy of beech and hazel trees, they followed a worn path, looking high and low for a dwelling. Just then, a majestic stone fortification came into view—a partial ruin with worn down watch-towers. Birds nested in the keep and large sections of the battlements were missing or ready to fall. They called out into the silence; only the wind answered.

They roamed deeper into the grounds past more carved mushrooms, this time painted green, red, and yellow. A quail addressed them. The air was rich with hyacinth and wisteria, and they stopped for a moment in an open space under a canopy. Sunrays slipped through the lush wooded vault and decorated the ground with dancing illumination. Mason and Winter paused to listen for voices then chose an uphill route past a shallow pool covered with nenuphars. Rounding a corner, they eyed a broad tower capped with a telescope. A set of anemometers whirled in the wind.

Their path led to the base of a large hill where it steadily ascended in a series of switchbacks and oxbows. Cherry trees, slender pines, and ferns lined the way. Halfway to the crest, they found a converted barn ringed in flower pots and artwork. Paintings of seraphs, lambs, and gates leaned against the walls. The cousins stepped over the threshold of the open door and at last heard a voice.

"Welcome! Come on in and mind your head down the stair," came the greeting from the heart of the structure. Mason and Winter were elated and relieved. Panning the space, they noted shelves of pottery, unfinished clay statuary, glasswork, and paint-splattered furniture. Down the helical they passed more paintings: doves in flight, staurograms, and shepherds. Everything about the place was cheery and bright.

"Help yourself to something to eat if you like,"

said the presumed owner of the house.

"Mister...Lokman, Sir?" inquired Winter.

"Oh well. Lokman or Lok is perfectly fine. I don't do well with formalities."

Lokman still had yet to turn around and face the men as he pottered about cleaning brushes, arranging bottles, and folding rags.

"I made the bread myself," he said, "and the wine I pressed onsite. You won't go hungry in my presence! I enjoy hosting and wanted to have something ready for your arrival. And there's more where that came from. We'll feast this evening."

Lokman, who some labeled a green martyr or an eremite, turned around and greeted the wayfarers with a warm smile. He was of average height, round at the waist, bald, and had a close-cropped white beard. There was a sparkle in his eye and a look of cheerful wisdom upon his round visage. He wore a simple painter's smock and a small wooden cross on a woven thread hung from his neck. A familiar looking peregrine falcon preened in the windowsill and appraised the visitors with a noble eye. Lokman pulled a walnut from his pocket and gave it to the bird.

"Her name is Mica and I wanted her to keep an eye on you. Did you know they can see things many miles away?" he asked rhetorically.

"Yes about that, Mr. Lokman, ah, how did you know, have you been in contact, and the, I guess...ah we were wondering," mumbled Mason in a feeble attempt to comprehend the chain of events, then simply gave in to total acceptance and trust. Winter could only laugh.

"Well, I am sure you would do well to get off your feet and rest. You've no need to watch an old man stain himself with paint all evening. Now then, Welcome to Rathcraddock! Allow me to show you our views," expressed Lokman. Through a series of short hallways, narrow rooms, and half staircases, Lokman led them back to the main door.

A fortified farmstead with an imposing gated entrance stood on the hilltop. As the party drew near it, they took in the impressive view of the Crystal Forest and surrounding countryside. Lokman pointed out the location of the suspension bridge. Past a quaint chapel with a turf roof, they entered the farmstead and immediately felt at home.

Through the gates stood a trio of buildings which were accompanied by a shed and a peel tower. A well and a firepit were centrally located. The buildings were constructed with hulking stones and beams and their oak doors were fashioned with ironwork. The cousins followed their host into the largest building's great hall.

"Make yourselves at home. The full guided tour followed by dinner in one hour. There is a room to wash up around the corner and please tell Fahriye or Hasbi if you need anything. I have matter to tend to," explained Lokman. After he departed, Winter and Mason let out bursts of joy.

"What luxury we've landed in!" exclaimed Winter.

Leather armchairs with carved oak frames flanked a fireplace with flaming sycamore. Wide bookcases filled with thick volumes, manuals, maps, and small artifacts awed them. A beautiful triangular guitar with fanned frets leaned on a chaise lounge. Next to it rested a hammered dulcimer with cross-shaped holes and a slit drum with mallets. Mason grabbed the guitar and Winter the slit drum. Here's what they sang:

I thought that I saw you driftin'
Far from the shore on a perfect day
Looking at me as if to say
There's no place I'd rather be

I thought that I saw you shufflin'
Down along the road where the willows grow
Looking at me as if to say
There's no place I'd rather be

The warm fire and the echoes of music freed them from fatigue. They could have sat and played songs for days basking in hall's nuances. It was nice to forget the dangers they faced.

Lokman returned and guided them around property. The peel tower, offering splendid views of the surrounding country, was equipped with sleeping quarters, a small study, and dining area. They climbed to the apex. During a purple and pink sunset, their host pointed out the distant peaks of the Black Mountains where Black River stood, a beautiful yet sobering moment.

The other large building contained Lokman's quarters and a dining hall where dinner would be served.

A thatched roof shed sheltered a blacksmith workshop and pens for chickens and goats. After the tour, the travelers were shown to a guest house where Mason and Winter each had a bed, desk, and large comfortable chair. They unpacked, regrouped, and rejoined their host.

Beneath a sloped roof, tapestries and wooden shields hung from the fieldstone walls. Ornate floor candelabras and a fire provided soft light. An oak table with long benches rested on a decorative carpet. There was seating for at least twelve. Dinner was served and all five ate heartily. Roast quail and goose, wild boar, quiche, citrus from local trees, sweet potatoes and vegetables from the garden, bread pudding, an epergne of cheese and nuts, and bottled wine covered the table. It was more food than they had seen in one place in years, and their faces showed it. The mood and conversation remained light; topics concerned wildlife, music, and art. When it veered toward world news and politics, Fahriye or Hasbi instinctively began to remove plates and asked the guests for any final requests.

"And now we must address a matter of utmost urgency, for which we must adjourn to my study. Well timed, my best thinking is done on a full stomach!" proclaimed the old mystic. Winter and Mason soon found themselves in an open space which resembled the nave of a church. It was quiet. The room featured frescoed ceilings, dark wainscotting, and checkered flooring. Wall to wall cabinets displayed rare volumes, navigation instruments of every description, planetary miniatures, fish skeletons, and other oceanographic curiosa. Shelves held chunks of azure, chrysocolla, and realgar—the products of some excavation.

The three men sat in chairs circling a low table. Logs crackled in the fireplace basket. Lokman lit spikenard incense and watched Mason and Winter admire the table's centerpiece—a bronze statuette of a winged warrior holding a shield and sword. It trampled a serpent underfoot.

"It celebrates the victory of light over darkness, good over evil," explained Lokman.

Right to the point, Winter asked, "Is there a way to stop Calon Du? The Overseers did not offer solutions in that regard, yet they explained you would be able to assist us in the undertaking—as absurd and hopeless as it seems."

"That word hope," began Lokman, "is the feeling of expectation and desire for a certain thing to happen, a feeling of trust. That's the first layer of defense. Think of it as a gambeson worn under armor. You must not prepare for the task without preparing the mind." Winter leaned back in his chair hand on his chin, appreciating Lokman's candor. "Calon Du's most powerful weapon, greater than any weapon of silver or iron or even his legions, is intimidation, and he intends to use it to its full capacity. It's a good bet he believes he will not encounter strong opposition. This you can use to your advantage. God will lead you in every step. He is your rock, your safe place, your strength. Hold fast your heart and remember the words 'take hope for I have power over the world'." Lokman's countenance lit with unearthly brilliance. He addressed the wayfarers again. "At no part of the journey will you feel secure. Surely your imaginations will run riot. You may very well face an army without one of your own, but do not be faint hearted. God is with you and Calon is guided by evil."

Lokman paused and let the pair meditate on the words. He arose from his bench, deposited a log into the coal basket, and retrieved a small walnut case from the mantel. It was handed to Mason who swung the lid open to find dark ribbon cut tobacco. The travelers filled their pipes with the mixture, directing praise and appreciative smiles toward their host. Winter passed a lit match and puffed just enough to draw the flame down into the tobacco. A warm, sweet maple essence soon filled the hall and the gossamer tendrils of pipesmoke hung suspended above them like early morning fog. In that moment the men felt a sense of clarity and initiative.

Winter peered into the embers of his pipe for some time and then spoke. "Those are words I needed to hear, and indeed they quieted my mind. As you said, hope is the gambeson under the armor. What can you tell us about the armor itself?"

Lokman paced the length of the mantle. "Yes, the armor—its worth is incalculable. Your struggle, our struggle, is against the firestorm of Calon's dark forces and his lust for the calamity of a war to end wars. You don't need to be reminded of his ruthlessness, determination, and cunning. Oblivion is all he desires. The pieces of armor that you must equip yourself with are the shield of faith (your certainty), the breastplate of righteousness (your purity), the belt of truth (your integrity), the helmet of salvation (your sanity), and the sword of the spirit (The Word of God). This raiment is essential for your confrontation with Calon, and will allow you to stand firm. Do this and you will be warriors without equal!"

Mason already had his roots well planted in these beliefs. He nodded during the message, but remained puzzled by what specific tactics, if any, could be used against an army of such magnitude and against the lofty stone walls of Black River. His faith was not perfect and, dismayed, he looked to the mystic and asked, "But what methods of attack might we employ to bring about the ruin of such obstacles? We are merely two."

This is where Lokman's message became recondite. All things considered, it was only natural for the men to want war room tactics, knowledge of a secret entrance into the city, or a large-scale weapon. Lokman did not offer those. He walked to an escritoire on the far end of the room and returned with a second case. He placed one hand on top of it and began his soliloquy. "If you've come here with preconceived notions, you'll be disappointed. We all have unique talents—bravery, focus, dexterity, and so many more. Mason, your gift of music will be a deciding factor in the conflict ahead, and I offer you this instrument." Their host opened the finely crafted wooden box and tilted it toward his guests. Inside was a shell trumpet. Its core was a conch shell wrapped in gold trim and studded with coral and turquoise. As it captured light from the fire it simulated shimmering autumn leaves. Lokman handed the trumpet to Mason and while it was being inspected, closed with what seemed to be song lyrics. Winter wondered if he wasn't addressing them at all, merely vocalizing speech-like syllables that lacked any readily comprehensible meaning. "This is not a secret, because I know you have heard it, maybe even lived it my friends. It's not a picture because you don't need to be in another place or time. Where you're sitting will be fine. This is not a puzzle because it's all right before your eyes. If you read between the lines on this one, you'll fall far behind."

At sixes and sevens, the cousins looked at each other trying to extract any meaning. They were mentally juggling hope, pieces of armor, individual talents, a shell trumpet, and now veiled verses. They were certainly no worse off than upon leaving their campground that morning, and it's true they were able to think and process better on a full stomach. But they expected clarity. Lokman knew hardships rarely came with step-by-step solutions. The two men had been so engrossed in their examination of the trumpet and the facts at hand, that they hadn't noticed Lokman perusing the bookshelves, tilting his head to read spines, stopping here and there and bending low, occasionally backtracking, and now and again mumbling about the need for a better classification system. There were so many books that one of Lokman's pastimes was simply to study their workmanship. At last, he corralled the most diminutive of volumes, perhaps the size of a pastry square. He returned to the fire and held the book out in front of him as he spoke.

"The information I have shared with you is much

more than meets the eye, and ear. When the right time comes, you will know what to do and how to do it. My last request is this: before sunset tomorrow, you must locate and consult the Sea Stars—three women who have knowledge as endless as the night sky. It's impossible to overstate the importance of this petition. In the pages of this volume, you will find a map to the Rhythm Tree. It's less than a day's walk from here, and though widely known, it's surprisingly elusive. The Sea Stars will find you there."

The old man handed Mason the volume, folded his hands, and blinked sleepily. "And now you must excuse me. It's long past bedtime, even for a night owl."

Chapter 5

The Rhythm Tree

Farewell to Lokman - The stream - Red stag - Gypsy camp - The Rhythm Tree - The Sea Stars - More intelligence

The travelers awoke amid gilded rays of sunlight. Uninterrupted sleep was a thing to celebrate. They occupied an intermediate realm neither, entirely in reality nor entirely in a dream, for the dialogue and drama of the previous evening seemed pure fantasy. Only the song of wrens and the comfort of the guesthouse grounded them in the physical plane. *What a difference a few days makes,* thought Mason. *Last week everything was at right angles and now the world is all wrong. Oblivion is a distinct possibility.* On the plus side, the previous night tapped into a deep reservoir of stability and resolve. Renewed vigor bubbled to the surface.

Mason was overcome with gratitude and, in prayer, he thanked God for even the most basic bodily functions. He was grateful for his friends and even for the challenge ahead. He reminded himself that, like a blade to the whetstone, resilience and mental toughness were best sharpened through catastrophe. He applied a verse: *Consider it pure joy whenever you face trials of many kinds, because you know that the testing of your faith would produce perseverance.*

Winter was in good spirits after a night of quality rest and a farm fresh meal, and he went about packing while keeping the mood light with absurd stories awash in exaggerated emotion, ludicrous expressions, and blindside humor. Mason wondered how one man could be so entertaining. Winter could outshine a troupe of jesters.

Under different circumstances, their visit to Rathcraddock would have been protracted and certainly more musically fulfilling. Lokman's residence had a full spectrum of comforts—a matchless view, an abundance of good food, savory tobacco, and plenty of fireside seating where books were meant to be relished and instruments were meant to be played. As it was, they needed to make the most of the day. Staff members provided provisions and bundles of food. After packing and extending thanks to their host and his gracious staff, they headed northwest along a shady road.

Sometime later, they gained the crest of a steep hill which offered full perspective of the wild uplands ahead. They waded knee-deep through meadows overrun with cardinal flowers, nodding sage, and foxgloves. Across the expanse of a cornflower blue, ranks of cottony clouds advanced west to east. Far on the western horizon, the sky appeared portentous, but even a scryer struggled to predict the active living patterns of rainstorms. Onward and upward they strode, doing their work with servitude and altruism. A thousand acts of charity would pale in comparison.

At an open tract in the forest they approached a primitive stone column—a recognizable waypost from Lokman's map. They had reached the borders of Tân Brenin, seat of the ancient kings of Carreg Haul. Now, only minor vestiges of their royal citadel remained. To the north, the terrain grew increasingly rugged and the cruel, ragged silhouette of the Black Mountains could be clearly surveyed. Far to the south was the guileless land of Archia, at peace in the present moment, but directly in the path of de-struction. This naked truth drove them on.

Northeast of Heddwich, in a forgotten ravine, a young woman with red-orange curls weighed her options. She circled the smoking ash of her campfire eating a handful of wild strawberries, their taste sweet and earthly after a lunch of cooked pheasant. The rushing hiss of the nearby stream helped her concentrate. Northgate Highway, she reasoned, was the quickest and most navigable route to Black River. Along that corridor she would watch for two travelers she knew only by name. When she reached the primary north-south road, Thornydale, she would either stay and canvas that area or proceed south. It was the beginning of a plan.

She cleaned her hands in the cool current and inspected her surroundings. Rocks in varied proportions and hues comprised the banks and bed of the watercourse, a tributary of the Black River. Upstream, all features were lost in the corridor's rich viridity. It was quiet. Suddenly, she caught a flash of motion near the bank, sixty to seventy paces ahead. Something moved slow and phantom-like out of the dark undergrowth; too close for comfort. She dropped to one knee, sitting tight as a toadstool, and pieced together the shape of a lynx—white chest, dark tufts atop the ears, long legs, and a stubby tail. It was well fed, she surmised, possibly forty pounds. Her pulse soared. Listless and unthreatening, the lynx examined her with pale amber orbs, but the stream won its attention in the end. She did have pheasant meat nearby. That was good and bad.

She knew a lynx could be kept as a pet, and she held firm to this logic while she eased toward her cache of the pheasant meat. Setting a small piece out on a rock, she gathered her gear and moved further down into the riparian woodlands. She sang the lines of an old ballad:

Emerald Eyes been asleep
Without a sound for twenty years
If I had a rattle full of beads
You know those sounds would fill your ears

Emerald Eyes been asleep
without a sound for twenty years
If I had a harp to play a tune for your soul
Would you sing along

No idea where I'm going, no
No idea where I'm heading, hey hey
No idea where I'm going, no
No idea where I'm heading, hey hey

And as long as I sing this song
Your Emerald Eyes will always shine

Around midday Mason and Winter approached the remains of a collapsed stone keep. The wooden roof was long gone, destroyed by the elements and reappropriated for firewood. Segments of limestone stood like immutable sails on a fescue sea bearing mute testimony to the victories and losses of a forgotten age. Notable for its high crosses and partial statues, the venue was highly regarded by poets, artists, and composers. They unpacked and prepared lunch. Winter commented that aside from its remoteness, it would be an ideal concert venue with its dramatic backdrop and grassy plateau quite fitting for a stage. On cue, the delicate sound of the breeze and the hissing of insects emulated an audience and they could almost hear the bowing of a crwth.

Conversation throughout the campaign had taken almost every turn and no topic was off limits. Winter inquired about Mason's bachelor status.

Mason responded. "One object of affection felt I wasn't in good enough shape. Another preferred spending time with friends rather than with me. One claimed my wardrobe needed serious attention. Some were jealous, others brought out the jealousy in me." He paused, took a drink, and examined the horizon. "Those with jumpy personalities seem to be attracted to my relaxed demeanor. Closed off personalities are attracted to my openness. It's hard to make sense of."

"I respect that," said Winter. "I've been counted

out due to a scratchy beard! I drank too much for one, and not enough for another. Several times I was never given a reason. I've seen couples try to change each other. I've seen the scales out of balance, unrequited love. Have you ever had a hard time forgiving yourself?"

"Yes. I was full of guilt; stuck and struggling; trying to dig my way out. I remember long days and nights, feeling weary and losing heart. I was truly sorrowful. Shame is the Devil's game and he was right in my ear saying, 'you will NEVER find something this good again'. What to do? Well, I began to heal after I accepted my mistakes and I realized my weaknesses. I repented and then it was time for an important thing: to let go and let God take over. I vowed to improve and become a better version of myself. It moved me onto a better path and prepared me for what was next." He paused and transitioned to a lighter tone. "How about relationship politics? Is a given situation or activity good for both sides? Some like company, others solitude. One felt left out of my life."

"I was once accused of being manipulative!" put in Winter. "Honestly, sometimes there are fundamental differences. It can be hard to compromise. Sometimes it's a mistake to give things up you love even if there's pressure, other times a sacrifice of some variety is worth it!"

Mason reflected, "There are couple dynamics. Sometimes the relationship gets intense quickly, perhaps from differences in personality. Upbringing plays a factor. Nurture vs. nature. Birth order. In some cases, there are unresolved issues from past relationships. One might crave acceptance. Momentum can be hamstrung by poor self-image. If needs are unmet, a conversation must happen or you're living on borrowed time."

They continued their exchange as the path flattened and broke north. Recollecting past events was at times melancholy but it shortened the route. Judgment was reserved and pure honesty liberated them.

Winter inquired rhetorically, "What happens when you lose your attraction for someone? It's pretty rough! There could be other turn-offs: occupation, table manners, or even their hygiene! Perhaps they lack ambition, satisfied with mediocrity. Sometimes conversation is challenging, as when someone fails to express adequate interest in you or ask questions. Some are too strict and some have lifestyles that are hard to mesh with. Compromise is important yet taxing if someone is unwilling to budge. So many challenges: lack of similar interests, controlling behavior, addictions, stubbornness, opposing priorities, selfishness, conflict avoidance, and emotional abuse! Love can trigger retreat."

Mason added, "Don't forget spiritual life. Progress is difficult when it lacks this fundamental component. I am looking for an awesome set of values, and a huge heart; one who is very considerate, in a good place with their life, and loves God as well as them self! It takes two people fueling the fire to keep it burning. When that fails, beware. I've seen it before and now recognize the pattern. Timing is a funny thing. I do believe in love, without a shadow of a doubt. And despite what naysayers say, true love can even bloom again."

They finished their meals and chewed the waxy cells of honeycomb as gum. Winter swore by its ability to diminish seasonal allergies.

The westerlies picked up and they doubled their pace hoping to find shelter before dark. Through a gloomy, unfrequented district, they followed the obscured sun. Sugar pines, five hundred years old or more, stood with their armored limbs reaching for lonely elevations. They noted scents of peat and phlox. The chirping, knocking, and buzzing of concealed creatures rose and fell like ocean surges.

Winter detailed his excursion through an exotic archipelago aboard a xebec. He paused mid-sentence and thrust out his arm as a barrier. He turned and pointed into a dark green sancyuary. Chewing but otherwise motionless, a majestic red stag regarded them warily head held high. Its seventeen-pointed diadem pegged it for a rare and stately variety known as a monarch. They looked on with a sense of alacrity.

"You're never really alone in the forest," whispered Mason.

Easily five-hundred pounds and sporting a coarse red-brown coat, it was rare to behold a more graphic illustration of primitive grandeur. The parties stood at a distance of a few hundred paces, and though they held few physical similarities, Winter felt they were kindred, migrants in a more sublime world. Often referred to as the king of the forest, the red stag (or hart) was deemed the defender of all other animals. Sometimes an auspice, sometimes an omen, it appeared repeatedly on crests, badges, and flags. To some, it was thought to be endowed with mystic power and had the ability to evade capture. To others, it symbolized good will, peace, and contentment. One ancient tribe of warriors believed it was a messenger from another world. Either way, it was an emblem for sympathy, instinct, and kindness. Boughs groaned in the wind and suddenly, green hues swallowed the stag whole. It vanished as quickly as it appeared.

The travelers reflected on any and all stag lore: symbolism; historical significance; and its many appearances in art and culture. The encounter inspired creativity. Mason skillfully crafted lyrics and Winter engraved the stag's likeness onto a piece of bark.

In the late afternoon, the men traversed lonely heathlands bursting with lupines, gorse, and fuschia. Rounding a many-colored granite outcropping, they discerned the high-pitched rhythmic clatter of instruments, raised voices, and horses. They climbed a promontory for a superior vantage point, remained low, and observed. One or two miles ahead were the unmistakable silhouettes of a caravan and a band of motley vagabonds. The travelers descended the peak and proceeded with caution toward the camp. An outrider spotted them approaching and turned his horse.

"Let's suppress any references to the evil eye, please," cautioned Mason.

The rider wore a buff wool coat with gilt buttons and a rise-and-fall collar. His waistcoat was a patchwork of beige, white, and gray remnants. A curved talwar hung from his waist. Five inches across towards the end, its watered steel blade shone exceptionally bright as if hours had been put into the business of polishing it. Drab breeches were tucked into his leather boots—somebody in the camp was a cordwainer.

"What ho travelers," announced the rider in an amicable tone. "Do you have business with the people of this camp?"

"We have recently had council with the Overseers of Archia and seek peaceful passage to the north," explained Winter.

Upon hearing this, the rider dismounted and gave them a formal bow. His countenance brightened. "If this is indeed true, please join us and share any news from the north. My name is Darsh."

"Thank you for your kindness, Darsh. I am Mason and this is Winter. It is true; we are en route to the Black Mountains. Strange and peculiar times are upon us and certainly we have a mutual enemy." Sorrow and fear mingled on Darsh's visage. He swiftly mounted his horse and asked the cousins to follow him.

Patchwork hogans, striped canvas tents, and a variety of temporary living quarters made up the outer ring of the camp. A few individuals were at work assembling a shadow puppet theater. Winter had seen such structures before, where shadows would be projected on an illuminated screen. The puppeteer made modifications to his collection of leather puppets. Beside him rested a wooden box full of items for which to charm the ear—rattles, plates, and other bric-à-brac. The inner ring of the camp consisted of eight or nine subgroups of sojourners each with a horse-drawn vardo. The ornate mobile transports, all variations on a common design, were best viewed close up. Each had flamboyant spoked wheels, mollycroft roofs, and smoking chimneys. Porches built at their front ends featured carriage lamps, intricately carved molding, and footboards from which step ladders could be deployed. Their exteriors were adorned with baroque doors and windows, colorful weatherboarding, and wood paneling festooned with artistry. A few of the vardoes were decked with gilded rails and hinges.

Mason and Winter, who thought they might have walked onto the grounds of an asylum, were escorted to the center of the camp. Several dozen gypsies were engaged in loud, animated conversation and it appeared a musical performance was in the making. There were dancers, palm readers, bare-footed children, and troubadours. Heading the cast, if only by virtue of her opalescent crystal ball, was a fortune teller they called Madam Nisha. She bore the expression of a disapproving mother. Her ensemble included a head wrap with an ouroboros sarpech, a loose-sleeved peasant blouse, and a long colorful skirt. Bells jangled on her wrists and ankles. The blithe demeanor of the community was replaced with cold curiosity. Many whispered and pointed. Some glared contemptuously. *Who admitted these interlopers to the inner ring?*

Darsh blew into a shehnai and the hubbub died down. All eyes were fixed upon the two travelers who now appeared uneasy. "Ov yilo isi! Strange and peculiar times are upon us! *Romale tai Shavale, Churara tai wi Lovara.* It is my great pleasure to welcome these volunteers from Archia who have the burtă to challenge the mountebank of the Black Mountains—Calon Du himself!" Darsh raised his fist and up went cheers and howls as well as goblets, flasks, and wood cups. A streamer was hurled through the air. *"A la sature!"* Darsh shouted.

"Baxt hai sastimos tiri patragi," bellowed a man in the back of the throng. His patchwork vest and billowing tunic gave him a clownish aspect.

"Devlesa avilan!" cried a young woman whose long hair was ran through a shabby burgundy scarf.

An older man in a frayed tophat leaned close and said, *"Te khalion tai te shingerdjon che gada, hai tu te trais sastimasa tai voyasa."* Darsh translated, "May your clothes rip and wear out, but may you live on in good health and in fulfillment," he says.

Winter acknowledged the man with a smile and bow. Darsh turned to the wayfarers and said, "Please be our guest as long as you like; eat and drink to your heart's content. You are our friends as we are yours. If you must go, do not let us keep you. *Zhan le Devlesa tai sastimasa.* This means 'Go with God and in good health.'"

A trumpet blasted, a rin was struck, and the performance commenced. Gypsies believed that festivity with music and dance drove out evil forces. A man with a qānūn played exotic modalities while women in carnival masks danced in belt rattles, clashed finger cymbals, and swung castanets. Flutes, pan pipes, and rare old violins joined in with careless precision. A tortoise shell served as a percussion instrument as the throng stomped their feet and clapped their hands. All the while, a group circled the fray expanding and contracting their music boxes. The music was jangly and melodious, and had a bizarre, enchanting impact on the listeners. The dancers near the center responded to the music instantaneously. When a lone balladeer stepped onto a footstool and began a solo, others took up the melody. Here was the gist of what they sang:

Out in the hills of gold when the world was new
The hawk and the dove they built their home
Where the angels flew
One with a broken wing fooled the world
You should all know now it's time to go

Are you a decent man? Is your body numb when the day is done?
And if it's a cloudy day do you wish to play?
Do you still have fun?
One with a broken wing fooled the world
You should all know now it's time to go

Down in a silver mine this man has a plan for you
So follow the moonlight home and you'll be alright
You can pull on through
One with a broken wing fooled the world
You should know by now it's time to go

A cohort of chefs began distributed meat pies still smoking from the fire pit. The Archians accepted these while deciding between wheels of cheese, cabbage rolls, and sa-varină cakes. Winter filled his waterskin, declining many an invitation for stronger spirits. They took inventory and prepared for their trek to the Rhythm Tree.

Near the edge of camp a youngster, no more than six, approached Mason. The child had a leg length discrepancy and walked with some difficulty.

She tugged on his sleeve then asked innocently, "Are you going to save us from the bad man?"

Half a butterfly had been painted on her face, and like some earthbound angel, her expression was buoyant with hope. In response, Mason couldn't hold back a laugh. *Would I not happily risk my neck for this little urchin?*, thought Mason. A young woman, perhaps her older sister, watched apologetically with paint brushes in her hand. Mason took a knee and looked into the clear eyes of the moppet. He wasn't sure quite what to say but words instinctually came. "Yes, of course. We are going to save you and all the people here. And when we do, you will be the first to hear the full story. How does that sound?" The youngster smiled and when shyness took over and she walked back to join her sister. And in some way, perhaps known to all living things, they drew strength and bonded through a collective trauma.

Few hours of daylight remained when the travelers quit from the camp. As the tents dropped out of sight, they enjoyed the faint melodies of one last enchanting gypsy chorale:

Hey hey tales the wind told me

Can our heroes make a recovery?
Looking back on early times
At Waterfront there hangs a sign
And they sing
Softer than the rain
Softer than the rain

Hey hey, tales the wind told me
Dig it deep, don't risk discovery
Untold and not yet a crime
Throw anything, just throw them a line
And they sing
Softer than the rain
Softer than the rain

The men passed through an empty rolling meadow pulled from the pages of an artist's watercolor book. It was clothed in bluebells, orchises, and saxifrages, dotted with ponds, and marked by stout cottonwoods. They paused to consult Lokman's volume. According to its map, the Rhythm Tree was eight miles ahead. This would synchronize their rendezvous with the setting of the sun. The palavered about their points of contact, the Sea Stars. Questions arose. What knowledge would they impart? What would they look like? What were their motives? Mason speculated about their alignment and Winter their origins. Excitement was a thin veneer over apprehension.

In the early evening, the sky darkened to the west and a gloomy nimbus cloud formed. They guessed rain would arrive by late evening; shelter would be a blessing. The forest dells grew steadily thicker and more ancient as rare flora appeared. Mason and Winter stockpiled the largest leaves they could find hoping to keep their food dry. Here and there, earthy banks and scarps bulged from the ground. Hollow logs and snags were the haunts of rabbits, foxes, and flickers. Winter sang a marching song.

I know a place down, down the onion road
And I think it's time that this dirty old season closed

Strands of running water snaked through the duff and red admirals pursued wavering courses. Spiders found their way into the dark pockets of the bottomlands, preparing for evening meals by spinning delicate webs. It was no exaggeration to say the place was a thorough spectacle of the fantastic. Mason and Winter inspected an overturned chaise clothed in creeper and moss. It had been reclaimed by the forest from which its materials had originated. Having walked the appropriate distance, they sensed their proximity to the destination.

Light dwindled on the horizon as the travelers climbed atop a drumlin. There, in primeval grandeur, stood a colossal oak with countless serpentine branches—the Rhythm Tree. Like astronomical bodies orbiting a stellar remnant, Mason and Winter felt caught in its gravitational pull. They circled it slowly, tethered in the elliptic. Perhaps five hundred years old, it was a fortress both high and wide. Any observer would have been struck with awe by its magnificence. Compared to the Raven's Tower, the five hundred foot spruce, or the sacred fig Ilhan, its age measured in millennia not years, this was equally impressive, if not more. The branches of the Rhythm Tree grew in complicated trajectories; some even plummeted underground then reemerged above the detritus. Witness to natural disasters, nameless battles, and the passing of kings, it dwarfed its lanky neighbors and usurped their water and nutrients. On that cool evening, however, it was the setting of a most improbable meeting. Mason made a reference to the spirits that were said to protect the tree. A darkness began to cover the land and the travelers found an optimal vantage point from which they could await the arrival of the Sea Stars. Like a bard of the old breed, Mason began singing:

Well I came out this far
Just to see what I could find
Dancing on the roadside
And no mean river's going to change my mind

I was given a chance to be free
And I'm looking away from the city
I was given a chance to be loved
So I'm working my way to you

And I'll be running to the shuffle of leaves
Until the world stops spinning
Swinging from the Rhythm Tree
Until it breaks that day

Winter, unsure how long they would remain in waiting, began gathering branches for torches. Just then, something caught Mason's eye. Two faint points of light flickered in the woodsy depths and approached with the speed of a hunting dog. Plunging through the landscape the points drew ever nearer. Winter wondered if it was some abomination whose territory they invaded. Vexed, the men took battle stances and unsheathed their weapons. The burning points, now rectangular, pitched back and forth like pendulums as the unknown entity closed in. They heard pounding hooves and snapping branches. After a harrowing moment, they recognized the shape of a horse-drawn carriage. Without moonlight, identification was unfeasible unless safe distance was forfeited. The carriage, sleek and stylish, squealed to a halt near the Rhythm Tree's great trunk. The horses brayed as the hooded coachman climbed down from his perch. He opened the door and three women stepped out in quick succession. They spoke quickly in a foreign tongue, then lit candles and searched the clearing.

Spotting Mason and Winter one of them said, "Well don't go on hiding in shadows! Let's have a friendly introduction."

Another added, "See, I told you they would be here waiting for us. These are men of substance and patience, that much is clear!"

The third one added, "Only a minor misalignment of time and space. Hello friends! Come on down, there is much to discuss!"

"Good evening," said Mason as he and Winter stepped toward the carriage torches alight. As faces emerged, it was apparent no danger was present.

"I am Mason and this is my cousin, Winter. It appears our map has otherworldly accuracy. Lokman deserves much thanks; as do you for meeting us here."

"You are more than welcome! Please let us introduce ourselves. My name is Asterina and I am honored to meet you." She was tall and thin and wore an elaborate pagoda-sleeved dress sewn from varied mediums. There were layers of ornate orange wool, white lace galloons, gold and burgundy cheviot, and frayed fringe work of bright yellow and orange. Rows of reflective stones, glowing in the torchlight, had been sewn into the sleeves and bodice. Her pleated ankle-length skirt in shades of pink was embroidered with flowers and coiled gold designs. It was a sight to behold even in the dim torchlight, and must be even more striking in the daytime.

A short, burly woman stepped forward with a glowing candle. Her dress had several layers, the outermost was a green chiffon with a hand-stitched gold ivy pattern. The cuffs, cummerbund, and binding were a metallic orange. Three gold buttons and a crystal brooch were centered on the red vest underneath. "My name is Brisingida, a pleasure to make your acquaintances this evening. I am also honored to meet you."

The third woman, lean and muscular, spun around and took a bow. Her dress was a folded fabric design of orange, red, and yellow linen. Short-sleeved with metallic yellow cuffs, her shirt was ornate gold, and from her waistband hung a small fan. Her oversized sash ran across an orange silk blouse. She wore a gold and pearl diadem and necklaces of gold, copper, and jade. "My name is Valvatida. Is it too much to shake the hands of heroes?" she inquired.

The three women exchanged looks then spoke in unison, "We are the Sea Stars." Neither Mason or Winter were used to this degree of formality, but they were entertained by it. The coachman who fed the horses from a small bowl introduced himself as Javin. The party moved to an area with fallen trunks of trees, more suitable for a conference. A fire was lit and viands were set out.

"We know you have been on the road many days and nights and you will be for many more. Take this porter cake, which will multiply your strength," explained Brisingida. She handed it to Winter with a look of wisdom and kindness. He wrapped it in the leaves of an empress tree and stowed it.

Asterina addressed the issue at hand, raising her voice as the wind picked up, "For some time, we have been following the rise of this dark-cloaked devil, Calon Du. We knew him decades ago when he was but an orphan. He troubled us then, but now the unthinkable has happened—the wanton destruction of two peaceful cities. What he may not realize is how many adversaries he has awoken. We have ridden many miles to assist you in every way we can."

Mason spoke. "It will take every bit of assistance we can find. We believe in our mission; we have a function. As we know, overthrowing his fearsome army is an unprecedented challenge. How can it be done?"

107

Leaves swirled and whipped about as Valvatida leaned in. "In search of your answer, follow the less traveled road. Feel with your eyes and look with your heart. Gusts will guide you. Rocks will roll at your command. A solitary bird with the voice of a lion will fly with you toward the mountain. You have a strong Faith. Remember the words of Lokman."

It was Brisingida's turn. "Through the ages, music has inspired and provided hope. It's an ancient art! Older than the landscapes, older than the waves. Music kindles love and soothes. But it can do much more! It has played a role on the grandest of stages. Great artisans have perfected the instruments through which its power can be wielded. It has an incalculable array of voices, from the shell horn, to the guitar, to the drum. It speaks to warriors and wayfarers alike in a language easily understood. You Mason, are a gifted musician. Draw on your talent."

Again, Mason and Winter sought a bounty of definitive tactics and actionable steps. The Sea Stars did not offer those but there was something powerful in their lexicon. They had faith the cousins would emerge as victors.

Asterina took a small silk bag from her pocket and untied its string. "As a guitarist, you know how vibration and amplification work. A pick simply amplifies the sound of strings. Depending on the material and what properties it's endowed with, a pick can magnify sound to unearthly levels. This is a gift for you, please accept it." She handed him a a guitar pick made of pure gold. It had one distinguishing feature: a cross cut through its center. Mason studied it in the firelight. It was thick, un-bending, and seemed capable of slicing straight through the strings of any guitar. He looked at the women and smiled, unsure how the item could be advantageous in the days ahead.

"Finally," continued Brisingida, "it will do you well to make a stop at Castle Rook and Falchion Forge. They are expecting you. There you will find additional aid and supplies before your last push up the mountain. Let's hope you can reach Black River before more chaos unfolds."

Both parties wished the meeting could last longer, but the wind howled and an open clearing was hardly the place to loiter. The fire was extinguished. Under an active sky, formal goodbyes were exchanged and the women boarded their coach.

Dark clouds swirled formless and frenzied as if mixed by a gigantic dipper. The men looked for shelter as the first fat drops hit their skin. More fell, and more still, culminating in an all out cloudburst. The derecho tumbled in, twisting and turning like a parade of colossal acrobats. Mason occupied his mind with the images and rhymes of classic verses.

I am the sunset. I am the storm in your crystal ball.
I am the rain song, make your flowers grow
Whoa five feet tall, yeah

I am the tin man, heavy parts but there is no heart
I am the face upon the moon you know,

Whoa, here we go!

I am the magic puzzle piece
Free from the frame that calls my name
I am the magic puzzle piece but you can't find me

Under tension, they dashed from tree to tree with their coats over their heads. One direction was interchangeable with another, and the travelers might have cut an enormous circle had it not been for Winter who spotted a cluster of lights. Like night animals, they set forth toward the settlement.

Chapter 6

The Dragonhead

**The storm - The Dragonhead - Open stage -
A conversation - Escape - The ranger station -
A wrangling**

Under the storm's anvil, bolts of lightning cut across the night like white veins through black marble. Thunder spoke in its many voices, from ethereal splinters to violent terminal rumblings like falling towers. As the squall line advanced overhead, the force and fury of nature was unleashed—elemental, overpowering, beyond wonder. Progress was sluggish. Trees and animals were whipped to the core while the landscape flickered between alabaster and silhouette. The rain fell dense and unwieldy and pools of water formed on a duff with no capacity to absorb more. Pressing through the wall of water, the men were like aquatic creatures navigating the stygian depths of a lagoon. Their clothing and packs were waterlogged and twice their normal weight. Mudslides swept away anything not deeply rooted as the primeval turbulence of the storm raged on, both creator and destroyer. The travelers lumbered past dark slick shades of purple and green, moving closer to the cluster of lights. Winter leaned toward Mason and with a raspy voice said, "Cutters and card tricks! I've neither seen nor heard the likes of this; I think my spleen washed away back there some-where!" Mason's visage was one of stern concentration as he stepped over and around downed branches. Listening to the hum of the copious outpouring he thought it ironic to be thirsty.

In due course, the travelers stumbled upon a slick muddy road bordering a hillside of modest homes and steeples. Thunder pealed from the sublunar plane. Breathing heavily, they disregarded a mercantile and a bakery and headed for a third building—a well-lit pub called The Dragonhead. They leaned into the massive oak door, tired and utterly drenched.

They gathered themselves at the threshold and took in the scene. It was a popular venue for a night beset with torrential rain. Patrons reveled in song, dance, and ale. Strange decor caught their attention.

"Based on the horseshoe over the door and the wall of catfish skulls, they take their immunity to witchcraft and enchantment seriously," muttered Mason.

The proprietor spared no expense on elaborately carved woodwork, etched glass, and highly decorative ceilings. A well-engineered stage sat against the far wall where a sign board read: OPEN STAGE EVERY WEEK—RAIN OR SHINE. To their left stood an inviting hearth; to the right ran a lengthy bar; tables, ornate booths, and a dance floor made up the remainder. An intense game of Nine Men's Morris was underway at one table and the soaring melodies of a madrigal prompted a group galliard.

The travelers drew looks ranging from quizzical

to neutral though someone had the kindness to hurl a dry towel their way. Rainwater pooled under Mason's boots and Winter wrung out his hat. With what strength remained in their legs, the cousins moved to the hearth to warm up and recuperate.

"Would think less of me if I fell facedown?" joked Winter.

They made their presence negligible and by instinct remained on high alert for Calon's thugs. They set their boots, tunics, and overcoats on a drying rack. A server brought warm bannock, vegetable beef stew, and dark ale at their behest. In time, a pleasant numbness of mind and body set in, and the cousins savored the musical performances and the rustic hospitality.

During the brief entr'acte, loud drunken voices and ro-guish laughter bounded from wall to wall while an acoustic trio stepped onto the stage. Possessed of aplomb and famous to more than just their friends and family, the trio adjusted their gear then initiated quick flashes of folk fingerwork. These words accompanied their romp:

Pulled into a bar in a mountain town
Music was playing, sun was going down
Her eyes on me and I mean eyes like a black-eyed crow
Dark cloud on its way son, take a good look around

Walked into a bar in Victoriatown
Music was playing, sun was going down
Draft in my hand and I mean a draft like a hurricane
A storm is on its way son, take a good look around

Stepped onto the stage in a fantasy
Music was playing and they remembered me
Blonde at the bar and I mean a blonde like you never seen
Now you know that it's desire
Stand back from the fire that's in me

When the tune ended, the minstrel at stage left unhooked her oud, stowed it, and replaced it with a fine purple guitar inlaid with a moon and stars. Her elaborate silver carcanet and matching earrings gave her an air of royalty. Shirtless under a black and silver paisley vest and donning tight black leggings and high heel boots, she flipped her blonde hair pretentiously. The males swooned, one feigning a blackout. A young man at the stage's apron placed a full flagon of wine near the minstrel's feet. The troubadour at stage right, decked in a white leather jacket and charcoal boots and trousers, arose from his seat and replaced his dulcimer with a horse head fiddle. He twisted its pegs and plucked its strings with his ear to the sound hole. The cavorters called out for another tune, impatient and ready to dance. An athletic young woman took center stage donning black leather britches and a dark flared-sleeve blouse. Her fuchsia jabot matched the color of her full lips. A long-tailed overcoat with silver embroidery completed her aristocratic look. With a bright smile she thanked the crowd, asked if everyone was enjoying the show, and complimented the previous performers in a strong even alto that easily reached the entrance.

"This is going to be a thrilling evening. My name

is Reina, and this is my talented sister, Karaliene." She paused for applause then added, "a multi-instrumentalist since she was five years old." More applause. "To my right, our talented troubadour, Gazi. Astounding vocal performance on the first number!" Someone threw a rose on stage and Reina laughed. A percussionist joined the trio and in his hand he toted a bodhrán embellished with rune symbols. "We are Little Queens!" A slow ballad with menacing minor arpeggios poured from Karaliene's guitar. The tempo was further established, and over beefy staccato chords, Reina cast her lyrical spell with inimitable power:

They burned down the castle
That I used to call my home
Even the meat that was left
Had been picked to the bone
I went down the village
Looking for a place to stay
Maybe I'll grace the Dragonhead
Since I'm down this way

The frayed ends of yesterday
Tying up my mind
A letter comes from tomorrow
Delivered sealed and signed
I went down the village
Looking for a place to stay
Maybe I'll grace the Dragonhead
Since I'm down this way

They sing the battle hymns
And hunt the Wendigo
Their hooves a-hammering down
In the valley below
They haunt the black pools
Cross the great divide
They seek the brotherhood
The Dragonhead provides

Mason leaned toward Winter, "This has to be one of the finest acts I've seen in years. Their talent and stage presence are extraordinary. And what a voice—do you recognize her?"

Winter shook his head and declared, "I do not! But what good fortune to have the storm push us this direction. 'Burned down the castle', indeed!" The third and final song from the trio was yet another grand statement and a host of patrons sang its infectious melody as the final notes rang out.

A few acts later, the travelers retrieved their dried clothing and relocated to an enclosed booth. Mason admired its carved flora, scale mail patterns, and cherubim—the unmistakable work of a journeyman. Winter made a comment about the rarity of a walled booth with a private door. Padded leather benches were a welcome luxury and the etched glass windows added further panache. The high walls of the booth allowed them to keep a low profile.

On stage, a tall man plucked the strings of a kinnor with confidence as he seduced the audience with virtuosity. Winter directed the conversation toward the exchange with the Sea Stars and the mysterious gold guitar pick they bequeathed Mason. Questions arose. What special power was in its design? Where should it be used? Why were the instructions so vague? Mason, the musician of the two, knew the responsibility of working out those details fell on him. They bandied ideas around but no solid theory presented itself. On the plus side, good progress was made on the day and the porter cake was still dry and in one piece. The next thing they knew, a middle-aged man with a pageboy haircut approached their booth and peered over the top.

"I'd be remiss if I didn't greet the two road weary travelers who were caught out in that bear's cage. I'm the proprietor, Quinn. Can you spare a moment?" He waited with a self-effacing smile.

The travelers sent telepathic thoughts. Winter believed some knowledge about the area would help; Mason sought a recommendation for lodging. It was a judgment call, but the man was invited inside. Quinn wore a crushed velvet tunic, a broad belt, cotton breeches, and boots of fine leather. A dirk and a leather sporran hung from his belt. By Mason's observation, he dressed the way a prosperous merchant or banker might.

Mason responded, "We appreciate your civility. My name is Wallace and this is Macolm. What can you tell two traveling musicians of our whereabouts?"

On stage, the tall thin man switched to a finely crafted pipa with silvery strings. His fingers produced exotic strains evoking imagery of far-away lands.

Quinn replied, "Ah, that question deserves a well constructed answer! Allow me to provide a spoken word tour. You're visiting a lonely part of the north. From the hill behind us, one can look over the forests of Tân Brenin to the south or into the heights of Dalton and Darkstone to the north. On a clear evening, it's possible to spy the faint contours of Castle Rook and Chessfield far to the northwest. The ridges and cirques of the Black Mountains can be seen if facing east. But as most know, that is a turbulent area these days." He paused to read the traveler's faces, but they offered no hints and told of no concealed purposes.

Quinn continued, "To the west is a friendly region called the Empire of Knorr, recognizable by graceful green slopes and farmlands that run along the Ichor River. The people there have a sweet sing-song dialect marked by glides in pitch from high to low. To the south is Utley where, in a lost age, King Tarik mustered his entire army and besieged its greenswards, plundered its silver and gold, and enslaved its women and children. We are descendants of those very slaves." Mason, feeling green, was impressed by this wealth of knowledge, and Winter felt it was the perfect sort of candor for a rainy night.

Quinn went on, "Continuing westward, one passes over an ancient trade route along which herbal remedies, fragrances, and woven fabrics traveled to and from what was known as The Crownpoint Exchange. Bending in a southwesterly direction, signposts point to Hunters-gate, where traveling musicians like yourselves can follow the 'Sacrum Cor' route to Whitecourt and Mountain Iron. One stop further is Roundfort, home of the famous songstress Síocháin. Erlewine, to the north, is an idyllic farming province nicknamed 'The Threshing Floor'. Cattle with bronze clappers walk single file through its sleepy hamlets and sturdy oxen drag ploughs through its fields. Jewelhead sits on the tranquil terrain of the westlands where strongholds of storied royal families are found every way the compass points. A few miles further west is the toymaking town of Logan, diminutive itself, much like its hand-crafted designs. There, spectators can watch toy races, listen to poetry readings, and participate in wood carving workshops. These eccentric toymakers produce a wide array of products with their sights set on the grandest scales!"

Winter and Mason wore expressions of fascination and reverence as their minds filled with scenes from the strange and wild hinterlands. The crowd had thinned but those made of sterner stuff continued dancing and singing as if there was no tomorrow.

"So have you lived in this area your entire life? Born and raised?" asked Mason.

"Forsooth, there is no place I'd rather be and no place more dear to my heart! Allow me to share a few more nuggets of knowledge. Past Logan, the town of Belltower was once the meeting place of the High Priests of Halcyon. There was a time when few visited the area, but today its chapels, styled with narrow clerestory windows, provide inspiration for artists and painters. The steep inclines just a few miles north of the town provide more panoramic views. It was here the famous scientist Adronicus, while peering into the upper sphere of the cosmos, laid claim to a comet. Drama ensued when the naming rights were ripped away and associated forevermore with a rival sky watcher. As it turned out, Adronicus was second to report it. Next up, head south via a narrow track to Moongate and the adjacent marsh-lands where The Queen of the West held sway some eight hundred years ago. More recently, it has become a fashionable locale for hunters of meteorites and other rare minerals. From the nearby crossroads, it's a short dash to a circle of quaint cabins. This is Bull Creek, named for the Bull of Bashkin, a warrior whose ancestry traces back countless generations, ultimately connecting two royal bloodlines. A ragged route leading south from Bull Creek cannot be found on any map, but those aware of it can save much time traveling to the cities of Meadowbrook and Birchcrest. Westbound, past traces of fallen empires, a giant carved eagle casts its eye over Archtop, a city known for its production of ancient stringed instruments such as the psalterion. Melody Lake, further west, is home of the famed library and research facility Parasol Park, so named for its domed buildings. Its neighbor to the north, Shaw's Pleasance, is the birthplace of Rowan "Hawk" McGrath, famous barrister from the House of Hands, who was taken up to heaven in a whirlwind. From here, well-maintained roads run to Copperhead and Camp Crow Wing—both world-class locations for trout and walleye fishing. Past golden blankets of wheat in Harvest Valley, stands Braemar, where Atakin defeated Ulu the Giant. It has the largest subterranean cave system this side of the Black Mountains and is also home to an international archery tournament. Its church tower was once part of a signal beacon network which included the belfries of Abbeyhill, Hamline, and Warroad. In the days of the Ghost Brigades, watchers in the lookouts sent smoke signals in the daytime or lit fires at night to warn of invaders."

A student of historical nuance and reference, Winter appreciated Quinn's spoken word tour. "We surely thank you for your insights and comprehensive coverage. Along the routes you mentioned, I imagine there are places where traveling musicians could find work performing in pubs and bialanns? I've heard farms and kitchens often hire migrant workers for honest wages or in exchange for lodging," he said with an enthusiastic tone, playing his part to perfection.

It was Mason who took note of an old rover through the booth's etched glass. Out of earshot and casually leaning against the hearth, this person of interest was the only patron who had a clean view into their booth. The rover's attention, however, was presently on his bent wooden tobacco pipe. He cleaned its chamber, packed it, lit the end with a matchstick, and took test draws. His long gray locks obscured his face and a sugar glider peeked out of his shirt pocket—perhaps to sell an air of benevolence. Mason thought about discussing Calon Du with Quinn, but momentarily decided against it; for now his attention was squarely on the long-haired stranger. Winter read concern on Mason's face.

The time had come for the final performance of the evening. A woman stepped on stage, opened a colorful horse bag filled with tabla and damaru drums, and busied herself in the preparation of a percussion station. Her beret, cape, and cambric shirt and pants were shades of deep green. A piper appeared wearing a red tartan kilt, a gold-buttoned doublet, knee-socks, and a bear skin hat. A sgian-dubh hung from his belt and the gaida he held was crafted from goat pelt, silver, and polished fir. A red-bearded blind man toting a nyckelharpa made his way to the front of the stage where he adjusted sheep gut strings. The instrument was a rare specimen. Narrow decorative purfling ran along its outer edge and the fingerboard was constructed of ebony and pearl. His apparel included a cloak, mechant cap, and puffy sleeved undercoat. Mason, who noticed a langspil slung across his back, was captivated by yet another multi-instrumentalist and the presence of so much elite talent.

The players kicked off a vibrant melodia, a true departure from the dreamy descants of the previous acts. Exuberant dancing ensued and soon it boiled over into celebration. The drummer's improvised lyrics described mythical marvels, the foibles of fate, and love's temperamental whims. Wails rended the air. The doorman broke up a sloppy drunken fight and sent two hooligans into the damp night still twisted up in a wrestling hold.

It was time for a prudent course of action. With a nod from Mason which held a dash of telepathy, Winter leaned toward Quinn. "Hold any sudden movements, but do you recognize the pipe-smoking rover near the hearth? He could be taking an interest in our conversation." Giving a wink, Quinn rose from his seat and moved to the bar where he used the mirror's reflection to obtain a clean view of the individual. *How resourceful,* thought Winter.

The proprietor returned with his report, "No one I have seen in the establishment before, but I'm picking up a slightly black bouquet—if you catch my meaning?"

This was the subtlety Mason awaited; trust flourished. Winter and Mason quickly gave Quinn an abridged explanation of their mission, correcting their aliases and revealing their true occupations.

The proprietor lit up. "Praise the Lord. That's the best news I've heard in all my days," he exclaimed, a tear welling up in his eye. "If the rumors are true, factions aligned with your cause are forming in Chessfield and Maple Hill West," he whispered excitedly. "You're sure to find collaborators there. If you choose to head that direction, ask for a man who goes by the name of Zero." Quinn provided the travelers with an alternate route to the cities, he insisted it was almost wholly unknown and typically free of raiders. It was time to take advantage of the jamboree and end the evening on a high note.

"An inconspicuous exit would be a prudent safety measure. Is there a second door?" inquired Winter. He tapped his carved whistle on the table top, a gesture Mason promptly decoded.

Quinn complied, "The window in the men's privy or through the kitchen behind the bar. As for shelter, there's a secluded ranger station just east of here; you are welcome to it. I will have supplies dropped at the door. We small town proprietors are all too often deemed swindlers and miscreants, I hope to break from those social mores. Now go Archians. Godspeed!" Their new ally excused himself.

The three men slowly dispersed into the room. Mason's exit included the theatrical measure of walking by the rover, passing the hearth, and ultimately pressing into the dancing throng before his closing gesture to the privy. Winter's retreat was methodical. He stood watching the musical performance with an empty mug pressed to his chest. He edged toward the servers' entrance to the bar awaiting the right moment—a magician can sense these things. Even under the most scrutinous vigilance, anyone could have missed him crouch, pivot, and duck step behind the bar, then swiftly gain the kitchen and finally the back door. Phantomlike, he vanished into the mesic forest. Mason was not far behind, throwing his leg over the windowsill and lowering himself to the ground. He crouched, listened for nearby footfalls, and moved away from the exterior wall. The hooligans who had been thrown out and continued their heated exchange in the road, made for a needed diversion. Mason took soft backward steps increasing his distance from the pub, then turned and sprinted for the tree line.

Winter moved stealthily eastward and listened. He filled the chamber of his carved whistle with water, then breathed into it softly. It produced a bubbly chittering—the likeness of a raccoon. Mason followed the sonic beacon and caught up with Winter near an old well. They took strategic positions a few hundred feet apart and canvassed the forest in search of the ranger station, all the while punctuating their progress with measured westward glances. There was no one in their field of vision.

After the storm died out, a quarter moon sailed behind frail rows of clouds and crystal light dripped down from the stars. With the help of this luminosity, the travelers discovered the secluded ranger station where they paused and took up the exercise of confirming they were alone. Succeeding an observational interval, they unlocked the door, stepped inside, and lit a small candle. There were two beds in the station, each equipped with wool padded mattresses—welcome upgrades from the packed earth they had been sleeping on. An assortment of bladed weapons filled a wooden crate but the rest of the room was empty.

Within the hour, Winter spied a rider on a sleek charger. The men prepared for the unknown, holding their blades in ready positions. But there was no reason for alarm; the rider dismounted and left a canvas bag near the door then galloped into the sylvan depths.

"Quinn is a man true to his word," commented Mason who retrieved the items. Inside was a carefully curated assortment of foodstuff and medical items— fat figs and prunes (good for the bowels), several kinds of bread and cake, a waterskin, apples, a cheese wheel, beans, a flask of ale, turkey meat, horsetail and moonwort (to staunch bleeding), ash tree leaves (for the bites of snakes), willow bark (for pain, fever, or inflammation), violet oil (to soothe and comfort skin), juniper (to counteract poison), lavender oil and mint (to calm the nerves), marshmallows (to ease coughing) and the leaves (for bee stings), primrose (for wound healing), several candles, soap, and bandages. They would take what they could carry and leave the rest. Tomorrow's journey would be of an unpredictable sort and they were intent on replenishing their energy. They barred the door and soon fell asleep.

BIn the crisp air of twilight, two death squads under Calon's direction prepared for a strike on the ranger station. Their mission was simple: eliminate the Archians. If they failed, they were instructed to never show their faces in Black River again. They racked up their horses near a copse of birch trees so as not to alert their opponents. Approaching from the east, the assassins closed in on their targets wielding pikes, maces, and throwing daggers. Crickets stopped chirping as they edged closer.

Mason and Winter remained in a deep sleep and by anyone's estimation, they stood little chance against the lean and muscular death squads. Clothed in black military gear, the assailants expected to easily dispatch the sleeping men with their vile brand of slaughter.

Suddenly, a feathered silhouette appeared against the deep blue vault, banking hard on a towering thermal. It was the director of downdraft, the sachem of the stoop, the overseer of the ozone—Mica the Peregrine! Gauging distance precisely, the raptor missed no detail as she surveyed from above. The squads were within a few hundred paces of the station when Mica made her move. Downward she plunged toward the small shelter and pulled up onto the windowsill on the far side. She pecked incessantly at the glass with her beak and let loose a distinctive, hoarse screech. Several more followed.

Upon hearing this alarm, Mason awoke and rolled to the floor griping his dagger. He moved fluidly to the west window looking past Mica and toward the horizon. "Good girl", he whispered. He saw nothing but dark tree trunks.

Winter had moved to the opposite wall, blades in both hands. He raised his head and peered through the glass, scanning the eastern woods. A moment or two passed. He spotted several approaching figures, then more appeared. In a blink, there was a force of ten, then over twenty. "Oh calamity!" he mumbled. His heart raced and his limbs became rigid. Leaning against the wall and looking toward Mason he wondered if his life had run its course. Fate had other plans.

Forthwith, the astonishing occurred, too profound to comprehend. Mason crouched against the bed frame head bowed, hands folded. Winter theorized. Had he forfeited? A man simply awaiting the death stroke? Winter heard him speak, but the sound was deep and plodding, like the voice of a giant; time seemed to decelerate, seconds fanned into minutes, extra memories were forged. Someone shouted, but the voice was warped. Mason lifted his head and rose like some fabled conqueror who, enshrined in legend, had survived a hundred battles and was eager for the next. There was a look of still confidence on his visage and a calm that could rock a baby to sleep. Each of his boot steps rumbled and shook the rude earth floor. Mason handed Winter the porter cake and instructed him to eat it.

In an altered state, Winter followed Mason outside to the woodland arena where large branches and blowdown were strewn across the terrain. Spiderwebs hundreds of feet away could be seen in fine detail and there was a strange sense of quietness. The squads, whose armbands depicted shields with three silver arrows, appeared as stationary as chess figures.

From the perspective of the assailants, the scene was beyond bewildering. The Archians bore down on them as if slung from a catapult. Amid fleet flashes of steel, the first two lines fell. The third line spread out, but it was too late. One assailant was hurled into a tree, and two more looked down upon mortal wounds. Winter defeated four in a beautifully choreographed maneuver, disarming them expeditiously and delivering catastrophic injuries. Another line was dispatched with swift precision. A motion blur was the only trace of Mason as he weaved through the ranks like a threaded needle. The remainder of the squad was left in utter confusion; the fight was over before it began. One man fled pell-mell into the woods while the rest met their end before the morning sun had fully risen.

In his sprawling fortress on the Black River, Calon Du studied war plans and crafted schemes of dark design. Circling an elaborate diorama, he evaluated the previous week's efforts. The first phase of his expansion, code named LANCEHEAD, had met with his expectations, aberrant as they were. The out-and-out ransack of Ft. Kerr had several aims: to showcase his military might, inflate his dictatorial power, and continue the campaign of horror and hysteria. After the raid, little of the village remained; its homes reduced to ruin, its palisade fences left in blazing shambles. The diorama reflected this. As for the capture of Heddwich, the justification was two-fold: to test how far he could push his might before resistance mounted and it was a strategic base for his military. The second phase of his expansion, code-named WOLFSBANE, targeted Deering and Silverbridge. The capture of Deering would provide his Greyguard additional room for manœuvres, while Silverbridge's nearby deposits of iron and silver ore would allow for the manufacture of new weapons. Finally, the securement of these towns would shield Black River from an eastern attack.

Calon left little to chance. Under his able rule, intelligence procurement was a long-established invariant. His network of spies, known as the Ice Ring, was a battery of well-trained collaborators—in myriad occupations— who used false names and addresses. They sketched arsenals, strongholds, and key leaders. They reported on the strength and morale of resistance forces. They created charts on a variety of economic subjects. The whole of the accumulated data helped Calon keep the upper hand.

It was through this spycraft Calon first learned of Mason and Winter. Day by day, the upstarts from Archia gained further support and became cause for concern;

but their defiance would not be tolerated. When he was informed the Archians were sighted at a pub off Northgate Highway, the demonic Chamber dictator was confident the two travelers would not witness another sunrise. One of Calon's top emissaries patrolled the area. Though his pet sugar glider might suggest differently, the aged rover was ruthless, calculating, and immoral. He had authorization to utilize Calon's death squads any way he saw fit; a favorite tactic was the pre-dawn strike.

Prone to crack under even meager pressure, Calon diverted his mind by taking up his brush. In his mind's eye, he pictured an unknown location. He began with a pale pre-dawn sky and layered in limbs of dark coniferous trees. A small structure took shape. With each even brushstroke, the scene grew in detailed: a gloomy landscape, frail rows of clouds, a solitary bird in flight, an open clearing, and finally two men—the same two who made previous appearances on his canvases. It was the Archians, standing with heads tilted skyward. Calon wondered if it was the past, the present, or the future. He worked quickly, never knowing when his inner-visions might vanish. Paint spotted the floor and colors ran together as he raced to complete the image. To him, the prescient talent was inexplicable; it defied logic. Even a theory was hard to design. To the old mystic Elymas, Calon was a clairvoyant despite the fact his second sight was unreliable at best. And most of his paintings held no links to future events at all. Calon moved his brush mindlessly, lost in a labyrinth of musings. The last detail made Calon's skin grow cold. Five, six, then seven dark figures took shape; they laid in unnatural postures in a clearing; eight, nine, ten more. The entire squad had been wiped out! He snapped his brush in half.

Questions flooded Calon's mind. How was it possible that two men could defeat squads of his best assassins? It was rumored that the Archians found their strength in God. Is this what is meant by being looked upon with favor? Was an angel fighting with them? It all seemed absurd. Vexed, then angry, Calon ultimately found himself in the grip of something he thought he'd conquered a long time ago: fright. He disdained it; it reeked of his squalid childhood. The sound of a wind-blown leaf would have sent him into flight. He abominated his foes, for deep inside, he knew their faith was more dangerous than any weapon.

In the aftermath of the conflict, Mason and Winter surveyed the clearing. Having wreaked havoc upon twenty-six men, they basked in a glow of optimism. The sequence of events, which Winter retold enthusiastically, was too astounding to truly comprehend. As the sun's golden eye broke the horizon and their adrenaline subsided, they directed their attention toward what needed to be done.

Mason took a knee and chronicled their blessings. Deliverance from the storm and victory against enemies were paramount, but the list was long: flowing rivers where body and clothing could be cleaned, good health, waking under a sturdy roof, the kindness of strangers, Quinn and The Sea Stars, and the food and provisions they had received. Mason was evolving, growing, and learning how to bridle his fears. The death of old ways produced new life. He gave thanks for the journey's many challenges and a bounty of satisfying conversation. His cousin Winter was a gift straight from Heaven. He felt truly blessed.

Mason recited his priorities in order of importance: God, family, inspired living, protecting others, hobbies, and friends. God's word was a lamp that lit his path. His family remained in his thoughts. They encouraged and built him up, and he vowed to love them, make a difference in their lives, and never take them for granted. When inspired, he was at his best and pain and sadness had no home inside him. Music, art, meditation, and prayer were his sources. The work he undertook was not easy. With compassion and integrity he endeavored to safeguard the lives of those who shared his desire for peace. He vowed to utilize his creative passions; never to forget, ignore, or push them aside. He appreciated these gifts and the sense of accomplishment they provided. They made him the person he was. He aimed to engage in fellowship with friends and acquaintances. He hoped to extend himself and meet new people with regularity. Interaction kept his mind healthy and fresh.

Mason rose to his feet and found Winter sitting on a toppled tree, humbly postured. If he didn't know better, he would have claimed Winter was saying a prayer of his own. Elation struck Mason as he walked to the edge of the clearing. Winter lifted his pack to his shoulder and joined him. Somewhere in the forest depths they heard neighing horses.

"Let's see if we can't find ourselves a steed or two," announced Mason.

"They would quicken the journey to Chessfield," added Winter, optimism shining through.

The travelers cut eastward, tracking the sound of the animals. In a quiet secluded grove, twenty-six beautiful specimens stood roped to a copse of birch trees. There were restless thoroughbreds, stallions, and destriers. Some kicked and whinnied nervously with ears drooped back; some danced and brayed; some stood warily motionless.

Mason produced an apple from his satchel and stepped closer. Eying this, a flaxen chestnut stallion swished its tail rhythmically while his head made small circles. Mason grasped the stallion's bridle-rein and fed him the fruit. He inspected the horse for flaws or wear and tear from the road and rubbed him on the neck and shoulder. When the steed's vitality and fortitude increased, Mason untied him and gently climbed into the saddle. He shortened the reins and urged him out of the copse. The brown leather tack was of high quality. Horse and rider made a few wide turns then slowed to a walk. After a mix of gaits, to work the horse's muscles, it was time for a speed trial. Mason clucked, squeezed his legs, and encouraged acceleration into a canter. Soft on the reins, he rode in half seat. When he gave the cues for a full gallop they surged down the path. Mason floated in space as if propelled by the wind, which is why he decided to name the horse Monsoon. They returned to their starting point for a rest.

Winter, too, made a selection: a muscular mare with a blue roan coat and light dorsal stripe. Her headstall, collar, rein, and saddle were made of soft black leather. He stroked the mare on the cheeks and forehead. In time, a connection was made, and they settled in as a team. As a departing gesture, Winter stripped the remaining horses of their tack, cut their ties, and liberated them so they could freely roam the forest. He stepped into the stirrup, sat atop the saddle, and joined Mason outside the copse.

"I've studied Quinn's map to Chessfield, and have a general idea of the route. It should take us a fraction of the time on the backs of our new friends," explained Mason. He directed Monsoon west, back toward the ranger station. "We can pick up the trail to the northwest. And let's stay well out of sight and off the Northgate Highway."

"After this morning's melee, our pace needs urgency. When Calon gets wind of this, his retaliation is sure to be horrific," warned Winter.

"Count on it!" returned Mason. "The day has held good fortune. Let's pray it continues." The riders passed the shuttered Dragonhead where no trace of the previous night's lively entertainment could be found. They directed their mounts to an overgrown trail.

Chapter 7

The Art of Navigation

**Passage to Chessfield - Winter's tale - The natural arch
The plan - Emry - Night camp - A visitor**

The riders carved their way through wild woodland, soggy and overrun with tall grass, where only a ghost of a path existed. Quinn's assistance proved invaluable; the tract bore no trace of traffic. Crickets sounded like clashing swords and a lone cicada whirred enigmatically. Off in a lonely glen, stood the remains of a stone chimney, part of a one-time dwelling now reclaimed by the forest. Elderberry bushes and saplings nearly hemmed them in and the horses' tack accumulated twigs and bunches of leaves. Winter grumbled while he cleared them away.

In time, the ground leveled and became easier to navigate. A proper well-shaded trail emerged. They heard moving water somewhere nearby, but it was obscured by trunks and green-garmented branches. For a duration, conversation surrounded a valiant cardinal with a bright red plume. Mason wondered if it might permanently join their caravan.

Sometime later, they drew up along a small watercourse languidly which rippled through the terrain. No more than a couple horse lengths across, it swirled and blended swatches of blues, greens, and browns.

Healthy flora leaned over its gentle glides. Here, the trail cut through the vegetation like a plough fur-row, straight and neat. It was well suited for riders in single file such as they were. They lived in the now.

"Once, when I was a boy, I became lost in the woods," recalled Winter in a forlorn tone. He took a moment to patch together memories in their proper sequence. "I was looking for our dog who darted off in search of some spectre only he could see. I must have searched hours before I found myself at the edge of a millpond looking squarely at a cottage. It appeared to be abandoned. I remember its water wheel creaked from lack of maintenance. I approached the door and peered inside. Spiders and moths besieged the countertops and part of the ceiling was missing. Golden-green light cast wild patterns on the floor. Strange shadows quivered. In that moment, bravery outweighed fear and for some reason I was freed from thinking of my own safety." Winter laughed and looked into the stream. "I went inside to investigate. The floorboards were soft from moisture and in a spot or two I could have easily fallen through. In that mill I felt something; a presence; something not of this world. The room seemed to darken and my mind went blank. I felt as though I walked into the realm of something ancient; a forbidding place I did not belong. Now, this I can't explain: for a fleeting moment, I saw the shadow of a powerful horned entity with stout shoulders and gnarly limbs. Its shape blazed in my brain like it had stepped between me and a bonfire. My heart leaped and I turned and ran with all the strength I had, not looking back once. I fell a few times but eventually found my way to familiar territory. Ever since that day, I have wondered about good and evil. I have wondered about the supernatural world where rules of science do not apply. Like that thing that inhabited the old mill, I wonder if demons can inhabit people and enforce their will upon them."

Pondering the account, Mason gazed into a growth of reeds where pelicans waded. Sometimes Winter merely posed a question, not looking for an answer. He already had one. Mason drew a line from his account and their journey. They were headed straight into the realm of something ancient, something evil. "Yes they do," said Mason from a dreamli ke trance. "Yes they do".

The last moments of morning slipped away and the sun seemed to stall directly overhead. They followed a tunnel of foliage, rich and green from its proximity to the stream, where boughs undulated in a sublime choreography. Gold and lime sun rays fell from the broken canopy and ochre dust floated and swirled away in the wake of the horses. Crawling things in the dark patches of the embankment raced for cover. Their primitive brains perceived the travelers as strange entities with elemental strength. Bleeding heart, dahlia, and heliconia grew in abundance along the shadowy aisle.

From deep within a zoetic colonnade sprang the song of a wood thrush. Its complex melody held a hundred meanings, all of which were lost on the Archians. The rest of the wood listened as if spellbound. Each crystal salvo was distinct from the prior; first mournful, then manic, and occasionally spiraling into lunacy. Its songbook consisted of lamentations, fanfares, and carols, ordered randomly, the better to hold its audience captive. The horses returned an occasion whinny.

The path widened and the air filled with the sweet fragrance of gentian. There was a conversation about lunch and the horses needed a period of respite.

"I've been thinking about names for my charger," announced Winter. "What do you think of Black Star?" Mason agreed it was a fitting choice.

The travelers stopped near an old boat landing where weatherworn pilings leaned at unstable angles. Here, the forest thinned out. Winter removed his boots and walked through the stream where the horses drank. The slight grade they toured provided an extensive view of country to the south. A footpath ran toward a drowsy broch which stood hollow in the sunlight, robbed for its stone and timber. Mason imagined a busy workday within its curved walls where each occupant mastered their individual trade; the blacksmith, the baker, the seamstress. The broch's very existence rested upon the coordinated efforts of a team. It was the same for their undertaking. Winter found oats in one of the saddlebags and fed the steeds. They looked healthy and strong. The travelers prepared sandwiches, cut up a cake, and reposed against the bole of a gigantic oak.

Winter digressed. "This looks like several trees merged into one. If crosscut at waist level, it could seat at least twelve!"

The task ahead weighed heavily on their hearts, but in moments like this, they drew up energy and stored it. As the shadows leaned further east, they mounted up.

It was midafternoon. They rode a mountain grade through a natural depression, descending by degrees. The stream diminished, dwindled, and soon was no more than a rivulet dribbling down from somewhere up in the tree lined heights. An insubstantial fence had been constructed in places where the path's shoulder was precipitous. Mason looked down over the edge and whistled. A hawk circled down there. Onward they pressed into the dream-drowned valley, past grassy swales, granite scarps with quartz veins, and dirt embankments where tree roots protruded. The sky was bleached turquoise from horizon to zenith. It seemed to fold up as they moved further down into the valley. Wayside hiking trails both advanced and moderate climbed up into the timberlands. Mason noted a kind of clearing about a half mile ahead where the elevation was lowest. He pointed it out to Winter.

"I remember it from the map", explained Winter. "From there, my guess is we are a quarter day ride from Chessfield. We should arrive around sunset."

"Good timing. Sequestering outside the city for another night would be justified. Tidings of our encounter at the Dragonhead may reach the city by morning, and our allegiances there have not been established." Mason, trailing, inspected Winter's horse and fixated on the hooves. "Black Star could use a good farrier, and the same for Monsoon. Let's find one in the morning. They should have nicer shoes than ours!"

The path had shifts and curves and it wound down

through the canyon like a great serpent. There were no milestones or signposts. A cottontail took a position of vigilance further ahead and gave a sidelong glance to the riders, half curious, half fearful. It sat upright gnawing on a leafy morsel, then sidestepped back into the brush as they approached—gone so completely to never have existed at all. Juniper and oak dominated the straightaway to the clearing and Winter noticed layers of violet and magenta in the adjacent ledges. He speculated they were amethyst deposits. *Perchance one day I'll return to build a quarry,* he thought.

Rounding a turn, a grand forested bluff came into view, its crest higher than a cathedral gargoyle. Mason scanned its rocky spine down to the horizon where it fell from view. *The valley must go deeper still,* he thought.

"The stream may have diverted down there," he guessed aloud. The horses seemed to know where to go and were just as eager to get there as the riders. The party followed an old fence and a barrier of hackberry and alder which obscured a ravine.

Winter and Black Star cantered ahead, took stock, then returned and found the trailhead. "The path must curve back underneath us. I can see it continue down in the valley on the far side. Must be a quarter mile long or so?" he guessed.

"The outrider has officially been elected," proclaimed Mason. "Add it to your long résumé. On we go!"

They descended into the evergreen gorge. Occasional stone steps and a fairly developed path helped the horses maintain their footing. To the left was a high travertine wall with saw toothed strata in umber, gray, and orange. They rode down, as if through time, toward a primeval place where the world began. There was a precipice to the right and both riders instinctively leaned away from it.

"That's a powerful long drop!" exclaimed Winter.

Silktassel and sumac bushes crowded the already narrow space. They switched back at a rocky landing and began to hear flowing water; then, a hollow rushing noise, like air moving through a hallway, or a conch shell placed to the ear. At a complicated portion, the riders dismounted and guided the horses around boulders and stumps. They determined it was best to proceed on foot.

When they reached the nadir, they followed the path along a creek to a place where they could fully appreciate the splendor of a towering natural arch. What was once the ground they trod upon, was now the roof of a tunnel. Stalactites, sculpted over millennia by erosion, decorated the cylindrical walls and hung from the arch's dome like fangs. The entire landform was easily two-hundred feet high and over five-hundred feet long. An eagle, indifferently observing, balanced atop a rock ledge and watched them advance. Mason had the notion the eagle might be one of Calon's familiars. At times caution verged on paranoia. The men navigated decayed timber, weathered rock, and flooded gaps. Tunnels and hovels disappeared into travertine. Mason stepped into a vast chamber, cool and cave-like in aspect, and swiveled his head in awe. Droplets floated down from high atop the arch forming the faintest of waterfalls. The clatter of hooves, movement of currents, and whispering wind echoed throughout the passage, weaving a fabric of sound that enchanted the ear.

"A choice locale for a short rest. We're out of the elements, and there's flat surfaces to lay upon," observed Winter guiding Black Star into the shade. "It feels like the haunt of a dinosaur. Perhaps it still is," he laughed. The horses dipped their tongues into a shimmering green pool. Mason knocked out a quick sketch and description in his journal.

"I'd like to design a woodcut from that sketch. Better yet, I'll make a cartload and sell them. Royalties split of course," offered Winter. Mason suggested a price tag much too low for Winter's taste, as many artists are wont to do. With some degree of compromise, they settled upon a figure before falling asleep.

Revived upon waking, the travelers made for the egress on the far side. Cascades showered them. The scenic marvels influenced their attitudes and tasks and labours seemed temporarily minimized; peace can be fleeting but they found good portions of it in that place. Mason greeted the scene with a traveling canto he penned as a youth:

There was a place in my mind where the sun shined
But now the rain's so thick I'm blind
There was a place in my soul where the sky was blue
What kind of blue, blew out kind?

So today just like any other day

The bright sun was out of view
Yeah today just like any other day
Was a dirty old summer too

I took a walk down on the beach (yeah)
And you can hide on the other side
You see the good Lord made her deep
But he chose not to make her wide

So today just like any other day
The bright sun was out of view
Yeah today just like any other day
Was a dirty old summer too

As he sang the last few bars, they cleared the landform and rode back out into the warm light of the day star. Winter made an inquiry into the lyrics of the song to which Mason provided a backstory.

"Strong melody line, that one. It'll be stuck in my head! Not a bad thing now," stated Winter. He looked off in the distance, then back to the arch and smiled. "You know back at that sheer drop off, it was funny. Reminded me of the time I watched someone climb a champion cottonwood. That tree must have been sixty or seventy feet tall and here was this young man scrambling up it in search of a toy. Barefoot too! I wondered if he was intoxicated. A few of us stood watching from the balcony of a house. My stomach dropped and I had to turn and walk inside. He was too far up. I couldn't watch," he whimpered. This was classic Winter. So much communicated in tones of concern, disgust, and silliness; ingredients he measured and adjusted as he gauged the reaction of whomever his audience happened to be. He was a true storyteller regardless of subject.

The path widened, the creek dwindled, and they began their gradual ascent out of the valley. Steady they rode the gulch's dry creek bed void of distinguishing features save for the occasional rocky outcropping. The deeds of the day were marked adventurous if not downright gutsy and the company remained steely visaged and set in purpose like heroes from ancient genealogies. The journey had cured them of a blindness and misplaced sense of purpose. They too, in a way, perished at the ranger's station that morning; died to their old ways, their selfishness, their idleness, their complacency. Hard living heightened endurance. Soft living, free from pain and fear, led to low tolerance. Fear, ill-shaped and many limbed, awaits where limits are pushed. It stares back from its own dingy corner all the while tethered to its host—all-seeing, all-reckoning, all-consuming. But that day the Archians looked straight and unwavering into that dingy corner and squared off. They thrust light there, they saw fear could be restrained—if not totally vanquished—and let fate's gears turn as they must.

Left and right their path rambled, each uphill turn laced with weariness. As the steeds picked their way over rough ground, a thin cloud passed the sun, wandering much like their own thoughts. There were periods of soaring hopes and periods of stifling terror when faith collapsed. On occasion, life-like figures appeared ahead on the trail, only to become mundane shapes of trees or bushes; atmospheric illusions emulated their uncertainty. They traded the security of Gardenwall for an unpredictable journey to Black River which weighed on Mason in irregular intervals. At times he opened up and spoke of his apprehension, other times he held onto them and they bored holes in his resolve; there was no consistency to any of it. As it was, he didn't speak for several miles, lost in abstract contemplation, an artist without a subject. He took a pull from a travel pack feeling sore and heavy, weighed down by the enormity of the task, set adrift by the lunacy of it. Arduous as it all seemed, he felt he was under the watch of an angel—a sentiment reinforced by the help he and Winter received from strangers. They were right where they needed to be, adaptation was the watchword.

At length, they came to a tableland where a shallow crystalline tarn was beautifully situated. Its still beryl waters fed the roots of crimson pines that cut spiked shapes in the sky, and boulders half submerged held down a setting that threatened to splinter and blow away. Mason leaned forward on his mount in a resting position. Sweating in the afternoon heat, he watched the movements of flame skimmers and blue dashers. Combing the cattails on glassy wings, they seemed to be legion. When an ample gust punched through the scene, they all dove headlong into the vegetation and Mason Ross lost sight of every one. *Well,* he thought, *may we be equally as hard to trace.* Winter climbed to higher ground where he spotted the muted angles of Chessfield's skyline and fortification walls, perhaps a two hour ride hence. Castle Rook stood further to the south, a labyrinth of fragmentary towers and bastions some centuries old, whose history had been obscured by the lens of time.

"We've earned a long rest tonight. And on the plus side, I see plenty of good cover in the high country. Our camp will be well hidden as long as we don't draw any attention to ourselves." Winter dusted off his attire and looked back into the tarn's mirrored surface, "Any idea how we might locate this Zero?"

"I've been giving that some thought," returned Mason. "My gut favors of a low profile approach. Start in the seedier establishments and try to pick up his trail. If we bluff, posing as Calon's spies, we have protection and might get lucky, yet we risk the trust of potential allies. If we play it straight and make an inquiry to the wrong clique, we could draw heat into the kitchen. The whole business is a gamble." He paused, dropping a fig from hand to hand. "If we pose as messengers from the midlands and play it neutral, certain doors could open. We must have our wits about us in that case. Yes, that could work."

Winter stacked on another idea. "We might inquire with the younger set. It's likely they haven't yet pledged allegiance one way or another: page trainees, magician's apprentices, and the like. Frigates and firewands! I do believe we have something resembling a plan, dear man."

"Yes we do," agreed Mason. "Let's add chapels and kirks to the list. And we better get an early start. Chessfield might be small in scale, but there's still much ground to cover."

The riders navigated the northern edge of the plateau then dipped down into an avenue of pines where deep green mingled with sapphire gentian. The song of vermilion flycatchers and summer tanagers provided a layer of beauty and nuance. They passed through a sleepy dorp where a grange leaned awkwardly on its foundation, in a sorry plight. A tin windpump squealed as it spun and Mason made note of the modest skeleton of a glasshouse. Branches swayed above a sign that read: EMRY, POP 4, "ADVENTURE STARTS HERE".

Mason pulled back on the reins and brought Monsoon to a stop for some reason unapparent to Winter. After a pause, he called out toward the grange but received no reply. As he scanned the property from one end to the other, something caught his eye. Out of place amid rakes, shovels, and other farm implements, stood a guitar. Winter shook his head knowing his cousin couldn't help himself and, sure enough, Mason dismounted to obtain a closer look. The instrument appeared in one moment both meek and magical. Weaving its enchantment, it soaked up afternoon light. Mason looked around and called out once more. Only the sound of tanagers and a groan from Winter who looked on from the road. Mason kneeled down aside the broken-down guitar, observing its rosewood, spruce, and ebony construction. Names were carved into the body and it was well-worn on the lower bout. *An even coat of dragonblood sap would serve it well,* he thought. Imperfection was the reason Mason took to it. He presumed something had fallen on top of it or it was dropped, as the neck had clearly been reglued. But most cruel of all was a three inch gaping hole straight through the top; off-center between the saddle and the sound hole. It caused him to wince. This flaw, however, had been shored up as well. Someone understood that you don't consign a guitar to the fire pit just because it had some wear and tear. He pondered its playability and timbre.

"You'll like the tone," called a friendly voice. "I was never any good at tuning those things."

"My apologies. I didn't see or hear anybody. Sorry to interrupt you." Mason stepped back awkwardly, and then respectfully stated, "We shouldn't have trespassed."

"S'no trouble at all friend. You appear to be quite capable." A white-bearded stepped out from behind the glasshouse. He was attired in a light canvas tunic, shabby green braies, and low field boots and his hands were coated in the grime of his toils. "Call me Shot." He pointed at the guitar with a gardening fork. "I suppose you wouldn't tune it up? My grandson would be delighted."

"Of course. I'm your man." Mason softly placed the guitar in the grass and tested the tension of the strings, all in working order. The tuning pegs squeaked as he spun them but proved functional. He slackened the strings and released them from ragged components. With the corner of his tunic, he cleaned the fingerboard, bridge, and headstock. Shot watched him work then nodded to Winter in the rural fashion. Balancing the guitar on one knee, Mason tuned up the strings as easily as if he were opening a letter. He formed a chord and picked out a cheerful melody. Adding diatonic base runs and grace notes along the way gave the tune further nuance. He appreciated playing a guitar again. He rose and approached the homeowner, handing off the guitar as though it were living precious cargo. "I hope your grandson can make use of it. And tell him to look up Mason Ross if he's ever in Gardenwall. I'm an instructor there."

"Gardenwall!" exclaimed the man. "Archia!? What tempest blew you so far from home?!"

"We have wondered ourselves at times, Shot. In truth, my cousin Winter and I have business in Chessfield, though we won't be staying there long. Thank you for indulging my musical curiosity."

Winter extended a compliment about Emry from the roadside.

"We must be on our way now. Good day," concluded Mason. He nodded, returned to Monsoon, and mounted up.

Shot acknowledged the random act of kindness. "Thank you for returning an old instrument to its former glory. It's amazing what a little tune up can do. Good day, friends." The man returned to his work with a strong hunch as to why they rode a back road to Chessfield.

As Emry disappeared from view, Winter strained to listen to the faint clang of a church bell—eight gladsome tolls in succession. Its profound music charmed a peaceful scene he was determined to enjoy. The sun slid to the horizon where it glowed like the jeweled end of a king's sceptre. On approach to the city the temperature dropped, as it does in higher elevations, and the Archians looked for a concealed site to overnight. Dinner entered the equation and Mason cycled through the options half aloud, half to himself.

Winter scanned the inner forest and pointed off to his right. On a patch of ground encompassed by moss-bearded logs, hidden from curious travelers, the men set up camp. The hills lost definition in the twilight as Mason fueled the fire. They cooked a potage from vegetables, jerky, and other odds and ends as the horses went to work on their oats. They all ate heartily as the last light receded and woodsmoke stole into the corners of the site.

"You know, we're still fully stocked with medicinal herbs. That's encouraging. Did you think we wouldn't have had a cut or bruise this far into the journey?" asked Mason as he dipped bread into his potage.

"Yes, good fortune on that front. And, in a way, I'm getting used to this way of living. There's something—a clear objective I think, and a large one at that—which keeps me from overthinking small tasks and frees me from despondency. It's strange," marveled Winter.

Night fell. An owl's fiendish laughter echoed through the gloom as the waxen face of the moon illuminated all with silvery light. Far away in the eastern heaven the nebulous light of gegenschein could be traced. Mason regarded its brightest concentration which reminded him of a gleaming eye—infinite and eternal. Further into the black apex he caught the afterglow of stars destroyed. In an astonishing display of the night's expanse, glittering particles flowed like a river down to the tree line. *The size of the universe is beyond all credence,* he thought. A song was delivered in a whisper:

Well, I tell you bout a treasure I could sing about
For all my time
Better than a diamond ring, Lord it shines
And even though this world of ours
Wants to steal our light
I can only see so far into the night

When it came to matters of the heart,
I thought I knew enough
I navigated ups and downs with experience
Then you reminded me of a few little oversights
'Cause I can only see so far into the night

Well history repeats itself in a different place
Or are we repeating history because it's safe?
And even though we're helped along by divining light
We can only see...

SNAP! Mason sent Winter a round-eyed look and brought a finger to his mouth. It was as silent as a lake bottom. Without warning, a large animal growled, startling the horses. The men stood bolt upright, shifting to fight mode. Mason thought he heard a footfall.

"We have strength for a fight... what will it be?" declared Winter, addressing a dark stand of trees. The men spread out and crept to the firelight's furthest edge, preferring to be on the offensive. They stood with weapons drawn like an ancient relief.

"You could have left a bit for me," said a soft feminine voice close behind them. The men whipped around to see a young woman kneeling by their fire. She, and the large lynx next to her, looked into the empty copper kettle. "She's mostly harmless, but I'm pretty grouchy when I'm tired and hungry." The young woman leaned back, smiled, and settled down by a log. "Well... manners gentlemen? Do you have names? And please, you won't need those blades." She said all this as calmly as if she were ordering tea and busied herself brushing the coat of the lynx.

A look with shades of cynicism passed between Mason and Winter as they sheathed their steel. They stepped back into the heart of the camp, strategically keeping the firepit between themselves and the formidable white cat.

"Let's peel the onion," said Mason submissively. Winter's arms were folded, but a smirk finally appeared. "Welcome to our temporary home," he said as he made a sweeping gesture with his hand.

"My name is Saoirse (SUR-sha). And my companion here is Ghost," she explained while her gaze alternated between Winter and Mason. "Quinn said I could find you on the back road to Chessfield. My parents know him. Well, knew him. They lived in Heddwich. I'm sure you know what happened there." Her light blue hooded cloak and multi-colored shawl were dusty from travel. There was a loose purple scarf around her neck the end of which she had the habit of spinning around.

The men sat down, not quite sure what to say next. This woman's parents were among the many poor souls who fell victim to Calon's brutal war machine. Yet here she was, with a brave face and a jaw set as firm as a statue after following them on foot and effectively tracking them down...at night. From these clues the men surmised she was a woman of great resolve and proficient in a wide array of disciplines.

"We're sorry to hear this sad news—truly sorry. My name is Mason and this is my cousin, Winter. We are from Gardenwall, many miles south of here. We have been asked by the Overseers to confront Calon Du, and put an end to his warring and madness. Our hope is that we can build up our numbers as we move eastward into the Black Mountains. Understand, we are hesitant to bring anyone into this perilous course of action. Maybe you could assist us in Chessfield for the next phase of our plan?"

"I may be small, but if I need to, I can dig my heels in and reverse the turn of the world. Allow me to join your crusade!" She narrowed her eyes and leaned forward with clenched fists to drive the point home.

"Brilliant! Three against an army is better than two!" said Winter with classic sarcasm and he wandered over to the horses mumbling to himself.

"Are you equipped with a mount?" asked Mason.

"Aye, a fine gelding. He rests a short walk from here. Even found tack and a saddle close to the Dragonhead. Funny how that all worked out," she explained as she gave Mason a knowing smile. "I was in no mood to watch the cleanup taking place near the ranger station, so I avoided it with a wide northward turn. Whoever was responsible for that affair must have been a prolific duelist and swordmaster, or the gracious hand of God was upon them."

"Praise God. He has been very good to us. He performs wonders that cannot be fathomed. Many times have I been awestruck on this journey, and many times He has given me courage to press on. It's simply well outside my sphere of knowledge. This imminent encounter with Calon seems almost surreal. Yet in my heart, I know we are doing what is right and that it must be done." confessed Mason. "We are gracious for your help."

Winter returned with food, drink, and a blanket for their guests. "Let us know what else you need. We've managed to adjust to life on the road. It's only natural with a shortage of options," he explained cheerfully. "The next phase is to seek aid in Chessfield. Quinn, our mutual friend, pointed us this way. But more on that tomorrow, even this cold ground appears comfortable after a long day in the saddle."

In the Black River camp, Calon returned to the silver mines having summoned of the Chamber of the Wolf yet again. He paced the throne room in a wide arc kicking up the bottom of his cloak with each measured stride. On his visage were hues of ill-temper and impatience mixed with a shade of trepidation. His four collaborators picked up on this oddity, looked around questioningly, and cycled through possible reasons why. Was he tired from the demands of conflict? Was his armor showing its first signs of wear? Had some new intelligence altered the landscape? Was he caught in the undertow of his own propaganda? They wondered how their merciless leader would proceed.

"Chamber members, it is a time of unprecedented change as we wage war on a common enemy and work around the clock to protect our hard won territory. Yet, it is also a time for celebration. So many are now unified under the red shield! So many are now in a more stable place! It's more than an orphan child from the trackless wastes could ever have dreamed of. In a span of six short months, the initial goals of this organization have been accomplished and we now stand on a new and stronger foundation—a foundation on which there exists chaos as well as order. There are those who have the desire to thwart our plans; this was expected from the start. It was measured as we drew up the overall design. And so the time will come when one circle will fracture," began Calon with typical pageantry. Laced with purple prose, his voice was like the cold and raw north wind. He avoided using the names of the emerging adversaries. "Our numbers are greater, our weapons far superior. Operation WOLFSBANE will conclude on tomorrow's dawn, and Silverbridge, with its rich lodes of ore, and Deering, with its strategic position, will be under our rule. Occupation of both will firmly shield us from any eastern threat." With each presentation, he left little doubt he was an exemplary orator and a military strategist of the highest order. "The Ice Ring continues to provide vital intelligence of any would-be resistance across the north from here to Chessfield. Many cabals have been blotted out, a trend which I have every confidence will continue. So, as you can see, very little transpires without the knowledge of the Chamber." He paused and studied the faces of his administration. "However, it is also important that we share our personal assessments. I would like to hear your sentiments on these matters," expressed the warlord in an oversimplified and slightly disinterested fashion.

Siol Dona, Calon's right hand man, head of security, architect of the Greyguard, and occultist, removed his wolf mask and held the grotesque gewgaw to one side. He looked unholy in his vermilion mantle. As second in command, he tended to echo the director's twisted axioms. "I wish to share the next phase of our grand offensive! As we are forced to circumvent the Lakes of Time, our next arena lies northeast of Lake Mjød and east of Chessfield, a plain known as the Mulga Lands. Eight divisions will assemble in that locale over a span of the next six days. Once securing this position and subduing any interlopers, we will capture Chessfield, then make the turn south and set up our final thrust into Archia. We seek to ride our current wave of momentum. Our first two military operations were successful as expected and esprit de corps remains high in our ranks," he stated with mechanical precision. His secret envy of Calon's position was growing by the day, but that is a story for another time. "We have sustained very few losses outside of a minor...setback...on the Northgate Highway. This was certainly due to our forces being fatigued and somehow squandering their element of surprise. It can be looked at as a positive. We have learned more of Archian fighting tactics and their choice of battle implements. We know they prefer a quick fight. We surmise they are severely outnumbered. And as they say, blood is the badge of victory..."

"BAHHH!" interjected Myrkrið, leading labor force organizer and director of manufacturing concerns. She reviled him. "You'd be a fool to dismiss this event lightly. Are you out of reach of all reason?" Her nose and mouth wrinkled to one side in a taut sneer. Outrage and dismay sprouted on Siol's face in anticipation of further incendiary remarks. Calon only observed, preferring to let his subordinates navigate verbal clashes without intervention like some gladitorial contest.

"These Archians are a severe hindrance to our so-called grand offensive and swift domination is chimera! The chronicle of their triumph will spread through the north, swift as a weaver's shuttle. Two men cut down our elite squads like sweeping a floor, and we stand here with optimism?! I for one will not simply whistle in the dark!" Her sharp tongue kindled a temper-fire as she stood bold on the flat polished floor. Her robe's silver stars and moons were in stark contrast to its midnight fabric much like her opinions contrasted with those of the others. She calmed herself and leveled her voice. "And what to make of last night's excitement? Two spies infiltrated Black River last night. Since our ramparts are supposedly impenetrable, some say they may have been assisted by one of our own. Then, like apparitions, the thieves vanished, plundering top secret reports and elaborate diagrams of the city's walls! Our men are still searching for them up and down the road and so far, they are nowhere to be found." She all but spit venom as she recanted the events.

From dark abysses the cave groaned and Viximar, spiritual leader of the Chamber, took a step forward and raised a calming hand. "There will be storms in this ocean of conflict, and these are sure to test our resolve. It's evident there is division in the room."

Standing in the throne room near the center of the cave, Myrkrið and the rest watched him, lean and sober-faced, eyes blinking fast, lips pursed, and gray hair and beard falling to the shoulders of his deep green hooded cape. His hands emerged from the folds, palms turned up, and they rocked like the scales of a balance. He attempted to unravel the Gordian knot. "Let's define the problem. There have been two known incidents carried out by four renegades—the Archians and the two spies. We might assume both duos have the backing of underground cells, adding perhaps fifty to one hundred more to the overall resistance. We have a possible internal defector, but this is still under investigation and we are in the process of gathering information. Now, we could treat this all very lightly, focusing on larger objectives or we could be very cautious of our next steps. If we run this through the rational and the analytical, the incidents would be easy to dismiss as meager efforts. However, would that action be consistent with our intuition? That's where I wallow, the solution confounds me." His divided position shone through. "Next, it would be wise to discuss all possible options, not eliminating any that seem hard to achieve or nonsensical. Are we making our decision based on fear?" *Impulsive behavior is a disease of the egotist,* he thought. And since it was a cruel dilemma, he preferred weighted analysis.

The econometrician Rhyfel, to one appeared dour, to another indifferent. The slow measured pace of his delivery was indicative of his advanced years; the falling leaves of autumn personified.

He began his analysis in a raspy voice. "Obtaining natural resources for arsenals, building strategic outposts, and securing defensive barriers are the three primary short term objectives. To date, the Greyguard under this Chamber's supervision has done this effectively and efficiently. It's no secret the rank and file act in deep-seated irrational ways; since the dawn of time it has been so. Therefore, we expected the temporary breakdown in trade, and station leaders have made adjustments within the walls of the city. Our GDP has proved healthy enough to sustain equipment manufacturing concerns. Our substantial population allows for a large army and the ongoing production of basic necessities such as bread and butter."

Firelight danced off the folds of his hooded green cape and he paused to make sure he covered all aspects. Then, he wore a look of anger as he applied vitriol. "The Archians, our rivals, have tremendous natural resources, which is the cause for some concern if this war is elongated. All the more reason to make quick work in the north and subdue the south."

Calon brought forth a set of leatherbound volumes and handed one to each member. "In your hands you hold The Chamber Handbook. It describes how to dismantle any institutions that pose a threat to our cause. Any actions taken in accordance with these programs are therefore supported, and under the aegis of the Chamber of the Wolf. As an additional resource, you will also find our Special Search List, complete with politicians, reporters, authors, artists, musicians, and scholars who must be arrested or detained expeditiously. The army will bring us victory in the larger battles; our administrations must win the smaller ones."

On those written pages, the minutia of precision management was laboriously spelled out by the hand of an egomaniac who, as sure as stars die, was letting his position of power take power over him. Paranoia, the lighthouse for fools, hell's red anchor, dendrite of doom, the annihilator of order and reason, the devastator of intellect, the haunting affliction that in turn leads to wasted energy, wasted resources, and ultimately wasted lives, had tightened its grip one more degree.

Chapter 8

Chessfield

**Within the walls - Mason's mission - The Spiral Arms -
Saoirse's strategy - Chessfield Cathedral - Winter's
wanderings - The marketplace**

Eager to embark upon new trails and new demands,
Saoirse, Winter, and Mason finished a breakfast porridge with fruit and nuts and broke camp. Bars of gold
brilliance, fresh from the morning sunrise, sliced up the
forest's wizardwork into neat segments and the travelers'
shadows stretched as far as their hopes. From this enchanted theater, the determined collective mounted up
and set forth along the winding road, where their preliminary plan was tested, questioned, altered, redrawn, eyed
anew, retested, examined, and finally advocated. Who
could devine if they would succeed in finding support for
their cause and truly set the fire of alight? Surely, design-
ing an offensive against the Greyguard was a high-risk
undertaking, and at any point the slightest miscue could
topple the whole thing over. Some would claim the riders' actions were conceived for the crypt, although, like
the aspen with its ability to sprout after a forest fire, there
could be life among death. Each rider held their own internal council and the descant of wandering orioles, both
passionate and proud, drowned all.

Mason wrenched his mind away from the supernatural pageantry of the landscape, reconnaissance calibration, and the devastating wastes of worry, regrouped, and turned his attention toward a more productive endeavor—morning devotions. Let Your hand be with us and lead us in every step, he prayed. Keep us from harm so that we will be free from pain. Please help us to not lose heart when we face the many pressures, anxieties, and troubles of this fallen world. Lord, prepare our minds to be ready for what we have not yet seen. Keep us from the evil one. Spread Your pro-tection over the people of the north, that those who love Your name may rejoice in you. Uphold our faith most holy, he prayed. Whatever is true, whatever is noble, whatever is right, whatever is pure, whatever is lovely, whatever is admirable—if anything is excellent or praiseworthy—help us to think about these things. Thank you for soundness of mind, courage, health, and the persistent efforts of my companions. Thank you even for this great test, which proves our faith, and teaches us patience so that we may be strong and complete and in need of nothing.

The riders emerged from a league of trees and connected with a primary roadway where they were greeted by a majestic panorama. Before their eyes stood the historic city of Chessfield. Encircled in defensive walls and resting on a hilltop like a crown, its contours caught the amber light of the midmorning sun. Interspersed along the wall, were square towers which provided omnidirectional views for archers. Mid-sized gall oaks and stone pines planted against that great barrier suggested a monk's tonsure, and were maintained with rigorous standards. The exotic configurations of the buildings were both imposing and impressive and Mason sensed that artists had a hand in its design. He noted the regularly spaced merlons and crenels—functional as well as beautiful—which festooned the parapets of the wall. This was the craftwork of another epoch.

"Wow is not enough!" exclaimed Saoirse, overpowered as if by a conjuring. The city's centerpiece, which looked down over one and all, was a medieval castle with a cruel vacancy on one side, obtained in some bygone hostility. Winter thought it one of the most breathtaking landscapes he'd ever beheld. He pictured himself the owner of one of its opulent estates, hosting carousels and music performances.

From the road's high vantage point they identified hazily distant massifs, munificent groves, a cromlech with a broad flat capstone, crisscrossing sheep tracks, here and there a straggling shack or shepherd's shanty, and handsome meadows running into infinity. The appealing symmetry of corn, bean, and wheatfields, tinged in dandelion-yellow, shamrock-green, and carmel-brown, formed the likeness of a chessboard which is where the city took its name. An extinct volcano loomed far to the south. In place of a peak was a bowl-shaped crater, scooped out as if by a giant's spoon. Away on the southern horizon, stood the unmistakable framework of Castle Rook, this too a remnant of another epoch, which left them feeling as though they had transcended time and space and now trod into a former age.

The caravan sallied through the city's outlying districts where plebeians built quaint cottages. Rose bushes, trimmings of choice, cloaked railings and lined foundations. A cat peered from the arbor of a gated graveyard where thousand-year-old headstones were on display. A mother and her children stood at the doorway of a bakeshop, waiting for its doors to open. The pleasant fragrances of pine, wildflowers and damp moss diminished, and were replaced by the scents of hay, cut wood, and production. On the whole, the riders felt a renewed vitality as they returned to the familiar sights, sounds, and smells of civilization. Mason noticed the ivory-coated lynx was no longer in tow and he looked down and around then back at Saoirse, who only shrugged and nodded.

"And now you know why I call him Ghost," she explained with a bewildered smile. "When we approach a town or city, he darts off to some far perimeter. But he's a clever one. I think it's survival instinct. At times I've wondered if he hasn't been called back to his wild homelands once and for all, when he pops up yet again like a jack-in-the-box. No, he stays with me for reasons I have not yet determined."

Winter pointed out a brick barn and stable where laborers were engrossed in equine commissions and blacksmithing.

"Looks like a friendly enough lot," he announced. "Black Star is due for shoes and some good-quality hay." He led the way to a reception area with a hitching post where a sign read: STABLE & PASTURE BOARDING. SHOES

AND HITCHES. FEED & WATER. FLEXIBLE SCHEDULING. RAPID RESPONSE. FULL SERVICE. Nearby, a muscular draft horse, upwards of twenty hands, had its teeth inspected, while a miniature horse, less than eight hands, received a thorough brushing. Two stable attendants with sturdy physiques and pleasant smiles turned and approached the three travelers; first, taking their horses' martingales and reins; second, helping them dismount; and third, initiating a conversation related to available services and tack upgrades. Winter had a notion to inquire about Zero, but on second thought chose to hold his tongue; a quick look toward Mason explained what was left unsaid. *All the better to ease into the situation,* he thought.

Saoirse made her own analysis and whispered to Mason, "I see you two have a gift of thought exchange. At least that's what my sister and I call it. We've used the technique."

"Friends," called a keen attendant as the convoy stepped away toward the road. "A word of warning. One should be cautious of allegiances within the city walls. Eh, rumors of an influential outside presence have bubbled up." Mason bowed and gestured with a wave of his hand in the traditional Archian fashion.

With determination high and profile low, they advanced along the paved road's incline and headed toward the ramparts. The travelers scanned the span of the edifice—the details more apparent with each step—and were taken by its precision geometry, tight joints, and raw tonnage. The wall was constructed of finely dressed ashlar stones excavated in unimaginable quantities and transported from nearby quarries. Chessfield's south-facing gate—the one they were approaching, with a depiction of a bear head carved in relief atop its arch—shone strange and pale in the sunlight. Uniformed officers at the entryway refrained from stopping or questioning any foot traffic and only stared absent-mindedly at the horizon. The iron-grilled portcullis, hoisted to an open position, was completely hidden inside the top of the entrance barbican save for its menacing spiked ends. They stepped through the mouth of stone, swallowed, and ingested by the city's rumbling bowels.

Winter suggested they explore first, learn the layout, discuss over a noon lunch, then separate into their respective investigations. There was agreement from Mason and Saoirse. They traversed a paved thoroughfare flanked by rows of upside-down trees. With swollen bottle shaped trunks and finger-like branches, they appeared as colossal forearms protruding from the dirt. The only thing needed to complete their limb-like look were rings and bracelets. Saoirse recalled the fermented juice of the trees was said to be a "perfect food" which balanced the body, reduced inflammation, and improved digestion.

They admired topiaries, royal apartments, an amphitheater, a luxurious palace and reception hall, guard fortresses, water transportation marvels, and raised iron walkways that seemed to connect them all. Nearing the north end of the municipality, the travelers heard a commotion. Some sort of political drama was unfolding in a square and they gathered it had something to do with the city guards' treatment of a particular prisoner. A protestor stood on a high wooden platform built for the occasion. Wool spinners, smiths, bakers, and hundreds of others converged on the spot and listened to the message with restraint. How long that restraint would last was uncertain for the environment didn't appear entirely stable. They circled back to the south gate and stopped at a lunch wagon where a man sold smoked haddock and grilled vegetables.

Winter kept his voice low as he joked, "I do not recommend recon work on an empty stomach. There is no shame in a double lunch is there?"

Saoirse was clearly on board as she gave instructions to load up her plate. Mason insisted on paying. He tipped generously, then had a brief private exchange with the merchant which piqued his companions' curiosity. He nodded to the merchant then bit into a large red potato.

"An acquaintance of yours?" asked Winter with a smirk. Saoirse raised her eyebrows and tilted her head as if to ask, "Well?!"

"Good catch!" Mason praised. "Pardon the play on words. Yes, I plan to start with the darker corners so I inquired as to where I could find someone to hire for an odd job. He directed me to a tavern on the east side of the city. My guess is it's just the kind of place we're looking for. And you two?"

"That demonstration on the north end sounds like a good place to ask some questions," decided Saoirse. "They didn't exactly strike me as Calon's crowd."

"The marketplace on the west side is as good as any," put in Winter. "Meet back here an hour or so before sunset? And remember the walls, floors, and ceilings have ears!"

Mason walked up a narrow cobblestone lane at the edge of the eastern quadrant. Tightly clipped hedges ran along the left and buildings of contrasting stone types ran along the right. Iron grates on windows suggested there may have been burglaries, and perhaps not all was as charming as it appeared. He passed the occasional curious walker or expressionless rider and noted the cleanliness of the streets. A wide avenue cut between two complexes of modest living quarters, the balconies of which were festooned with yellow awnings. Their vermillion bricks were welded together with joints of creeping ivy. Further afield, snapdragons erupted from a compact garden offering unique color and fragrance to a sweeping calm. He could go no further at a cul-de-sac with a bell tower and had to double back.

Mason recognized it was difficult to become truly lost in a walled city even though all the corridors were curved like huntsman's bows and straight lines were nowhere to be found. The wind carried the glissando of a zither to his ear, but it faded when he rounded another turn. After an interval, he reached the southeast section of the rampart where couples and small groups mingled in an artful garden. He purchased candied chestnuts from a street vendor and ate handfuls as he scrawled directional notes in his journal.

With no time to waste on sightseeing, he hiked back uphill into the maze of passages angling east where the looks were more suspicious and the places more dilapidated. Here and there, horses were tied to posts idly waiting for some greater task that lay ahead. At one point, a heavy white dog blocked his progress and poured forth a moody growl which rattled its collar. Mason retreated pell-mell over a wall; he was unnerved by canines since receiving a bite to the knee more than a decade ago. At the top of a staircase, a tatterdemalion was asking for coins. Mason dropped one in his cup.

He continued under gloomy arcades, past an audience of urchins, and followed a winding corridor where the buildings leaned so close together that residents on either side could shake hands. Some passages were crowded, others were vacant. He noted elaborate stone pillars and crownwork dating from late antiquity. The route led to a sunny plaza where poplars whispered like scheming sprites and a stream of sapphire droplets rose and fell from an ornamental fountain. Nearby, the patio of a cafe received a brisk sweeping. All was finely balanced like the choreography of a dance routine. So much so, that Mason struck up a tune.

There's a wise old tree
Been here a long time
Seen a lotta changes
Many more than mine
There's a dirty brown river
I'm stepping my feet into

It's washing away
The dust and the highway hues

Yeah the Gateway
The gist of my communique
Yeah the Gateway
And there's gold every single day

You don't have to say a thing
My indigo sees your blue
My love is a new song
It's a rush just to play it for you
And the freedom rings
And a new voice sings
And the strength it all brings
It could break everything

Yeah the Gateway
The gist of my communique
Yeah the Gateway
And there's gold every single day

At length, he entered a maze of blighted alleyways filled with the dissonance of uncouth language, the sobs of children, general discourtesies, and an aggressive style of panhandling, bordering on panhassling. A monkey in a cavalier hat looked to be in on the action. Broken furniture and refuse lay heaped in piles and a busker with one leg reaped an insistent fantasia from a rebec in a frieze where all had run to riot. Mason worked his way through tugging hands and dirty bodies, weathering the occasional bump that was most likely an attempt at pickpocketing.

At the far end of one passage, a battered sign leaned over a doorway: THE SPIRAL ARMS. He looked back over his shoulder catching a few poisonous glances, then entered the establishment. Inside, malcontents as grimy as the floor suffered in the prisons of their own making. These were the spiritually shipwrecked. They bent over their steins and contemplated the miseries caused by the very thing they desired. No music was presented here; the commotion from the alley was the paltry substitute. The barkeeper, who stood with arms folded in a gesture of out-and-out boredom, was quick to initiate conversation when he noticed Mason belly up.

"Can I help you young man," he inquired as he leaned on the wood surface.

"Apologies. I needed a place to sit down for a bit," returned Mason. "And I'd better make sure I still have all my valuables. I am happy to make a purchase though."

"Uh huh," was the response that carried a hint of suspicion. The bartender studied Mason with a dubious expression, half smiled, raised an eyebrow, pressed his tongue into his cheek, glanced at the doorway, then back at Mason. He waited another moment.

"So...you came all the way to the east side, turned down a questionable alley, and navigated that foul lot just to take a rest?" He adjusted his apron trying to hold back a laugh. "Suuuure." A shoulder shrug followed and the man began to walk away.

"Maybe you can help me," inquired Mason. He slid two obls across the bar where they clinked into a trough. The men eyed each other like chess players. Mason lined up questions in a neat row like the posts of a fence while he explored how he might conceal his inquest. For an ante, he offered some background about himself and Archia which he believed would cast him in a nonthreatening light. There was no disengagement from the barkeeper and Mason thought he noted a softer expression. Both men leaned in subtly, a good sign.

"Tell me how the people of the city have felt lately. Any safety concerns?" During the response, Mason nodded repetitively—a display of empathy and an attempt to garner more detail. What the barkeeper did NOT say was equally important. Mason listened and stretched the silent gaps hoping to elicit further commentary. He didn't want to cut him short. As the exchange continued, the man grew more amicable. There were no rehearsed phrases, inconsistencies, or darting eyes. There was no subterfuge, peppered speech, or evasion. In no time, Mason had a solid picture of his allegiance. The barkeeper was no loyalist to Calon and deserved credence.

The Archian took the leap of faith and lowered his voice further. "I'm looking to connect with a certain individual I know only by name. Zero. Like the number. Since I'm an outsider and in an unfamiliar setting, I wonder if you could help me locate him?"

The barkeeper leaned forward and brought a hand up to cover his mouth. "We all know of him, but rarely see him. His domain is underground—quite literally. Our city sits on a network of subterranean passageways to which there are many entrances. The one I know of is off the main courtyard, behind a red grate. Easy to spot, though I recommend you enter after sundown. Stay sharp, devisers of wicked schemes are always near. And friend, please don't mention me or The Spiral Arms?" The two men shook hands formally, exchanged departing words, and Mason headed back through the passages wondering where he and his companions might stay for the night.

Saoirse contemplated her reflection in a long rectangular pool embellished with gurgling waterfalls. Goldfish, black moors, and fantails swam in wavy trajectories while a small family of turtles reposed on a log near the center. She felt rested despite having slept only a few hours the prior evening. A satisfying lunch, good company, and her excitement about being on the front line gave her motivation and energy. A man in a straw hat lowered clay pots filled with gravel and water lily tubers into the pool then fussed over their exact positions.

Departing from these placid surroundings, she walked under a series of pergolas toward the heart of the city's northern quadrant. She followed the interlocking stonework of the thoroughfare which curved neatly around the bulbous trunks of up-side-down trees to a corridor running between buildings. The occasional potted plant or tree gave an air of domestic tranquility. A hosta plant spilled over a wall and she ran her fingers through its smooth heart-shaped leaves. In the doorway of a shop, a well-fed goldsmith, whose eyes were buried between apple-like cheeks and a thick brow, stood waiting for clients and he smiled as she passed him. Her wandering led to a bustling plaza where royal banners of red, blue, and yellow rippled in a breeze. She followed the bouncy shimmering tones of a hammered dulcimer, curious to find their origin. A woman wearing shades of pink linen and a fishtail braid sat behind the instrument, lost in her performance. She played with great dexterity, and the notes blended with exaggerated sustain to form a melody gushing with exotic beauty. The enchanted onlookers swayed in appreciation, and someone dropped a well-earned obl into her woven basket.

Around another turn, food and drink were being served under the umbrellas of a street cafe. These were ordinary scenes, yet surreal under the circumstances, as the residents tried to go on living day by day knowing of the imminent threat of Calon Du. She felt responsible for all of them and it weighed on her heart as she navigated a crowd of shoppers and then approached an elegant cathedral. Austere statuary lined the curves of the archivolt and lions with shields topped a row of pilasters. An inscription near the door read: CHESSFIELD CATHE-DRAL—HELPING YOU FIND YOUR WAY.

She noted the ornate columns and gothic entablature of its entry surround as she walked through it. She crossed the narthex and accessed the A-frame nave where two other visitors sat quietly in a pew in welcome contrast to the clamour of the outside world. Behind the altar hung a tall geometric art panel depicting a grapevine, dove, lamb, and blessing hand. Its light blue tone nicely complimented the scarlet carpet. In lancet windows, stained glass was cut to likenesses of swords, trumpets, crowns, and fish. She paused for a moment, enjoying a moment of serenity contemplating her route, when a gentle voice behind her inquired, "Nice and quiet in here, eh? Can I be of assistance?"

Saoirse turned around to find a short woman in a habit. "Oh good day," she returned. "Beautiful church, um, cathedral here. I wasn't sure if you were open to the public? I was wandering and thought I would pop my head in."

With a broad smile the woman returned, "Of course! We're always open to wanderers, especially to those who need help finding their way. Call me Ruth, and please stay as long as you like. Can I offer you a cup of tea?" That sounded perfect to Saoirse and she accepted graciously.

The woman returned with a platter of tea and blueberry muffins—an additional generosity. She seemed content to go about her business, but Saoirse touched her arm and asked, "I wonder. Would you like to hear a yarn?"

Saoirse shared the unabridged version of her escape from the Black Mountains, how she met Ghost, the way she tracked down Winter and Mason, and her troupe's crusade—however deranged it all sounded. Saoirse didn't realize it until finishing, but it was a story she was compelled to share. Ruth nodded calmly all the while and, in response to an inquiry of Zero's whereabouts, submitted only a concerned expression and some words of consolement. War and espionage were clearly not her forte, but faith and strength were, and she went on to equip Saoirse with a radically new outlook. Thus it was, when Saoirse left the cathedral she felt as though buckets of ice water had been dumped on her head. The accumulation of fear and doubt which plagued her life, interfered with her decisions, held her back, made her physically ill, made life lousy in general, and even affected her posture at times, had been washed away like so much filth. *And to think I almost walked by that holy house. To think* anyone *could walk by it!, she thought.* Prior to that conversation, it seemed as though she had completely forgotten her worth. Now it was up to her, with a little help from God and whoever else He might work through, to rise to greater heights.

In due time, she approached the congested square where the morning's uprising now seemed to be in recess. City guards monitored the loitering mob with looks of impatience. She cautiously approached a band of sign-wielding protestors, who were engaged in a spirited discussion, their faces in all attitudes of displeasure, impatience, and discord. Tensions ran high. She was unsure of their political motivations, but made a play for information by complaining loudly about the animosities of the Greyguard. The tactic worked and a conversation ensued from which, as luck would have it, she gained a possible lead. She logged the information on a compact scroll then tucked it away.

In pursuit of a more advantageous view of the rabble-rout, she studied the walls and archways and took interest in a balcony which wrapped around the whole of the plaza, one story up. Taking advantage of the general confusion, she proceeded to a winding staircase and gained the upper level, drawing her hood to conceal both her identity and her gestures of surveillance. The balcony's commanding view of the plaza offered up an equitable target—a female street performer whose accoutrement included stilts, fire batons, knives, percussion instruments, and a python. Down the stairs and zigzagging through the throng went Saoirse to a ring of spectators where the performer could be viewed with more scrutiny.

A dark bandana held back her iridescent blue hair which, along with rainbow lipstick and white face paint, added to a free-spirited presence. Her cool smirk threw in a dash of fearlessness. The performer removed the snake from her shoulders, placed it in a large basket, then pulled the lid down tight. She procured several clubs from a canvas bag then turned to Saoirse and challenged, "Don't tell me, you are either lost, looking for lessons, or have an important inquiry?"

"Probably all three, but the inquiry takes priority," explained Saoirse. "Although, trust and honesty seem to be on their way out in this place."

"I don't know where you get your optimism," returned the performer with a droll delivery. "There was a time when it was not so. Yes, there was a time. My father would say it was before the madman carved up the mountain."

"He sounds like a bright man, your father. Times certainly are strange. Unstable, verging on combustible.

You know, I'm curious. A movement based right here in Chessfield seems to have gained attention as of late. Some say they are leaderless, but I've heard an unusual name in association with it, which escapes me now. So I'm looking for help in an attempt to locate this individual and learn more about his goals. My allegiance is to him." Saoirse would have fabricated a counterfeit scheme if she suspected the woman of harboring Greyguard sympathies. Now, whether this individual was willing to assist Saoirse was a different matter entirely. The performer walked to the center of the ring of spectators, then raised her hands and shoulders in apology. It was all she could offer.

Saoirse was vexed by her own faulty intuition. She pressed into the mob, pondering her route back to the south gate, when she heard a voice call out. "Zero. You're looking for Zero." Saoirse looked back. The performer had left her post to deliver this important message. Her face at first waxed diffident, then she gave a look of approval.

"Know where I can find him?" inquired Saoirse. Her countenance grew bright with anticipation and hope. "He can probably use all the help he can get."

"Not exactly, he's a moving target. But I know where you can start. The tunnels underneath the city. There's a grate off the main courtyard, but it tends to be closely watched."

On that cooperative note, they exchanged valedictions of goodwill which led to Saoirse's final query. "How much would you take for your batons?"

Winter's trek to the interior of the western quarter began at an ancient well. The water break, part smokescreen, allowed him to examine his surroundings in a furtive fashion. He cranked the bucket down through the oak-lined shaft, past strata and fossils, where it sank into the pool far below. Labor and leisure activities were under way. A woman wheeled a stone carrier, an artist painted earthenware, a crew repaired a doorway, and others lingered about unremarkably. Winter retrieved the bucket and revived himself with cool, sweet water. This preliminary concluded, he pursued the aroma of boiled apples. An array of varietals—including Sugarboon's Nonsuch, Cosmic Crunch, D'Angelo Spice, Queen's Estate Pippin, Rockport Beefing, and Archer's Bonny Moffat—were sliced up and condemned to a bubbling cast iron kettle. Winter thought the outfit might be in need of a product testimonial. Chessfield had been a favorite culinary destination for ages, much like its sister city Creekside. He approached an assembly line where apples provided raw material for jelly, butter, cider, hand pies, pancakes, galettes, and other items of sugary flamboyance. After purchasing several hand pies he considered interviewing one of the merchants, but a small crowd had gathered so he opted to continue his efforts elsewhere.

He wended through narrow streets lined with wrought iron fencing and artistic brickwork to a common where stately ash trees provided shade for cafe queues. Two guards in the midst of conversation held the bridles of their steeds. A monastery rose up from the next junction and Winter promptly decided it was the city's tallest structure. It was dressed in ornate pinnacles, lifelike gargoyles, and the handiwork of adept gardeners. For a moment, Winter stood in its shadow, simply in awe, the feeling which it was designed to evoke.

Shortly after, Winter paused to fill his pipe at a scenic terrace. He savored a view of the region's undulating hills, refuge of the fox and lark. The rise and fall of the landscape, bathed in teal spruce, purple globe thistle, and cerulean brunnera, reminded him of vast mid-ocean swells.

"Hard on the lungs!" came a serrated croak, disembodied and seemingly produced by the wind. The Archian released a puff of smoke and spun on his heels to account for the interjection. No one emerged its fitting source; no one at nose level, that is. Seated in the cool niche of a stairway was a gray-haired woman accompanied by a myna with azure wings. "Too much smoke!" screeched the passerine, continuing his castigation. A guffaw burst from Winter's diaphragm, mostly from shock.

"And what is your name, feathered creature?" quizzed Winter as he raised his brow submissively.

"Vow of silence," testified the bird and it settled at the end of the woman's outstretched legs.

"He recites mathematical formulas and ancient proverbs with equal dexterity," put in the old woman who lifted her head to reveal her impaired vision. "He also seems to be flowering in palmistry," she added.

Winter greeted her in a formal fashion and then said, "Tell me cultured friends, during your tenure at this terrace, have you heard of a certain faction, a resistance force, that is growing locally?"

"Mmmm, one that seeks to thwart the ghastly objectives of a...Calon Du...Perchance?" proposed the woman in a voice now slightly hoarse.

"Polluted mind!" jeered the myna.

The woman enlarged on the theme, "There is a faction, traveler. Embryonic they say, yet growing. Disciples of an enigmatic leader who goes by the name Zero. He is not far, but well hidden." She became absent for a moment, lost in a doldrum, then recommenced. "If their efforts fail, I fear it will spell the ruin of us all!"

"Yes. Where can I find this man? Or his faction?" urged Winter.

"The labyrinth below the streets!" she howled as she slapped her hand against the pavement. And then in a quick whisper, "Seek the entrances in grates low to the ground." Winter swiveled his head in vigilance. "Often there is more than meets the eye, is there not?" advised the woman with the charm of a mystic.

The myna repeated, "More than meets the eye."

"As grim as the picture is, hope still remains strong. You've been most helpful," emphasized Winter. He split his remaining hand pie, set half in front of the bird and half in the hand of the old woman, then departed with a word of gratitude.

"Vade in pace," was the bird's final soliloquy.

Winter followed a cobblestone avenue in deep reverie as puffs of smoke dissipated behind him. What luck to have happened upon such a pair, he thought, and the added bonus of a health warning to boot. *Perhaps I should commit the pipe to the dustbin someday soon,* his thinking went. *Not bad advice.* As he threaded a slender corridor's brickwork, he discerned the hum of the marketplace. Foot traffic increased and many carried burlap bags of recently purchased commodities. In time, the triumphal arch of the civic market revealed itself, decorated with yellow and green voussoirs and exhibiting a sturdy iron gate.

Upon entering, the upsurge in energy and burst of colors and aromas gave the setting a life of its own—clearly, it was the heart of the city. The mix of traders, overwhelmingly diverse and from all points of the compass, included family businesses, long standing enterprises, local farmers, and new ventures. The offerings were as varied as the clientele. A small group of women pointed at rows of poultry and beef while a patient butcher looked on. Pots and cruets of healing herbs and spices formed neat rows and one merchant's table overflowed with henna, nard, saffron, calamus, aloes, and cinnamon.

Winter stopped at a stand where a merchant sold genuine dragon eggs, or so the sign alleged. With the objective of obtaining insight about the mysterious Zero, he struck up a conversation with her using light generic topics, but was derailed by a paying consumer. He drifted past tables weighted with cob loaves, barrels of cherries and peppers, a cheese booth, a fish counter, garden vegetable displays, and a chocolate shop. These were all situated under a boisterous dining mezzanine.

He carved his way through pedestrians absorbed

in deeds of responsibility and enjoyment and looked for the right opportunity. A covered passageway with clothing and novelty shops led back out to the main gate so he circled back through the market for a second pass. Just then, a man with a bucket and broom sped by and drew his attention. Winter guessed he dealt with building maintenance so he turned and followed, waiting for an opportune moment. When the man stopped at a clogged drain, he interrupted him with unrushed courteous tones.

"Pardon me, I can see you are busy. But, are you well acquainted with the marketplace sir?"

"Sure am," replied the facility worker as he took a knee. "Been here for years. As long as things keep breaking," he pointed to the drain, "there'll be work to do. Something I can help you with? I can listen and work."

"Well, yes there is. It's an unusual request though." Winter paused to look over his shoulder and shape the inquiry. "There is a certain individual, well-known to some, who I'd like some information on."

"Oh?" replied the worker as he initiated the repair.

"His name has been popping up more often, used in association with a certain clique that I know very little about." Winter paused to look over the other shoulder. "It is said they harbor in the passages under the streets. Have you heard of a man named Zero? Our motives seem to be aligned."

"Ohhh, indeed! You had me worried there for a moment. I could be of some assistance to you, but here in the middle of the market...there are too many prying ears," cautioned the man. He rose, collected his tools, and gave a quick nod toward a narrow passage. "Follow me."

Through a doorway, they descended a half flight of stairs, rounded a corner and entered a brick corridor which, further down, exited to the street. Winter thought it strange how quickly it became quiet. He followed the man into a blind alley with maintenance equipment, storage crates, and tables strewn with parts in disuse. The man set his tools down and removed his gloves.

"You've brought up one of my...our...favorite people of interest. He is...I suppose you would say...a most dire threat to our agenda in Black River," pronounced the facility worker with slow deliberate precision, not yet performing an about face.

Much to Winter's chagrin, two other men had entered the alley and now stood in the access way looking bad-tempered. A sinking feeling overtook him, he was outnumbered and surrounded. *I sure could use a slice of porter cake,* he thought with anguish.

"We'll take him apart piece by piece," boasted one of the men with a smile as crooked as his teeth.

"A fresh filet for the market," declared the other, revealing a cleaver.

"We can't have this feeble resistance causing any more concern. And we DO have our orders from the top. Now let's not have this get too messy boys," sneered the facility worker. Looking completely unhinged, he closed in waving a rusty planting hoe.

Winter stepped back toward the wall. Think. What would Mason do? "Anyone for tea?" was Winter's feeble attempt at humor. This was met only by taunting and further encroachment. He drew his weapon. *That's right! Pray!* The gap closed again.

Just then, the laughter and chatter of men could be discerned. Focal points zipped from face to face, faster than arrows. The assailants hesitated as the chatter grew closer. Weapons were momentarily stowed.

Four city officers appeared in the doorway and stopped. They took note of the men's positions and their body language. "Anything wrong?" inquired an officer with an air of suspicion.

Winter took advantage of the confusion and bounded toward them. "Great to see you chaps! Having a terrible time locating a restroom, such a maze. Thanks for the help!" He didn't stop to look back.

Chapter 9

Zero

The Red Lion Inn - Underground - The crossing -
The Diamond Mine - War room - Introductions -
Music and magic

Completing their respective assignments, the travelers reconvened near the south gate as planned. Winter appeared more frazzled than the others, though they all looked in need of an intermission. There was a brief recanting of events and pooling of field intelligence which led to the question of accommodations. Mason had made note of a guest house on his return loop, which he offered as an option. The others agreed and after a short walk they were admiring the facade and entrance of The Red Lion Inn. To the west, the setting sun oozed a deep honeycomb gold, which added a spectral brilliance to the inn's red and green ivy walls. Nearby, a stately alabaster fountain, intricate in design, spoke in a bubbling tongue. A staff member greeted them as he held open the door.

The party secured two rooms with balcony views, a welcome change from the cold, damp forest floor. Crossing the lobby's chessboard tile, they paused at the threshold of a barroom named The Kingfisher. Its patrons enjoyed dinner and drinks while a xylophone player planted dreams in their heads with a bewitching and virtuosic nocturne. Whispered observations and gossip echoed off the walls while a fireplace was being prepared for a night of entertainment. A faint bouquet of orange and cinnamon came and went as Mason urged his companions onward.

In an upstairs chamber, Winter reclined on a bed and gave an account of the hostilities he encountered in the marketplace, sparing no detail. The faces of Mason and Saoirse exhibited fright and dismay and subsequently all agreed to submit no further inquiries to the locals. The consensus was the place crawled with spies and was too unpredictable. Moreover, they had come so far and prudence was best for the sake of all involved. Saoirse handed a news bulletin to Mason which she procured from the square's crier. Headlines on the page included: REQUIEM FOR DEERING, SILVERBRIDGE SACKED, IS THIS THE END?, and CITIES IN FLAMES.

"Ahh, news," lamented Saoirse, "where do I even begin?" She was repulsed. "The headlines draw you in, the rest is ridden with editorial commentary that spoils the real flavor. We're forced to pay attention to it, yet there are so many downsides. It induces mob hysteria. It causes anxiety and wrecks a good night's sleep. All too often it's one-sided. Can't we just have the truth in its distilled, pure, and neat form?"

Mason looked down from the balcony taking in a view of a burial ground. He drew a deep breath, cherishing distant hopes. Dusk fell. Headstones, hawthorns, and a ruined chapel with a missing roof lost definition as night flung its arms around the territory. Saoirse lit tapers and as a unit they reviewed timelines, assignments, and objectives, breaking down any presumptions along the way.

Winter produced an iron pry bar from his tote and explained, "Hammered by an Archian smith this is. I did see a second grate on the way back from the market, further up the road from the other. That one looked more concealed."

Mason shrugged and checked the window again while Saoirse clapped her hands softly.

"Why don't I keep an eye out while you two enter and descend," he said, building upon his proposal. I'll follow when all's clear. That road must be in shadow now. I only noticed a few lamps."

"If," Mason corrected himself, "*when* we find this Zero, it's a good bet he'll be suspicious, doubtful, or even hostile toward us. The truth is all we have now, and we must stand by it. The truth will protect us." Mason began snuffing out tapers until only a three-arm candelabra remained illuminated. The shadows on his face danced in the amber light. He went on. "We go armed, but force should be a last resort. We go with haste, though it may take hours. We go with intention, as this is our opportunity to build an alliance. We go with confidence, though we must be watchful." The entire room seemed to revolve on an axis, so intensified was the moment. "Forward in faith," were his last words before he led the cadre from the chamber, down a stairwell, and out the inn's side exit.

The moon, secretly sailing behind purple clouds like a magician exploiting the brain's limitations, burst forth and clothed the countryside in a magic silvery fabric. Under this pale glow and the radiance of scattered wall torches, they worked their way through dim passages while echoing voices punctured the silence. At the quoin of a building near the main boulevard they paused, noting two guards and a man leading a horse. Like night hawks, the travelers passed unnoticed on the far side of the fountain. Past an intersection, a pocket park stood on slightly elevated ground. Winter, head on a swiveled, garnered quizzical expressions from Saoirse and Mason.

"Well, you're just about standing on it." He pointed to a short brick retaining wall. Fastened to the brick and no more than two feet across was the aforementioned iron grate. "No magic here, it's gonna take some time to unfasten that thing. Keep an eye out." He took a knee and began prying the edge while Saoirse and Mason positioned themselves on opposite ends of the pocket park and let him work.

There was an occasional grunt mixed with sounds of scraped brick and stressed metal. A barking dog elevated Saoirse's pulse. Hurry up, thought Mason. When the grate clanked against the cobblestones, they joined Winter at the opening.

Mason, clutching a length of rope, entered feet first with a lit candle between his teeth. He inched his way down, navigating complicated turns while whispering descriptions back to the others. The task was tedious and there were multiple occasions when a spider was reluctant to give up its delicate web. He wedged a candle in a gap and lit it. At length, he lowered himself down a steep shaft which emptied into an ancient cistern. The air was heavy with humidity. Magnificent stone columns disappeared into the blackness, giving it the aspect of a submerged cathedral. Water dripped, echoing.

Saoirse snatched the rope and vanished in the blink of an eye, feeling like a burrowing rabbit. Halfway down, in the pale orange candlelight, she counted a positive: Mason had cleared out most of the debris upon descent. She was nimble and handled the turns with relative ease, but she wondered how Winter would fare. A wretched odor turned her stomach as she approached the final drop. *I'm actually moving toward it!?,* she said to herself. Down she slid awkwardly, like an amateur gymnast, yet managed a three-point landing.

Winter squeezed through the gap and positioned the grate back into place, all while gripping the rope he tied to it. He pulled it firmly. Distinction between bravery and foolishness was gone. *This is ridiculous,* he thought as he descended the chute. He took slow deep breaths to stave off claustrophobia and at one point burned his finger catching the tumbling candle. After the first turn, something crawled over his shoulder and he shrieked. Saoirse cupped her hands over her mouth.

"I'm fine," came a whisper laden with frustration. Near the bottom, he became stuck for a moment and wondered if he should tie the rope to his ankle and have the others pull him down, but that vision had a grim outcome. He twisted his way through the corner and shot down the slope. His expression said it all, and when he had landed safely, a levee of much needed laughter burst from everyone.

With only a bit of dirt and dreck to brush off, and otherwise none the worse for wear, they edged further along the damp ground of the cistern. Somewhere a rock fell, sending an echo into the void. After an interval, Saoirse called for a pause. Outfitted for the occasion, she retrieved three juggling batons from her pack, doused the ends in vegetable oil, and handed them to the others. The upgrade quadrupled their light.

"Capital!" marveled Winter, his voice bouncing off damp walls.

The vaulted tunnel curved, ascended, became decorated with arcane drawings and doggerel, then dropped again before leading to what appeared to be an impasse. Here, the ground dropped sharply to the edge of an underground lagoon.

"How do you like to swim?" asked Winter in a jovial tone. The sometime sailor was positively unaffected by the complication. Mason looked unsettled. He tapped the water's surface with his boot as if challenging its very existence, sending ripples into the inky maw. The lagoon only murmured back with indifference. The men propounded the idea of hand traversing the brickwork to the other side, but after a bit of reasoning they determined that route would likely result in an unwanted swimming exploit. "I'm happy to go first," chuckled Winter as he began to untie his boots.

Saoirse, standing near a mound of rock and dirt, raised her torch to illuminate what lay beyond. She bent down and lifted up a small paddle.

"Why don't we use these?" she said elatedly, and proceeded to drag a coracle into view with her free hand. After a fully merited cascade of praise from the men, there were some cargo securement considerations. The troupe maneuvered the basket-like boats around half-buried columns to the water's edge. There was no telling how deep the water was and no telling what lived in it. One by one, they pushed themselves away from dry ground. Winter's coracle heeled with every figure eight paddle stroke and the waterline nearly touched the lip, so maximized was its load. He was almost certain some kind of bloated catfish followed him for a stretch.

Reaching the opposite bank, they disembarked and climbed to a corridor where the ground leveled and the passage branched in two. Mason was quick to open his travel journal and sketch the course, preferring one path's barely perceptible glow. The travelers followed torch light toward their target. Mason recalled a madrigal from the old bards' songbook and began singing its bright melody:

Leave it unsolved
I don't need to know the how, the why, or the when
It'll be fine, If I keep on won'drin
I see the hawk, the hawk sees me
Let's leave the rest a mystery

Leave it unspoiled
So that enchantment someone can feel, and heal
I see the hawk, the hawk sees me

Pebbles crunched underfoot and smell of petrichor and decay mixed in tunnels well acquainted with the winged and the blind. A deep rumble of shifting earth frayed their nerves. They passed piles of animal bones and brick arches to more branching passages. Following each navigational decision, Mason journaled the route line. In one area they squeezed through a snaking crawl space. Irregular shapes were draped in dust like things forgotten in an attic. Three zealots were they, moving through a mazeworld.

"Shhhh," Saoirse held up a hand, "Voices!"

Mason, mildly benumbed from prolonged wandering, lit up. Indeed, words could be vaguely discerned and Winter doubled his pace, seeking their origin. The passage, now well outfitted with burning torches, led to a spacious vaulted stockroom. Casks were stacked high, wall to wall. Two men rolled another barrel into the area, noticed the observers, and nodded dispassionately. Mason guessed they were below a tavern or brewery and recalled how some brewers preferred subterranean storage as they reduced damaging temperature swings.

Human presence and a general lived-in look became more apparent; the haggard tapestry or two decorated walls, tables and chairs were situated in antechambers, and articles of clothing could be found here and there. After wandering the imposing and complex underworld for hours, another conversation piqued their curiosity; the voices droned deep and sturdy like rolling boulders. In the bronze-orange obscurity of a long passageway, they distinguished two figures standing at either side of a massive door. As they advanced so did the two figures, who now, upon closer inspection, were lightly armed troopers.

"It's good to finally see a human face!" expressed Mason, finding a friendly tone. "We must be on the proper course."

"Good evening travelers!" one trooper announced as he took a position in the center of the passageway. "What brings you to The Core?"

"Good evening to you, sir. Fortune has led us safely to your doorstep. We come in good faith and by the grace of God. I am Mason and these are my companions Saoirse and Winter." The troopers remained affixed to the ground, their faces indicating a need for further convincing. "We, who have been selected by the Overseers of Archia, and directed by Lokman, come in search of a man known as Zero—one who re-portedly shares our ambitions of defending Chessfield and the cities of the north. Would you guide us to his headquarters?"

The troopers nodded and the iron door swung wide on its rusty hinges. Two more troopers, muscularly built, appeared behind them and two more ahead as they crossed the threshold into yet another distinctive setting. A tall woman in a supervisory role asked them to remove their weapons with the understanding they would remain under lock and key and could be collected upon departure. The Archians put up no argument, feeling hos-pitably treated thus far.

The retinue, now consisting of the three travelers and six troopers, continued into The Core. The hubbub of festivity could be discerned. Along the main channel, now wide enough for two or three chariots, was a series of small sub-caverns, alcoves, and nooks. In one, an aged man with wild, wiry hair, scribbled on a clipboard against a backdrop of sextants, astrolabes, and other navigation equipment. In another, a trio of youths leaned over a wide table as they created maps and wrote upon scrolls. A tortoiseshell cat examined the proceedings. In addition to these business endeavors, there was a healthy dose of leisure activity and good clean fun. A group assembled around some sort of multi-player board game that Saoirse set down for a version of Mehen. An off-duty trooper stood behind them playing riffs on a rustic gittern decorated stock to bout with akoma, denkyem, and aya symbols. There were several private quarters, sleeping rooms, and even a modest kitchen, similar to what is commonly found on a schooner. By all accounts, it appeared to be a self-sufficient barracks.

They passed through a second iron door and entered a massive tunnel which one of the troopers referred to as The Troll's Bridge. As they traversed its rocky terrain, the hubbub of festivity grew in strength. Somewhere ahead, a throng was carousing and the sounds of singing and merriment echoed into infinity.

"It's always worth the trip down," said one of the troopers as Mason, Saoirse, and Winter took their first steps into the subterranean tavern called The Diamond Mine. A sprightly hostess welcomed them and joked with the troopers. Along the entire left wall, an oak bar served as a meeting place for clerics, war veterans, politicians, city officials, scientists, knaves, shopkeepers, freedom fighters, miracle men, farmers, and an armored collective called The Mad Knights.

"Looks like my kind of place," jested Winter. The furnishings and decor included landscape paintings, barrel racks, plush couches, table and chair sets, a crumbling floor-to-ceiling mosaic, and a goliath bronze heron. All were bathed in flickering lamplight. The travelers were shown to a gigantic farmhouse table where an assortment of characters sat. One raised a drinking horn like some ancient warrior. Another bit into a greasy turkey leg. Additional seats and benches were pulled up. With cymbals, harps, and lyres, the musical troupe sprang into their next number—an anthem with verses delivered in a foreign tongue. Here's an approximate translation:

Out of the box and I'm on the move
Won't get my boot heels stuck in a groove
Breaking it down, I'm on the case
Just trying to match up a name with a face
I'm not sure what it is I desire
I'm walking to Chessfield, and the sky's on fire

Away from the box, it's never too late
Watching the bulldogs race to the gate
The sun's in the dust, the moon's on the rise
Even the ones that you love are disguised
Maybe next time we can avoid all the pain

I'm walking to Chessfield, and it looks like rain

Back in the box, setting the clocks
Some things are low and some things are stocked
No good to dwell in the days that are gone
Better to just keep it moving along
For my last trick, can I get a volunteer?
We're walking to Chessfield, we've got nothing to fear

The travelers sat mute as they endured neutral expressions, whispering, pointing, and a general lack of friendliness. It was Saoirse who injected the right amount of humor.

"Not the most lovable lot, but I'm sure there are at least a few worth saving!" she announced with an irrepressible grin. There was a release of tension followed by the approach of a cordial gentleman. He was thin, pale, and cloaked in a long green zupan.

"It's my understanding you are here to see Zero?" asked the gentleman. Nods of agreement all around. "Follow me if you please."

In the war room of his riverside stronghold, the soulless Calon and his fellow dementors calibrated their grand strategy, while the Greyguard continued to contaminate the northern borders with calamity and fiery doom. Ruthless strikes, which drove misery before them, razed villages to the ground and wiped nameless settlements from the map. Resisting was to stand in the path of an avalanche. The atrocities committed were too grotesque to describe in these pages.

Complete triumph over the north still eluded Calon and he reasoned Chessfield must be captured next to accomplish this goal. It needed to happen swiftly and decisively to crush the hopes of resistance factions which continued to mobilize against all odds. The maestro of malice took up his stylus and ranked his primary concerns on a wall board, composing a prelude to his symphony of terror. The list was topped with two things: Failure of the Ice Ring to locate Zero, and Mason Ross's charmed advancement.

Zero was a master war strategist in his own right, Calon's thinking went, but past his best years of swordcraft. Mason was an able fighter but lacked battlefield experience and military prowess. Together they could be a formidable combination. Would these two be able to piece together an army of any sturdiness? Calon could not say. Would they be in a position to mobilize soon? Another unknown. There were rumors of an underground barracks, but it was yet to be discovered. There were too many question marks for an already disturbed mind.

Calon spoke. "Operation FIRESTORM. This offensive will be carried out in the Mulga Lands northeast of Lake Mjød, east of Chessfield. The army, siegeworks in tow, must not draw any nearer to the city or it risks detection. Eight divisions, under Siol Dona's meticulous watch, will be en route soon. Our outriders plotted a course with the fewest topographical obstacles. The invasion of Chessfield, where our combat superiority will be on full display, completes the offensive. No prisoners are to be taken; no building is to be left standing. It will be made an example of. The cities to the south will see I do not tolerate opposition." His optimism was tinged with madness.

The dictator took a languid lap around the table looking down at his battle plans and scale models, then paused to peer through a pointed oriel window. He appeared distracted and restless. Outside, a wistful thin-horned moon was carried toward its zenith in the talon of the night. Calon had fantasies of holding the entire known frontier in the palm of his hand, but was haunted by this inscrutable Archian whose diamond hard determination would not splinter. The alarm in his brain wrought havoc and caused time to tumble in reverse, making him feel less stable and returning him to an earlier more immature version of himself. It pushed him further from the calm shores of sanity.

He collected himself and turned to face the four chamber members. "Our foe is ill-prepared, vastly outnumbered, and minimally equipped. I have every confidence in our victory. Go. And do not fail me," he stated in a malevolent tone. The council of war adjourned.

Calon continued to make public appearances preferring each monthly rally to begin with the city's uplifting anthem. His entourage and quantity of bodyguards increased in step with his delusions. His myriad speeches, to some clear and unifying and to others egotistical and insincere, were ridden with deceit and misdirection. They left the population mystified and unsure of their safety. Like a parasite, he fed off their fear. Local newspapers, supervised by the Chamber of the Wolf, described neighboring villages as hostile threats to freedom and regional security, thereby justifying occupation and use of "mild force". Often, it was impossible to extract even a portion of truth from the pages. Articles continued to warp reality by pointing the finger at Chessfield, claiming that its governing body was standing in the way of the general policing of the region, making it unstable for everyone.

Saoirse, Mason, and Winter followed the cloaked gentleman into a long narrow room on the far end of the tavern. It was a quieter setting. Four men sat in a booth in the back corner and the travelers made mental predictions as to which was Zero. No conversing took place until all were seated and troopers had taken positions to secure access to the room. Onlookers were politely shooed away.

"Welcome to our table, friends. If we may call you that?" inquired an intelligent looking member of the party. A censor effused thin fragrant fumes.

"Good evening. Of course, please consider us friends, and protectors. We are believers in freedom and believers in your cause," explained Mason. "Your troopers have been gracious to trust and lead us to this establishment. We come under the protection of God, with humble and determined hearts. Two from Archia and one from Heddwich. I am Mason and these are my companions Saoirse and Winter." The four men listened attentively with sympathetic expressions. Mason went on, "In response to the developing situation in the Black Mountains and all across the north, we're on an expedition organized by the Overseers of Archia. We identified your location through the help of Lokman and some cooperative Chessfield residents. May I ask which one of you is Zero?" Mason was urbane and enthusiastic.

"These are unprecedented times. Please excuse the table manners of our party. They are watchful, well-trained, and can spot cohorts of the Ice Ring a mile away," said the deep, smooth voice that, like wine, had mellowed with age. "I am Zero." His rhythmic, measured accent contained well enunciated words with few contractions. It was evident it could, like a lion's roar, intimidate when necessary.

He was perhaps fifty years old and of a medium height and build. He had a round face, a rich dark complexion, placid eyes full of wisdom and confidence, a slight courteous smile, and the hint of a moustache. Surely, he was trusted by all who were hard-working, virtuous, and ethical. His clothing was eccentric. He wore a dark green floor length robe adorned with delicate metallic fibers that seemed to glow in the dimness like starlight. Equally striking was the gilded scale mail underneath. A chain surrounding his neck held an oversized lion's head pendant. The piece threw off light and Winter wondered if its mark-ings denoted an orison in some lost alphabet. Resting against his shoulder and neck, held loosely, was a crosier. The word UNION was written upon it.

Zero continued in an unrushed tone. "I was born

in M2214, on the day of the new star—the tenth year in the reign of Ade. I'm the son of Andrago and a babe of the Cahaba. Early on, the volcanic fires of high adventure bubbled inside me. Astrologers believed I possessed special, sometimes supernatural traits. In my former years, I was fascinated by the natural world, witnessed many strange phenomena, and often walked the painted road along the Warrior River. Archery and swordsmanship were once my greatest strengths, but I've had less interest in those activities in recent years. You'll often find my nose buried in a volume of folklore, history, or devotions. I have children and a wife and I have lived in Chessfield for more than half my life. My wife and I love to cook, entertain guests, and listen to music. I am not a big drinker of ales and spirits, though I pass no judgment on the actions of others. I like to remain informed, though I steer clear of news and gossip as much as possible. I go to church on The First Day, and like to volunteer and care for the poor. God gave me a courageous heart and a strong back. I served honorably in the Lake Wars and I recognize most of the names on Chessfield Veterans Memorial. Now enough about me, these are my longtime friends and fellow veterans, Dex, Bara, and Ahina. Together we are known as The House of Ahl. It is written: one who has unreliable friends soon comes to ruin."

Dex completed the portrait, his expression somewhere between gracious and humble. "Zero, as you might expect, is modest to the marrow. Allow me to expand upon those words. The name Zero is a story in itself. It fulfills a central role in mathematics. It can't be divided, it can't be split. It symbolizes that which is open to change, ready to be born, a child in the womb. It's the end of a countdown; unrecorded on calendars; neither negative nor positive; leaves nothing to be counted, and nothing to be counted out; an empty space; green on the gambler's wheel; the circle of eternity; an enigma, yet approachable and here in the flesh. He is the chief officer of our brotherhood. He speaks seven languages and fought with a general's rank in the famous naval battle of the Lake Wars."

"It's quite an honor to meet you Zero," declared Mason. "YYour history is a thing to be revered. I have read and heard tales of the Lake Wars. Certainly they were a dark chapter in our collective history, but the outcome was a good one, and tens of thousands were ultimately saved through the heroic efforts of many good men and women. I'll let my friends introduce themselves." Mason motioned to Saoirse.

"Indeed thank you for your kindness, hospitality and any help you can offer. Ah, and for showing us this fabulous tavern, with peerless musicians and incomparable cooks who tempt us all with delicious aromas!" she proclaimed. The hint was taken, and plates of salad, baked cheese bread, and sweet meats were delivered soon after.

"And who is he," Zero asked dryly, "Your muscle man?"

Winter and the rest let out hearty, well overdue laughs.

"I'm Winter, yes, I'll put up my fists for my two

companions any day. Although it seems they are very good at taking care of themselves. Thank you. Your words and your welcome are a remedy to many tiring days of travel."

"The hour grows late; let us discuss the urgent matters at hand. The two spies who were sent to Black River have obtained confidential information including reports, calendars, and structural diagrams of the walls. They've also drafted maps of landscape features near the target area. Through their efforts, we are also now aware of an imminent attack on Chessfield. All this has aided us in planning our next course of action. Workshops and basic training are taking place west of the city on a rural farm. The people you see in this establishment are committed to our objectives and each one knows at least a handful more who are willing and able to fight. That gives us a foundation of at least five hundred, though thousands of others have pledged. Once recruitment efforts have been completed our force could reach roughly 15,000. And now we have three courageous and dedicated new friends!" said Zero as he panned the table. "Mason, your reputation arrived before you did. News travels faster the more desperate the time. We understand that in combat your skill is preeminent and some say you have the ability to defeat physics."

Winter nodded in agreement and gave a brief rundown of what took place at the ranger station.

"What else can you tell me of yourselves and your travels?" inquired Zero.

Both men looked toward Saoirse who explained,

"I was once a candle bearer and witness to ceremonies and meetings led by Calon Du. This is where I first learned of Mason and Winter. When my parents became victims of one of the Greyguard's brutal acts of aggression, I decided to take action. It was a time of mourning, but also a time to develop courage and resilience. Wishing that it didn't happen to me was only being selfish. I came to realize that it's not what happens to us in life, it's how we respond. And it was time to release my mind from that dreadful day and prepare my heart for battle." She paused for a moment, as if some memory tugged at her. The men noticed she was handling a precarious situation and a vortex of emotion like a champ. She resumed, "I tracked these two on foot, deciding I would join their cause before they knew a thing about me. I can confirm Calon's plan is to attack within one week. Their force is nigh on 100,000," lamented Saoirse.

Ahina stabilized the room as she chronicled their advantages. "Indeed the odds appear to be against us, but fighting in familiar territory works to our advantage. These curtain walls were designed to offer the best possible protection. We can utilize the element of surprise. We are defending our very own homes and safe-guarding our families. We know they are coming and we now know when. And most important of all, God has put confidence in all of our hearts. He will help us fight our battle."

The travelers were so engrossed in conversation they hardly noticed the musical interlude, though it wouldn't last long. A new ensemble prepared for their performance wielding an arsenal of instruments: guitar, mandolin, violin, bodhrán, hornpipe, and xylophone. Someone delivered a flagon and full wine glasses to the foot of the stage as whistles and shouts in support of the group grew to a genial crescendo. The mandolin dripped minor arpeggios, the guitar and xylophone chimed in, and the lyrics, an homage to the old country, followed:

The reflection of an ancient ruin dancing on a pool
And her late afternoon shadow is long
Who once was her keeper? Who looked from her tower?
Who sang her oft requested evening song?

We are staring into a window in time
We count blessings and drink wine

Throw your past in the dust
Roll the barrel down the hill
If you don't take some action now
Somebody else definitely will

Rise today strength of Heaven, radiant fire
It's raining but the sun is shining through
The river is swollen it turns on its way to the sea
It's like it says "I'll see you soon"

We are staring into a window in time
We count blessings and drink wine

Throw your past in the dust

Roll the barrel down the hill
If you don't take some action now
Somebody else definitely will

For the better part of an hour, topics flowed around the table. Backgrounds were elaborated upon, specific concerns were vocalized, relaxed humor was seasoned in, cohesion was built, and hope was instilled in what amounted to a kind of therapy. And so it was that the travelers acted out the proverb that said 'plans are established by seeking advice; so if you wage war, obtain guidance.' At one point, two guitarists took the stage for a presentation of an instrumental tune introduced as "Knuckleduster". Politicians and shopkeepers danced.

Bara refocused the group. He spoke with liberal use of hand gestures and lip movements and his dialect was strong and guttural, in the fashion of the moorlands to the north. "They are a crowd favorite and may play for at least another hour. Although, you'll do well to get ample rest tonight," he cautioned the travelers. "Tomorrow will be a busy day and we have our work cut out for us. Castle Rook and Falchion Forge & Range are five miles southwest of the city. You are welcome to join us for lunch. Training will follow." He spun a small, circular coin of copper color which depicted a kinnor on one side and the iconic contours of Foxfire Castle on the other.

Winter immediately recognized it as local currency, an obl. "May I borrow your coin?" he asked. Bara handed it to him with an amused expression. Winter rolled the moneypiece over his knuckles several times, then held it outstretched in the tip of his fingers with the back of his forearm against the table. He dropped the coin out of sight into his palm and immediately it reappeared in his other hand near the back of the top of his forearm, all within a fraction of a second—leaping, as if by magic. Smiles and gasps spread around the table. A few applauded.

Having had his fun, he revealed the hidden prop—a second coin. After a few long sighs, he performed the legerdemain at half speed to show how the coin appeared to leap.

Preparing to depart, all rose and bowed to one another in the traditional fashion, with one hand over the heart.

Zero offered a final piece of assistance. "Rather than spend the next few hours backtracking, our troopers will show you a swift route to the city's entrance fountains. We enjoyed meeting you." As they vacated the Diamond Mine, the band burst forth into a final number with the singer in top form:

So today the tide has changed
On a wave rides something strange
Common courses through the age turning like a page

Draped in satin, ribbons, bells
Truth the only words it tells
Under shadows of a church
Pray when something hurts

Mmm, yeah brave we love and cry
Names upon our crest electrified
So tonight the world it glows
Comfort like the things we know
Voices up they rise from the deep dens where they hide

Richer than the greenest earth
When the arms they rescue me
Like a time so long ago returns eventually

Mmm, yeah brave we love and cry
Names upon our crest electrified
Oohh yeah brave we cry and heal
Fly the Royal Banners, rows of steel

Mm, yeah brave we heal and learn
With a passion, hearts they will burn

In the morning feel a shift
Find your mark and race for it
When change and tears are passed
The safe and blessed meet at last

The grate near the fountains popped open easily and
the travelers found themselves in familiar surroundings.
The Red Lion Inn was only a stone's throw away. They
returned to it, walked through the silent lobby, and entered their rooms. It was then the travelers finally and
deservedly released the ropes that tethered them to the
waking world and plunged headlong into the harbor of

Chapter 10

Castle Rook & The Isle of Dolls

Castle Rook - Training - Mason installed - A Conversation - The Isle of Dolls - Visions - Lake Mjød - The Greyguard - A plan - Battlegrounds

Dreams are a spectrum of unsolved riddles, productions of the slumbering brain at once wondrous, vexing, and widely contrasting. From witchery to whimsy, from death traps to delights, from the grotesque to the gorgeous, and at times indistinguishable from reality, they are inclined to swift dissolution like ice in hot liquid, unless captured in writing upon waking, which is what Mason undertook as the midmorning's gilded sunlight leaked through the drapery.

Resting a quill on a blank journal page, he could only resurrect fragments: the remnant of a song chorus, an exam, awkward attempts at communication, rushing water, and horse's hooves trampling gear. It was a fluid story at one point, but now seemed like incoherent ramblings. He set the quill down.

As for the tasks of the day, he had a much clearer understanding of those; a good night's rest will do that. His morning prayer was one of gratitude for health, safe travels, companionship, last night's accomplishments in finding Zero and the House of Ahl, the breath in his lungs, and the steady beat of his heart. He made his requests known to God: guidance, protection, clarity of mind, retention of new knowledge and skills, peace of mind, patience, and strong friendships.

The aroma of baking bread and something lemony graced the room and roused Winter to stirring, stretching, and finally the day's first conversation about, as might be expected, how quickly a table at The Kingfisher could be obtained. During breakfast there was talk of training and traveling and how the events of last week seemed like they occurred months ago. Certainly, the travelers were on tenterhooks and formed their own solicitudes of the setting and the troopers which they would soon know much more about.

After filling their stomachs, fresh legs carried the travelers off into a profound unfathomable blue. The solar barge plotted its course across the sky and the doomsday clock kept ticking. Castle Rook and Falchion Forge was only a moderate walk through forested hills. They hiked under leafy arcades decorated with snags, logs, and brush piles. Crystal palace and elfin blue, beloved constituents of the rolling hillscapes, put on a show as resplendent as sea surf and the full wilderness seemed to be embalmed in sweet mystic fragrances. After an interval, they stopped to appreciate a stately maple tree dappled in mint-colored lichen. It stood alone at the center of a shady bower, hemmed in by smaller varieties, like an actor delivering a prologue to an audience. Far from the bustling city streets, it grew vigorously.

An amber phantom appeared on the scene, taking them from one reverie and delivering them into the next. It weaved its way through thick-leaved branches, along an erratic and half crazed flight path, then came to rest on the cloudy blossom of a hawthorne. There, slowly beating its wings, the creature had a mythical quality all dressed in crystalline faery-like regalia. Saoirse took soft steps toward it, reaching out with her hand. For a moment, the phantom touched down on her arm, then whirled away toward a league of shadowy columns. Observers of the natural world tell us a butterfly's unusual flight style is actually a tactic that makes it difficult to capture. The same could be said for the three travelers as they continued to evade the long reach of Calon Du.

They passed close enough to Sutton Pomegranate Orchard to warrant a quick visit and purchased three oversized sharp velvets, enough to make multiple jars of jelly. As they pressed on, Saoirse entertained them with stories from her youth. She was a tomboy and enjoyed climbing trees and playing games more physical in nature, the kind boys normally gravitate towards. Her friends were quick to point this out but words never swayed her. On she went, feeding large wild animals, fist fighting with boys, throwing knives, building elaborate forts, taking dangerous leaps into swimming holes, and accumulating an assortment of bruises and scars which confounded the neighbors. Her parents on the other hand, encouraged her to be herself and to follow her passions, loving her even more for her individuality. She recalled her favorite weekend activity, a sojourn with her father to the glass-paneled laboratories of the

Pomologist Society of Heddwich. In sophisticated workshops, they created fruit hybrids through constant trial and error. Hybrids of coconuts and limes were dubbed cocolimes, combinations of pumpkins and mushrooms, both rich in earthy tones, were aptly named mushkins, raspbarbs were the merging of raspberries and rhubarb, and a favorite of hotel and tavern owners, were champagne-infused gumdrops featuring an array of varietals and once again, the pomegranate.

Off the path, moss and gold maiden grass transmogrified a dolmen with a precarious capstone. It took a keen eye to spot it. Soon after, Winter handed out dried beef and handfuls of cashews, thinking they must be within range of their destination. Mason pointed into the canopy far ahead. The stony roofless keep of Castle Rook steadily revealed itself, a beacon for their party and the gathering army known as the Chessfield Defenders. Bits of conversation could be heard somewhere beyond the thicket, and upon closer inspection, their origin proved to be troopers angling in a nearby stream. Troopers lined a stream, indicating they were close. In time, shouting, cheering, and the clangor of weaponry drew them toward valor unknown.

The woody region thinned and finally broke open entirely to reveal an expansive flat field with tents and tables positioned all along the boundary. From the entrance to the far horizon, swallow tailed gonfalons of dark blue linen hung from stout poles. A hive of enlisted men and women engaged in preparations and workouts, all against the backdrop of an ancient fortress which spoke of power and glory. Many had previous military training, but the vast majority worked as cobblers, smiths, and farmers and had abandoned everything to join the cause. With a doomsday clock ticking, urgency and enthusiasm rode high in the cool wind.

After entering the grounds proper, the three travelers were greeted by administrators, checked in, screened, and instructed to fill out documents. These formalities completed, it was off to a brief orientation, followed by lunch.

Falchion Forge, rich in history and subject of innumerable rhymes and refrains, stood along the northern boundary of the swath. Mason watched as at least three dozen blacksmiths clad in leather aprons and heavy work boots manufactured, repaired, and polished weapons and armor. Soldiers had their choice of a variety of standard swords: rapiers, broadswords, falcatas, shotels, claymores, flamberges, scimitars, and of course falchions. Many carried their own arms, which was encouraged. Longer spear type weapons were a popular choice as well. Pilums, tridents, angons, xystons, fauchards, guisarmes, and voulges hung on display boards where soldiers made their selections before retrieving them from bins. The order and magnitude of the operation brought a tear to Saoirse's eye.

The archery range, on a downward slope adjacent to the forge, was configured so errant shots would sail harmlessly into a hillock beyond. Tutorials were underway, though many had the ability to hit a swinging grain sack at a hundred paces or snuff a candle at fifty. They took aim at eggs, haystacks, and flying breadboards. Battle added another element though, as equipment sustained damage, calm hands could rarely be counted on, and no target stood still for long.

"THREE LAPS AROUND THE WHEEL AND REPORT TO MEDICAL!" shouted a woman with a deep voice. The man being reprimanded wore a bright orange sash signifying that he either had an attitude problem or was falling behind his squad in training. A caravan of six-wheeled lorries was parked along the southern boundary of the grounds, weighted down by great stocks of clothing and gear. The military jackets of the Chessfield army, dark blue with gold braiding across the chest, were distributed and armored items such as cuirasses, pauldrons, gorgets, brigandines, and hauberks were being customized to fit the wearers.

Basic training was highly structured and conducted with the utmost earnest. Recruits were awoken before even a hint of dawn's pale arrival, and moved clockwise along a circular arrangement of stations, the sum total nicknamed "the wheel". To simulate the battlefield, the wheel included intense physical challenges, a competence course with wood, water, and rope obstacles, martial arts instruction and matches, weapons training, archery courses, and rappelling down the keep. A new language and culture were taught, which broke down old habits and reprogrammed minds. Pain ran through the body and lingered. Roughly one tenth of the soldiers were selected for the amphibious assault force; Mason was in that group. And though his combat skills were middle-of-the-road among these fighters, his running and swimming abilities placed him in this elite echelon. He placed third in the triathlon. The full course, traditionally designed to last months, was greatly compressed as the sun rose and set three times over Castle Rook.

It was on the evening of the final night that Zero made his appearance and gave a rousing speech, unequivocally moving, which readied the hearts and minds of the armed forces. He spoke of war, its undertow and unpredictability, of fear, how it petrified and paralyzed the mind, and even threw in an apologue for good measure. His final chronicle, the true tale of a protagonist who stood his ground against overwhelming odds, was a set-up for naming the leader of the entire military campaign, someone in their very presence who would guide the ranks from Castle Rook to the Mulga Lands northeast of Lake Mjød, and onward into the brooding Black Mountains. A soft drum roll and the drone of deep horns set the mood and amplified tension in every nerve.

"Chessfield Defenders, good evening. Thank you for taking the oath to defend our great city and for participating in this abbreviated training program at Castle Rook. It is with great pleasure I give to you your new Chief Defense Commander, hailing from our sister province to the South, a man of many talents, unequaled in mental strength, a master of the blade, Mason Ross of Archia!" A roar from the multitude rattled Mason's bones and sent an electric pulse down his spine as if he had stepped onto hallowed ground. He rose, waved, and soon became lost in a sea of back slapping and brotherly shoves.

Later that evening, Mason was summoned. Several men led him along the quiet edge of camp to a large round-topped shelter system, easily forty paces long. Inside, Zero and the House of Ahl sat around an ill-lit table looking like men who had just found hidden treasure.

"Welcome and congratulations again Mr. Ross. Please be seated," began Zero in a formal style. "As the hour is late and rest is critical, we won't keep you long. We have one final bit of intelligence to share, gifts you could say, and perhaps a challenge," Zero explained as the others eyed him with admiration. "These gifts belong in the custody of the Chief Defense Commander. A hammered mail shirt and a sword, dubbed Zafer, made on these very grounds hundreds of years ago. The undulating blade, forged by legendary metallurgist and blacksmith Málmur of Bryncir, is said to be unbreakable, capable of cutting meteoric rock like bread, and light as a pond reed. The shirt can withstand a thrust or slash from any weapon and can halt the speeding tip of an arrow. Both items were blessed by the High Priests of Halcyon."

Now there have been many famous swords throughout history, some with glamorous titles: Vorpal, Excalibur, Tyrfing, Ridill, Fragarach, Moonmetal, El Cid's Tizona, Beowulf's Hrunting, Edward the Confessor's Sword of Mercy, Charlemagne's Joyeuse, Roland's Durendal, Kraki's Skofnung, Gungnir also called The Swaying One, and Attila's Sword of Mars. Others were nameless: Napoleon's golden sabre, Timur's kilij, The Black Prince's broadsword, Trajan's gladius, Maximilian's Zweihänder, Erik The Red's Ulfberht, Genghis

Khan's scimitar, Surt's flaming sword, and countless other examples of metalwork from scriptures, folklore, and mythology. This sword was second to none of these and deserves a book of its own.

Mason's pulse doubled as he leaned in closer and crossed his arms on the table's edge. "Where might I find these...gifts? Are they here on the premises?"

"Not so fortunate. The relics rest in a strongbox on the Isle of Dolls, just southeast of Oakenholt," explained Dex in sanguine tones. "The isle itself is a wooded quadrilateral no more than the size of a riding arena and wedged in a narrow loch. A footbridge on its western edge offers access. Bring excavating tools; the strongbox is most likely buried or at the least heavily overgrown. It is said that all seekers of these relics are vetted in some way, though this assessment is unique to each person, and we've only heard rumors. This is all we know."

"We will be praying for you and the entire campaign Mr. Ross. You offer your lives for every hearth and home," testified Zero. "Remember your gifts and put them to use: integrity, resilience, positivity, courage, poise, patience, intellect, purpose, and self-confidence. Keep God in your heart and mind, and you will be where you need to be and where the others need you to be. Rest well, friend."

Mason bowed to Zero and the House of Ahl and departed. As he walked to his tent on a moonless night, vast star patterns rotated against shades of deep violet. Within them, his mind built imaginary test obstacles, creatures of legend, baffling riddles, and physical danger. Like a ship unevenly loaded, he listed for a period of time, dragged under by the weight of a terrifying unknown. He wrestled with it, then let go and corrected by releasing these false expectations. He remembered each day had trouble of its own and that tomorrow would care for itself. In these calmer waters, he was able to quiet his mind and find rest.

The clatter of the assembling army began before dawn and, like the rising sun, it grew in intensity and strength with each passing moment. Mason armored himself upon waking.

"God, thank you for waking me, giving me energy and vitality, caring about the smallest details of my life, and bestowing this great challenge on me, so that I might remain close to you. Thank you for the assistance of Zero and the House of Ahl, for my companions, and for a unified group of troopers." He asked that an angel walk with him and protect him.

The divisions set out under their standard: a gold lion with a silver sword. Mason, Winter, and Saoirse set the pace just behind a vacant traveling carriage. Their refusal to ride inside demonstrated a belief in absolute equality. The cavalcade was, however, missing several key constituents which a trip to the Chessfied stables resolved. Black Star, Monsoon, and Saoirse's yet nameless gelding galloped in an oversized pen. They met their riders with loose jaws, swinging tails, and ground pawing. The horses were taken by the army's finest hostler and remained under his care, tackless, until the imminent engagement.

The war parade traveled west and north of the city on a broad, familiar road. In an act of gratitude which left the troopers awestruck, early rising citizens had assembled along Chessfield's ramparts, some even atop the battlements, dreamlike against the sunrise. A hymn, which seemed to abolish all doubt and distress, was sung to the bright heartfelt accompaniment of stringed instruments. Dark blue banners were waved, fists were raised, many cheered, and others were moved to tears. A young boy holding his mother's hand was dressed as a trooper. The thundering sound of applause was sent up and the clash of swords on shields was returned in recognition.

The city fell from view as the Defenders rumbled onward through colonnades of evergreen and ash trees which received rays from the morning sun—swallower of stars, perfect and flawless like refined silver, fawn-like in its purity, and indifferent to the melodrama transpiring under its watch. Wildlife moved in the cool shady depths while troops recited epic poems of fearless warriors, wandering mariners, and legendary knights; themes of old days and of new, some fictional and some rooted in fact, some tragic and some light. Any time a comment sunk the mood, humor quickly offset it. The forest, like an emerald, changed color under the changing conditions of light. A shallow valley divided by weathered fence work and dry stone boundaries gave way to purple hillscapes dotted with barns and storehouses. A captain from the rearguard began singing and soon others joined in. This is part of what they sang:

Look up in the mountains, hey hey
The mountains of your mind
They've got you by numbers, hey hey
Their legions swarm the hillside
Be careful where your words go
Somebody may know what you know
Now they ain't gonna stop
No they ain't goin' down until the clouds roll

Say look at you now, hey hey
Still runnin' for your life like a child
And all his mystic music, hey hey
Is makin' those hounds go wild
So we be careful where our words go
Somebody may know what we know
And they ain't gonna stop
No they ain't goin' down until the clouds roll

Entertained in this fashion, they traveled along the southeastern edge of the Honey Meadows. A ploughed field, the ruins of a triangular fortress, a pasture of grazing sheep, and a gated church and graveyard drifted silently by as the distant hills turned from olive green, to gold, to copper, and then back again. The paved road yielded to a dirt path and then totally surrendered to a pair of wheel ruts through grass. An outrider silhouetted against a powdered sky reigned up at the top of a knoll and confirmed the route was navigable for an army. At one point, the coachman whistled and pointed earnestly into a heath blanketed with orange hawkweed. Saoirse jumped up to peer through the carriage window. Her countenance immediately brightened; they both spotted a familiar white-coated lynx. Ghost, at times appearing only as a gliding tail or tufted ears, was keeping pace.

The day wore on. A series of spectacular sandstone formations crept into view, rising abruptly from the surrounding plain like the half-buried skeleton of some fallen behemoth. They were several times the height of the treeline. Situated atop the southernmost formation, like a seagull perched on a moonraker, was the dreamlike and seemingly inaccessible Cill Bhríde Hall & Castle. Its turrets burst up from the rock in a precarious configuration that astonished the viewer. To add to the majesty, a late orange-yellow sun dramatically lit the entire design. These were the remains of a once great empire that one could now only read about in history books. Born from the dust of a torn land, it took a century to build and posed great architectural challenges, but in the end, it became the watching eye of the east, stood safely out of arrow shot, and gave its inhabitants the ultimate vantage point over opponents. Within its walls, grandiose ceremonies took place and famous history altering documents were authored.

Not long before the sun kissed the western horizon, the cavalcade was ready to camp. A lowly glen, east of Thornydale Road not far from Oakenholt and the mysterious loch, offered suitable terrain and fair protection from the wind. Specific assignments with detailed instructions streamlined the set-up. A delegated company marked out the space, cleared brush and logs, built stone fire pits and hitching posts, and assembled tents. The area of the camp totaled some fifty acres.

From the Chief Defense Commander's quarters in a centrally located position, Winter and Mason witnessed the proceedings. A sea of burning torches offered light for the evening meal. *So many mouths to feed, yet so efficiently managed,* thought Mason. Nearby, Saoirse fed Ghost. Not long after, the din subsided and one by one the travel-worn troopers prepared to rack out. Against Heaven's violet arch, the moon took its celestial throne and presided over countless dreamers.

During the night, howling wind and rain buzzed the edge of camp. Mason awoke to booming thunder and watched electric skeletal hands reach across the black night as a storm pounded the adjacent valley. One clap was so loud it shook the ground and caused horses to rear. Further afield, ferocious gusts whipped tree limbs and hurled heavy drops and hail. The worst of it lasted for the better part of an hour, and then it rolled on to harass more southerly regions. Mason watched it all from his storm chair. *Anyone without a solid roof, hold on,* thought Mason as he sealed his tent.

When the new day dawned, the camp and hills emerged slowly from a thin straggling mist. Visibility was limited to a half mile. Storm debris littered the camp and Saoirse retrieved a delicate glass pendant from the wet grass, wondering how it withstood the severe weather and the traffic of heavy trampling boots. During breakfast, she noted the troopers were unusually quiet and they refrained from laughter and horseplay.

Mason, steadfast in his morning devotion, trusted the door to be shut and locked against any cruel and wretched abomination intent on devouring him or his army. Perseverance took form as he shielded and focused his thoughts. He prayed, "Ah Sovereign Lord, you have created this magnificent land and all that lives and grows on it. Scenes, sounds, and smells which poetry can only attempt to capture. No task is too great for you. You have given strength and courage to these thousands of men and women. Your deeds are awesome and you have triumphed through miraculous wonders. Protect us and build us up on every side, God. Let your Holy angels be with us, that the evil foe may have no power over us. Keep hope and peace within and keep sorrow and distress without. Strengthen our bones, muscles, hands, and hearts. Thank you for doing these great things. Thank you for blessing us even in the midst of trials. Thank you for listening and answering our prayers."

Mason, Winter, and Saoirse convened around a campfire for a breakfast of eggs, bacon, and porridge. The smells of cooking food mixed with smoke and the earthy smell of damp leaves. Winter had an outrider's map rolled out near his feet.

Confidently he spoke: "According to this, the loch we seek is on the other side of these hills, very close. The three of us can be there and back by midmorning. I'd prefer a small convoy to avoid any unnecessary attention." He looked to the others for thoughts and reactions.

"Gentlemen, this is straight out of some folktale. A real treasure hunt, of course I'm ready when you are!"

put in Saoirse who needed no cajoling. She moved with a surplus of energy and began packing up foodstuff for the expedition.

"Yeah, I don't want to miss this. I mean, you might not be able to carry it all!" laughed Winter. "I'll find shovels and meet you at the hitching posts."

After mason handed mission details to the colonel, the three travelers mounted up and trotted into the misty hills. A waterfall was first heard then seen. It rushed around and between mossy boulders and a wickerwork of twisted trees, formed a pool, and finally spilled under the bridge they crossed. Stands of silver birch and sessile oak rose skyward on a steep hillside where the roof of a lonely farmstead was still wet with rain. The convoy ascended, following a stone wall with miniature battlements. Never limited to a trail, Ghost bounded off toward the hill's airy summit. Past a tract resplendent in mossy ground cover, the path split and there, on a column, someone had carved the word "LAKE" with an arrow pointing right. The muddy road to the summit switched back twice through the lush hillscape where white-grey boulders lay. Sheep fed on grass under a blue-gray and faded rose cloud cover which exaggerated dark spaces and dulled the greenery. Slate walls and ferns led the way to a flatter terrain where the travelers reigned up between two rock outcrops.

Great hills and low mountains wearing a misty mantle loomed over the loch and the Isle of Dolls in what looked to be the handiwork of an inspired watercolorist. Each traveler valued the scene as they hoofed around the western shoreline. When they reached the footbridge to the isle, temperate winds rose and rain of the lightest possible variety dampened their raiments.

Mason dismounted and surveyed the footbridge. He shook its rope railing a few times, took his first timid steps, then looked over his shoulder. "Wait for me here. I must do this alone."

Winter untied a shovel and tossed it to his cousin. "It's a good job you're prepared!" he grinned. Mason spoke softly to the bridge as if words could strengthen its construction. He tested each soggy plank. On the far side, a lone redstart sang from the heights of an evergreen. A profusion of balderbloms, in a raging bloom, led into the wild thicket like a white carpet. Mason cut down branches as he sunk into the isle's woody depths. Then, a boggling scene. Inside the first ring of trees was a motley menagerie so startling, so madcap, so outlandish, it hardly seemed tangible. It was closer to a hallucination or the theatrics of some stage production. In a fairy-realm where silence was vague and awful and there were no sundials to mark the hours, hundreds of dolls festooned tree trunks, hung from bits of twine, had been skewered on posts, lay half-buried, or had been pegged to a weather-beaten shelter. Some were eyeless, some headless, some painted, some naked, some in rags. Limbs were all that remained in some cases. Whispers and vacant eyes seemed to follow him, and more than once he thought he detected the twitch of a head or arm as he walked the white trail of flowers.

Soon, Mason stood in a ring of trees with a telltale

earthy mound at its center. The wind rustled leaves and bones covered the ground. He thrust the shovel's end into the soft earth and struck something solid. Digging quickly, he cleared dirt from around a rusted strongbox. He pried off its lid and then stood beholding two relics: a hammered mail shirt and the legendary undulating sword they called Zafer. He wasted no time in pulling them from their dark domicile.

AAs he turned to leave, a man stepped forth from a dark space and blocked the way back. He dressed, moved, and bore arms identically to Mason who thought some magic mirror was reflecting his likeness. Even the stranger's voice had a familiar ring when he formally spoke the words, "Hello Mason. My name is Nosam". Mason unsheathed his sword, regripping the handle rhythmically as he crouched and stepped closer to the doppelganger. "Sheath your sword, Mason. The fight isn't between you and I. To be more precise, it's between you and yourself," explained Nosam with the cold composure of a viper.

The shape-shifting clurichaun, using wit and witchery, proceeded to describe in detail every ugly deed from Mason's past: every failure, missed opportunity, disloyalty, lie, insult, and aggression. The doppelganger hissed reminders of Mason's rude and discourteous words. Every act of pride, cruelty, ignorance, envy, lust, gluttony, and abandonment was recanted. He added every wretched and hurtful word that cut into someone's heart, the ridicule and judgment of others, work paid in full yet only half-completed, self-indulgences, and every bit of avarice. Through sorcery, a list of Mason's boastful quotes appeared. Most cruel of all, a compendium of his mistakes appeared in a tempest of smoky visions. Plumes and murky haze wore him down, crushed him with an immense weight, and left him gasping. His balance fled and blackness crept into his periphery, threatening to toss him into a void. Then, as if aided by a comforting paraclete, Mason was guided toward the solution. He suddenly remembered a vitally important key to life, a must for any resilient mind: to forgive oneself, completely and totally. He remembered grace superseded his failures, and embedded that thought firmly in his core. He fell to the ground and the last thing he remembered seeing was the shade walking away, diminishing in form and structure until it simply was no more. Exhausted, Ma-son passed out.

He awoke on the far shore of the lake. Winter and Saoirse spoke to him in calm tones, asking if he needed anything to calm his nerves or if he wanted to be left for a moment.

Suddenly, a horn wailed. The signal to move out came from an outrider of a horn from an outrider silhouetted on the hilltop.

"No rest for the weary," lamented Saoirse.

During their return trip, the outrider informed them of the Greyguard's position which called for an immediate response. Mason's strength, aided by the fresh air and smooth strides of the perceptive Monsoon, noticeably improved as the convoy reached the path's final bend. The view opened up to a greensward that seemed to run endlessly through the valley's swirling mists.

They were greeted by a grandiose spectacle: rank upon rank of troopers, mostly volunteers, stood at attention ready to be led toward the plains of combat and a fate unknown. Nearly fifteen thousand strong, some mounted, some on foot, and some bearing dark blue banners, the impressive and imposing Chessfield Defenders looked toward Mason and his companions. To this, the Archia native and the newly appointed Chief Defense Commander, pointed Zafer skyward and rode southeasterly with Saoirse and Winter at his side.

Hamlet after hamlet drifted by, their designs handsome, their names lyrical: Haymarket, Whispering Well, Silky Plot, and Martinbridge. These shy societies, overpowered by a sense of doom, kept their doors and windows closed while the troopers marched by. Their trepidation was understandable, thought Winter. These remote settlements were extremely vulnerable to an attack from the east. By midday, the sun had burned a hole through the cloud layers and dissipated the mist.

The name simply fell from her lips as she sat atop her dapple gray gelding. "Kelpie," she whispered, and then said it louder and more confidently closer to the horse's ear. "Kelpie, that's your name," she said as she rubbed his neck. It fit like a key in a lock. A conversation about horses ensued, though it was the last bit of joy they would experience until one of the two armies yielded.

When they crested a hill and looked out upon the vast plain, a cohort of captains joined the vanguard. They remained in discussions for some time while troopers awaited orders. Mason studied the landscape from the elevated vantage point and made notes and sketches in his journal. Lake Mjød, filling a caldera, rippled in the distance. The land surrounding the oval basin sloped steeply down toward the plain, reminding Winter of an anthill. Mason studied two things: a smallish watercourse flowing down one side of the landmass and a blackened patch of ground. They transfixed him like a passing comet and he smiled for the first time since leaving Chessfield.

Sixty thousand Greyguard soldiers approached the Mulga Lands from the east, led by Siol Dona and his powerful blood bay destrier. He was flanked by regiments of towering, brutal figures known as The Greyguard Giants whose feet were like the foundations of buildings. Their own strength was their god. Behind the front line, a sea of infantrymen chanted ominously as they marched: Uun! Ha! Uun! Ha! Uun! Ha! The din, reinforced by the beat of deep war drums, rolled through the still plain like a temblor. Special care was taken in the crafting of each war drum, either a low slung side tom or a shoulder-harnessed bass drum, as they swiftly raised morale while simultaneously demoralizing the adversary. Drum rolls were the simplest and most precise way to convey orders to the Greyguard in the case of physical obstructions, atmospheric effects, or any other unpredictable element a battlefield might exhibit.

The Greyguard's standardized, distinctive attire echoed unity and pride, differentiated them from the opposition, and was suitable for many climates. Each member donned spiked leather jackboots, grey sleeveless surcoats that fell to the knee, spiked silver belts, light mail for the arms, grey leather gauntlets and high collars. The helmet was visor-less with a "Y" shaped opening for the eyes and mouth. The standardized weapons were pikes and long daggers coupled with red shields that bore the insignias of the Chamber of the Wolf—three silver arrows.

After crazed conquests that decimated one peaceful town after the next, the confidence and arrogance of the force soared. As they stepped in unison, they had one singular sinister purpose in mind: to lay the whole of the north to waste. Uun! Ha! Uun! Ha! Uun! Ha! The doomsday clock ticked.

Mason could not yet see or hear Siol's soldiers, but he felt their presence. He gave an order for the Defenders to set up camp on the hilltop as night fell and star formations emerged. An outrider returned from the plain and a lengthy discussion, rampant with hand gestures, ensued. Throughout the evening, Mason blocked out everything but his journal. His stylus dashed madly from page to page. Off by himself, tapping his foot rhythmically, his face took on different forms in the dancing firelight. Some wondered if he was cut out for the task, others reasoned he must be some kind of spectral genius.

Approaching midnight, Mason called for his most seasoned farmers; he knew they wouldn't be sleeping much anyway. After they gathered, he handed out pages from his journal, duplicates of the same image: a schematic. One intuitive man looked down at the parchment and said, "He's going to divert the river." It sent a shockwave around the circle.

"If timed right, the water should cut their legions down the middle...if only temporarily." Mason paused and looked into the depths of the night. "But that's all we need. Two parts are more manageable."

Next, he configured a crude diorama on the ground using stones, sticks, and a mound of dirt—but the visual was enough to show how the terrain could be augmented to suit their needs. He made a deep imprint in the earth with his boot heel. "This is a tar pit. It's dry now, but it becomes something entirely different when drenched." He poured water into the imprint and lowered his stance looking all the more like the seasoned agronomist he was. "Tar behaves much differently than mud." Those in the circle caught on. In short order, the crack team of farmers moved toward their target like nocturnal birds of prey.

The farmers worked and slept in shifts outlined by Mason and by first light, the trenching and dam construction had been completed. Upon inspection, they estimated the handiwork doubled their chance of victory.

The Defenders assembled into four separate defensive positions while the sun bled red. The farmers, joined by one full brigade, assembled on a hilltop in the shape of a fishhook, blocking a retreat to the south. Mason guided a second brigade to the brow of a hill, northeast of the tar pit. Saoirse and a brigade of archers took a position west of the tar pit. Winter and a fourth brigade were the bait. Positioned just west of the trench, they would be the first resistance the Greyguard would see. From these separate locations, the brigades could communicate with flags waved in set patterns.

By late morning, a deep pounding of drums signaled the close proximity of the Greyguard. With swiftly beating hearts and tightened muscles, the Defenders watched the forms of soldiers and towering horse-drawn siegeworks take shape on the dusty plain. Their formations approximated lengthy rows of sturdy trees. He leaned heavily on prayer. *If I wind up in distress, answer me Lord. Hear my plea. As I'm cast into the wake of war, and the waters close in over me, hold me up. I shall always look upon you to be my rock. If my life faints away, I will remember you Lord. Remember me. With deep gratitude, thank you for these men, this landscape, and my strength. Salvation belongs to you Lord!*

Many miles to the east in a quiet war room, Calon looked upon a vestal section of linen that he tacked tightly to an oak frame. His confidence had shriveled, his nerves were frayed, and his extremities were trembling. He couldn't remove the image of Mason from his sick mind. Desperate for news from the front, he began to paint a scene. A red sunset took shape, followed by low lying hills and unique landforms. He closed his eyes and lost himself in the project.

"Awake! Awake! Rise up for battle!" roared Mason to fire up his troopers. "Sharpen your swords! Take up your shields! Clothe yourself with strength!"

Siol called his front line into position as he examined the three Defender brigades now within an arrow's range. Like his other ruthless campaigns, there would be no negotiating and no discussion of terms. With the rise and swift downward slice of his sword, the Greyguard's first volley shot skyward. The flag bearers cut a signal pattern telling the troopers to take cover. The battle had begun with no other formalities. Two other volleys were sent with little damage done. The Defenders responded with a volley of their own. The Greyguard Giants sustained losses as they struggled to evade arrows and slung rocks. The Defenders held their ground, shielded by the hills. No matter, thought Siol, they can't hide forever.

The proud Greyguard commander was prepared for trickery, but he had lost his patience with preliminary salvos. With the goal of taking the hillscape and swiftly and brutally ending the battle, Siol signaled the entire Greyguard Army to attack. Careening over the plain and bearing down on the Defenders in deep ranks and horse drawn chariots, Siol's soldiers were like demons bursting from Hell's gate. When half of his army had crossed over the trench—cleverly covered with sticks and leaves—time stood still.

Chapter 11

Knockout

The torrent - Second sight settled - Winter's brigade -
Against a wall - Entr'acte - A painting - Night camp -
Dawn drive - Meteor crater

With one well-placed blow of a sledgehammer, a lanky farmer let loose a deluge. Shattered parts of the makeshift dam were violently swept away in the raging torrent. Down the hillside it gathered strength and speed, both much more that its builders or its architect could have predicted. Some Defenders lost their footing and were sucked in as the outpouring devoured everything in its path. Like a pulled tub's plug, the entire lake began to drain. Siol stood in awe as the whitewater bore down upon him like a wall of pale colts. It was too late to react, he could only move forward—his army cleanly bisected by the unexpected surge. Thousands of his soldiers were drowned, their heavy uniforms opposing buoyancy.

In a sudden sortie, Saoirse's regiment took aim at the heart of The Greyguard Giants and the leading half of the army. With less space to operate in a bowl created by hills, the delirious Giants were pierced by spears and arrows. In horror, they realized the extent of their hasty gameplan. They had dropped knee-deep into the ground, stuck like flies in honey. Siol could not see the cannons of his destrier as it whinnied furiously trying to free itself but only worsened its plight. Down they went, horse and rider together, into the sticky black tar. Over fifteen thousand were buried, half-buried, wounded or rendered immobile, tipping the momentum in favor of the Defenders despite the initial disparity in numbers.

Mason's hammered mail shirt gleamed as he strengthened his grip on Zafer and rode Monsoon to the hilltop. He and his garrison looked down upon the tumult and realized their extemporaneous engineering efforts had leveled the field. It was an unpredictable blow that sent waves of panic through Siol's remaining divisions. The celebration was only momentary, however, as the Defenders descended the hill with the aim of striking the Greyguard's northern flank.

Something caught Mason's attention, and in a vivid flash of imagery, like light from spinning crystals, he was certain he'd been there before. He struggled to reconstruct the past from its familiarity. *Could I be reliving this event?*, he wondered.

Flash! Off balance for a moment, he spun around. The next series of events felt prewritten. *Flash!* He connected two points in time. It was the vision he had in his kitchen in Gardenwall! *Flash!* It all appeared before him now, again: the desperate yelling, the indiscernible shapes, the opaque and fuzzy chaos. It was then he saw that a trooper—an armor-bearer—had sunk chest deep in the black tar and was being swallowed alive.

In one motion, Mason dismounted and bolted toward the treacherous quagmire scoring a spear on the way. At the edge, he dropped to the ground and distributed his weight as one might on thin ice. Knee to elbow and pushing with his feet, he crawled steadily forward. At the limit of his reach he bridged the gap, but as he pulled the man toward him with the spear, he lost all leverage and became fixed himself. Pushing down into the muck failed to provide results, and in an instant his arms were buried to his shoulders. Suddenly, he felt pressure around his ankle and realized he was being dragged toward his starting point. He looked behind him at two troopers testing the limits of their muscular endurance. They heaved the two men out, helped them to their feet, and all four rejoined the fray.

The flag bearers cut another signal pattern and the Defenders raced away from the blackened dregs. A barrage of burning torches spun end over end like burning wheels, and in one cataclysmic *WHOOSH!*, the pit was lost in a blinding firestorm. A column of blistering air hauled fuel into the inferno and fed it further.

The back half of the Greyguard hesitated when they saw their commander and frontline consumed. Mason's brigade took immediate advantage of it in a calculated sortie. The Defenders formed a human blockade with one goal in mind: to contain and cut down the enemy line before it could retaliate. A fierce bit of fighting ensued on that sodden quarter of the Mulga Lands. Swords whirled madly as horses reared and arrows flew. Mason and Monsoon moved with sure swift steps and seemed to be in multiple locations at once as they split the northern flank into smaller and smaller pieces allowing their captains to finish the work.

Mason's hammered mail shirt felt as light as linen as he swung Zafer with balance and control. In alignment with the old maxim, he held his sword like a bird: not so tight that he crushed it, but not so loose that it flew away. His combat techniques and bladework were at their peak and he could feel a verve building inside. He functioned at a faster speed than those around him, as does the dragonfly, and gained confidence with each small victory. With fluidity, he evaded the sluggish movements of his opponents as they swung shotels that appeared too heavy and too awkward for their person. Down they fell, ten here, ten there. Mason was a constantly moving target with a far superior weapon. Clash, volta, thrust, parry, riposte, balestra, moulinette. Zafer sang as it sliced and danced like the burning core of a fire whirl. These things he realized as he picked up steam: he had not truly lived and he had not truly known who he was hitherto facing this kind of adversity. Determination found a solid resting place in his heart.

In the thick of one skirmish, the Chief Defense Commander partnered with one of the volunteers, a schoolmaster. Back to back, in the boar's tusk stances, they slowly revolved feeling the moment and timing their strikes. Using this method, they held their ground and dispatched scores of Calon's combatants who realized they were outmatched and were able to submit only wild and reckless swings. The schoolmaster noticed that fighting alongside Mason elevated his fighting spirit.

Across the field of slaughter, the brigade under Winter's able command rolled south where they faded into eucalypt woodlands. Racing along a hidden trail, the only resistance they faced was from the occasional brush of gimlet gum branches. They approached the crude plankwork their carpenters erected the night before. Upright during the river's initial surge, they were safely lowered and used as drawbridges. Over the rushing water they charged—men, women, and horses.

Barreling out of the woodlands and approaching with the force of a battering ram, Winter's troopers struck the Greyguard's southern flank in an ambuscade, sandwiching the soldiers within. Black Star and Winter moved back and forth parallel to the enemy line creating an imaginary border which immobilized the enemy. Many of his troopers were dual wielding specialists, unconventional on a battlefield, making them unpredictable and difficult to defend. His small agile squads of axemen were having great success up and down the flank. Their strategy: short ferocious attacks followed by line changes. Like a shark replacing lost teeth, fresh Defenders constantly rushed in to replace the lost, fatigued, and battle worn. Swift and often flawless, the line changes of the axemen took a heavy toll.

Mica had a far grander view as she looked down upon the shifting mass from on high. Feathered fauna appeared to have few luxuries—no armor, no camping gear, no forged weapons— yet their extraordinary inheritances could have changed the outcomes of innumerable campaigns. Flight and superior vision gave her an unbroken view of the Mulga Lands, making the advantages, opportunities, and quandaries of the Defenders easy to spot. She heard the muted war cries, the brittle clash of arms, and the dim beat of drums with the utmost clarity.

Mica also picked up the cutting shriek of Saoirse, who had fallen from her mount in the melee and lost her arrows. Loose silt and clay hung in the air reddening the sun and turning the landscape to foreboding sketch work. She tasted grains of sand and salt from a bleeding lip. Collecting her body from the ground and finding her balance, Saoise became cognizant of an eroded hill behind her. She retrieved her unbroken bow. Kelpie was off a short distance struck with panic and shaking his head on the verge of racing away. She made a move toward him when several figures appeared in the churning dust. Terrified, she looked upon a series of disembodied heads flying in arced paths around her locus. She scrambled backward to increase the gap then sized up the dune-like wall behind her. She sized it up for climbing. The heads took form and shape and revealed themselves as sword-wielding Greyguard horsemen. With haunting dynamism, they fanned out to corner her, a hunting tactic favored by wild dogs. The wall appeared to be mostly gravelly soil and a chunk slid away when she tested its firmness. The horsemen advanced, gearing up for nasty deeds and help was nowhere to be found. In their helmets' "Y" shaped openings, she saw darkness like freshly dug graves. Her heart sinking, she searched frantically for a large rock or an implement to sling but found nothing. All seemed to point toward her undoing as she held her bow sword-like and waved it in front of her. The lead horseman sprung to the ground and edged toward her with a stained sword.

She sent a few desperate words skyward, possibly her first attempt at a prayer and the world hung still for one intolerable breath. All at once, the shadow of two great wings appeared overhead setting off some fantastic improvisation. Mica dropped her cargo, a full quiver, at Saoirse's feet. The leader dodged the furious flyer's open talons, regrouped, and lunged forward but too late. He'd been arrow-pierced. A second horseman dismounted but froze staring down a drawn arrow. A third, a dagger artist, was now in her blind spot. He rushed to close the gap when a screeching white blur spooked him, ensnared him, and brought him down. Ghost went for his throat and held fast with stabbing canines. The cat's wriggling body was awkward and hard to grasp and its claws cut with the ease of broken glass. The mauling was met with a frenzy of flailing and kicking as the soldier slapped the ground frantically in search of his dagger. Saoirse released the arrow, a narrow miss which nevertheless kept the last soldier rooted to the spot. She drew another and moved quickly to Kelpie's side. With the smooth and sure motion of an acrobat, she was up in the saddle and gone.

Further ahead, flying wedges of Defenders smashed into the rectangular mass of Greyguard soldiers the way a sculptor's chisel breaks down a marble slab. Small units using hit-and-run tactics and other spontaneous maneuvers were successful in carving away ten here, ten there. With all that metal and leather, speed, mobility, and some aspects of vision were compromised. Intimidation from greater numbers no longer had its effect and the Greyguard began to falter and lose its structure like a weather-worn barn in a tremor. Harassed on three sides by swarming Defenders, it fought to hold its position, but could not. Its trailing line suddenly shifted east in an effort to evade the relentless attack and regroup in open space. What followed was a full blown evacuation. Soldier after soldier turned and ran, some even discarded weapons and equipment. This was a needed shot in the arm for the Defenders who thrust their weapons skyward and released howls, whoops, and colorful screams. They were like an unquenchable fire burning up chaff. The hub of the battle was undoubtedly moving eastward, away from Chessfield. The momentum shift put the Greyguard on the defense and triggered further withdrawals, retreats, and pullouts.

From their saddles, Mason and Winter signaled the edges of their brigades to turn inward and converge, forming a vast bulwark five or six troopers deep. It was as if an immense gateway closed off access to the west. A regiment led by Saoirse and Kelpie moved in to reinforce the line. The three leaders marched their entire force eastward in a display of strength and prowess. The Greyguard attempted to restructure itself but leadership seemed to be in disagreement and all looked to be systemless and frayed. After falling back to a safe distance they assembled into small groups. Mason drew nearer to determine their numbers, then held. It was a standoff, however temporarily. For the first time since the torrent, there was stillness. Mason could hear Monsoon's breathing. A thin dust devil zigzagged on the horizon.

During this unexpected and strange entr'acte, the two armies squared off and measured each other from either side of a thin tract of land. Some soldiers hunched over to catch their breath, some checked their wounds, some just looked dazed. Under ordinary circumstances, the retreating army might have capitulated to spare lives and thereby become prisoners of war. However, this was far from ordinary and this was the Greyguard. They would do everything possible to avoid crawling back to Calon with anything less than a sterling report. Mason knew he had no choice but to continue the valiant errand and push the opposition further east until it finally submitted. He waited. The dust devil lost shape and dissolved.

All that led up to this point, all the trials and all the savagery, all the preparations and all the hopes, came down to this moment. One last push. Remarkably, the final outcome would not rest upon muscle strength, athletic ability, or weapon proficiency. Rather, it was the passions of the individuals and their belief in a common cause. These factors, typically unaccounted for in historical descriptions of war, could not be measured, could not be planned for, and could not be targeted. The Greyguard was driven by their mad leader's lust for power and domination under a mandate to suppress any that stood in the way. They were mindless clones with hateful and prejudiced hearts who were obsessed with Chamber loyalty, glorifying violence, and instilling fear and dread into the small and the weak. It was a dark path that, in the end, robbed many of sanity. The Defenders were propelled by goodness and peace and fought passionately for the freedom of every upright person from Black River to Archia. If they failed, Calon would tighten his stranglehold on the region and bring down ruin upon all they knew and loved.

When his men appeared rested enough, Mason gave the signal and the hostilities began anew. The Defenders fought with boundless heroism using their reserves of strength. The Greyguard continued to lose ground and soon they were in disarray and on the run again, heading to the far eastern perimeter of the Mulga Lands.

Far over the east horizon, Calon rumbled through the corridors of his stronghold, the nightmare realm he had constructed. He pushed open the door of his studio and looked over his painting supplies with spiritless eyes. The late sun's oozing motifs emblazoned the chamber as though it were a quarry of ruby-violet eudialyte. But poisoned minds are numb to nature's elegance. Amid the smell of cut wood, amber, and white sage, he dragged his easel to some specific spot on the floor. He repositioned it, then one more time, restless and uncomfortable. Even the smallest decision he questioned. His minions would say "the fret" was over him. Examining the poplar board, he cycled through subjects hoping to trigger the magic yet again. Dark sea caverns, white crows, cromlechs and dolens, sheogues and corrigans, elementals and spirits, fairy glamour, and phantom funerals. He scanned his work table: flacons of colored water; jars of flaxseed oil;

wax molds; stacks of tracing paper and feather quill pens; brushes and sponges; clay figurines; rulers and protractors. A clay bust of his own head stood on a corner pedestal.

He pulled a floor candelabra in close and lit the tapers. The tall ceramic piece was painted a deep sapphire blue and ornamented with imps and long tangled witchscapes. He stepped to the easel, called for his resident musician, and filled his goblet with shiraz the tint of a dried up rose. Underlayers began to cover the board along with an adhesive and a lamina of silver dust. Through desultory strokes of red, burnt umber, and a trace of goldfire, a dreamlike sky emerged. He used burnt sienna and orange on a fan brush to shape barren hills and shrublands. Green pigment was used for the surrounding bleak woodlands. The brush touched down softly at first, then harder; back and forth, up and down.

His musician arrived and unwrapped a small worn fiddle. He twisted its pegs to alter the tuning then stuffed it under his chin. Under a tight hank of horsehair, the strings whimpered with woe, like the strange and fiendish dirges of red caps.

Calon went about stirring dirty water, lost in his own musings. He straightened up at the easel. In tones of cobalt, cyan, and gray, a caldera and a river took shape. The silver dust complimented all. He softened the edges to create realism all the while experimenting with color and shape. Candlesmoke lingered in the air as the room's corners faded to shadow. He took a step back for a fresh perspective and dried the brush in a scrap of wool.

The fiddle moaned with minor scales and flatted fifth triads, made all the more menacing with dramatic slides. A freshly rosined bow gave the notes clarity and sharpness like a mouthful of teeth.

Picking up the pace, Calon added a mass of Greyguard soldiers, their postures complex and varied. Some appeared to be struggling, others were in agony. The brush moved like a horsefly from the board to the palette's arrangement of mixed colors. With each stroke, came more detail. *What was this!?*, he thought. His own men in a burning black bogland!? Awestruck, he contemplated the canvas.

The fiddler picked up the tempo, fingers dancing along the neck, and seemingly bent upon cutting the instrument in half with the bow.

In that dreamlike sky, a band of winged warriors took shape. They wore elaborate headpieces and carried shields, spears, and swords of blue flame. A band of holy angels working with the enemy in what appeared to be an all out route.

Calon lost all focus and seemed to shrink down in size before the fiddler's eyes. His head teetered as if on a fulcrum and could not hold his brush hand steady. *How could my perfect machine be overpowered!?*, he wondered. His brow, eyes, and mouth were configured into something completely graceless that defied description, their interrelationships somehow wrong. The whole visage hung limp like melted wax, aging ten years in one expansion of the lungs. With a sense of impending doom, he attempted speech but it came out a dry stutter. Ma-Ma-Ma. The words would not come. He stood there detached in silent dread while his mental faculties caved in.

The sudden stoppage of music brought him out of his state of shock and he realized he had lost his sense of time, utterly absorbed in divination. He gathered himself. Yet another picture that flowed easily from his hand to the board as if he'd created it before. He opened and closed his hands hoping to feel them again and, a moment later, stepped away from the easel and set his brushes in a tin of water.

He beckoned magicians, herbalists, enchanters, sorcerers, and astrologers. Though he already knew the answer, he went straight down the line questioning each one on the possible meaning of the painting. Their eyes reeled around sharply, flashing white in the corners. After each appalling answer, he returned abuse and condemnation, all the while his face reddening as though he'd just eaten fire. No one could offer succinct advice. When their council had failed to quiet his mind, he sent them away to meet some unspeakable end. From that moment on, Calon lived in some other world with a fixed belief that what he had witnessed and heard were merely the enemy's hexwork. He caught a whiff of conspiracy in everything.

Soon, Black River began to unravel. Officers disobeyed orders and broke long standing procedures, telling many to leave for a day of reckoning was near at hand.

During a pursuit through the day's longest shadows, the retreating army was pushed eastward along the Northgate Highway. The sun and moon, trading altitude on opposite ends of the world, played on a seesaw. Deep blue surrendered to black all along the horizon. Tired, hungry, battered, outnumbered, disoriented, and leaderless, the Greyguard soldiers huddled in small groups awaiting daybreak. Vespertine battle being impractical, this was their opportunity to rest, regroup, and prepare for perhaps one last stand.

Not far away, the Defenders gathered at the base of a hill and established their night camp. A bundle of old blue and red stars silently revolved overhead. By torchlight, Winter and Saoirse organized a makeshift hospital. They delegated tasks, one of which was preparing bog moss dressings for the wounded. Saoirse, surveying this process with a tireless intensity, had a manner of zealousness.

"This absorbs just like a sponge," she explained, pushing into a handful with two fingers. She moved her hands here and there to show the curious and unacquainted. "Squeeze out the water and it's good as new. Use it over and over. It sanitizes wounds and prevents infection. A little miracle isn't it?"

The night watch moved into position, some at the crest of the hill, some along the shoulder. Others patrolled major compass points well past camp's edge forming a wreath around their locale. They installed trip wires with bells to stifle intruders. They built fires with dense eucalyptus branches which burned hot and gave off sparks. Erected tents, they hammered guylines into place. The cooks prepared scores of sandwiches with salt-cured meats and pandemain.

Mason bit into one, swallowed, then addressed Winter. "We're a short distance from the meteor crater." He paused and arranged the parts of his sandwich with the same care one might take if sitting at a king's table. "Those sheer cliffs. They might serve nicely as a pen for the rest. Fairly long way down though...so I'm told." He premeditated, rationing the details as he spoke. His weight on one leg, head down wearing a vague smile, far away yet present, he was confident and composed. On the whole, he spoke less and believed more. Untrammeled, his instinct was sharpening.

Winter's countenance beamed as his cousin's compact illustration triggered a clear picture. "Sheer and a long way down...indeed. I don't expect they'll stand to give up much more ground or surrender without a fight. At any rate, it's ours to win or lose." Mason was nodding rhythmically as he chewed, as if listening to a nocturne no one else could hear. "We should get an early start," added Winter.

They angled back toward the fire pits where troopers entertained each other with the details of the day's skirmishes and entanglements. "Yes. Before the dawn. I'll give word to my brigade and inform Saoirse to do the same." Mason took a final bite, gripped and shook Winter's shoulder firmly, then disappeared among flickering orange faces.

Saoirse watched him approach the hospital with a quick gait and a look of resoluteness across his visage, his hand fastened to the pommel of Zafer. They walked the perimeter of the tent city where she apprised him of the lost, the suffering, and the saved. Rows of trooper laden cots could be seen through dim openings. It was a scene common in the aftermath of battle but nevertheless hard to come to grips with. Saoirse cleaned her hands on a piece of cloth and her words were painted with a touch of gloom. Her summary, however, was better than expected. She and her staff had done a fine job. The vast majority responded well to treatment and improved by the hour.

"A strange thing happens when a person believes they are near the end," she lamented. "All the details become... inconsequential. The things they said reminded me of messages on headstones. Most wanted to feel as though they made a difference; to be remembered for what happened today. Some asked to hold a banner. Some spoke of their families and loved ones. Others feared they hadn't done enough. Some apologized, felt they were a burden...to think. One was simply sad to leave his friends. Another saw the beauty in everything, even her last moment. That one got me."

Compassion was something that rested within every Archian heart and Mason had it in abundance. He grieved for the fallen and the wounded, and he prayed aloud for them, perhaps the most eloquently constructed lines of verse Saorise had ever heard. She seemed to study the words and phrases, measure them, and commit them to memory. She inhaled and exhaled slowly and deeply. The picture was reframed, her gloom transformed into something wholly tranquil.

After a moment, Mason said something to raise her spirits, but only a portion registered, so in a trance was she. They drew up to a whipping torch where he motioned for her to stop. Then, in the fashion of a mapmaker of old, he pulled Zafer from the scabbard and scored the ground. A landscape took shape, first the highway, then the meteor crater. All this was explained as he carved the scrimshaw. "Now here's what I have in mind for a knockout blow."

In other parts of the camp the atmosphere verged on celebratory. Troopers who had pulled through with only mild scratches and sore feet described the battle's most calamitous moments. With a comedic approach, the bridge builders recanted the prior night's events as they endeavored to raise the structures with scarce light and a sorry assortment of tools. There was laughter where there had been so much horror. Others basked silently in the peace of accomplishment. Many nodded off to sleep were they sat, hypnotized by the arrhythmia of glowing cinders. When only night owls remained, a soft strain slipped up with the smoke toward those old stars.

Twist of a shadow on fresh fallen snow
The road it is narrow so the riding will be slow
Down comes a blackbird and up goes his soul
He hangs his head over just to hear the wind blow

I guess I need some time
To say what's on my mind
I guess I need some time

To say what's on my mind
What is on your mind?

A meaningful journey in an all but hateful dream
I was standing right next to you but I never heard you scream
Sometimes I think that you just like to scare yourself
Is everyone a doll upon your little bedroom shelf?

"Already?" mumbled Winter, shaking off dreams of frigates and false transfers. It was yet dark and Mason was nudging his boot to rouse him. "Just when I got comfortable," he grumbled. The waking party was dressed, armored, and tearing into slices of scrapple.

Saoirse offered one to him and whispered, "It's showtime."

The full corps of Defenders followed a fiery violet star named Tychonus, known the world over as "the scorcher", which sat low on the horizon over the meteor crater. It gazed back from its aerial throne room with silent kinglike authority and imbued with passionate interest, lifting their spirits and somehow urging them on. They traveled afoot to ensure a stealthy and muted approach in an arc one thousand troopers wide and several deep. The formation was dubbed "the net" as it was similar in form and function to a fisherman's net. At length, the fingers of dawn lightly traced treetops, highlands, and eventually enemy lookouts. Their strategy was partially efficacious, and three lookouts were eliminated while three others fled on horseback in the direction of Tychonus. Mason's signal launched a pursuit and full-blown attack, the sound of which was like an ocean wave sweeping a beach. The abrupt appearance of so many adversaries put the enemy camp in defensive postures as they scrambled desperately for arms. The use of timing, the gaining of momentum, and the exploitation of any advantage, however superficial, can pay large dividends as military leaders are well aware; and so it was that many of the Greyguard were dispatched before they could organize or take saddles.

The mad discordant roar of battle surged in erratic tangents. War cries and clashing swords mixed with trumpet blasts and deafening drums. The Greyguard realized they could no longer hold their position and hustled to a neutral plot to the east. They held briefly then gave ground, resisted for a turn, then withdrew. They were hedged in here and cut off there by the steady tempered Defenders who with dogged determination began to assert their dominance. As speculated during the evening's council, the opposition seemed unaware of, or at least unaffected by, their position in relation to the enormous hole in the ground. Eighty horse drawn carriages in single file would not span its width, so great was the cavity. The action rattled uphill toward the raised jagged edge of the crater which appeared rusty orange in the early morning luminescence. Across the plain to her left, Saoirse watched a curved rank of Defenders maneuver itself in an effort to close the gap and thwart an eastern retreat. A clockmaker would have said the movement simulated a second hand racing across a dial. And so it was, within moments, the configuration was recast once again.

The Greyguard, pushed to the precipice by these ragged and hastily trained troopers, appeared mystified. Their ominous chant no longer rang out. Many stole glances into the abyssal cauldron now crosscut by a lambent lightplane. Below that, it was jet black like a hole where a star had collapsed. Baylor's cavernous mouth, a channel to oblivion, would have been more welcoming. Fortune's careening wheel began to flatten them with its forbidding payload as the steel hearted worked the ground with their boots to prevent backsliding when contact was made. "It'll be your grave," one cried out. A volley was sent toward the approaching Defenders who stood firmly behind shields.

Winter and Saoirse knew their adversaries were still fueled by acute conditions of evil and corruption, and this was no time for a misstep. *The most dangerous animal is a wounded and cornered one,* thought Mason warily. He recognized the gravity of the moment. The Greyguard was facing him. There could be no honorable negotiations. There could be no exchange of logic. An extension of Calon himself, they were malevolent, ruthless, and callous. And forevermore, there would be no abatement of their grotesque and vicious agenda until they met their complete and irrefutable end.

A second volley sailed toward the planted Defenders. It triggered an aggressive and dramatic response which would be reconstructed in history books, encomiums, threnodies, and epic poetry as the centuries spiraled down. The two armies engaged on that precarious plot without faculty of time or place. There was only the hideous fervor of swords and pikes. Prayers were sent toward the permanent sphere. The Greyguard caught the full force of the vigorous charge and many with no ground to give were sent tumbling from the dizzy height, their arms pinwheeling as they descended like maple tree seedlings. Here and there an entangled Defender was hauled over the brink, in a dreadful and horrific avalanche.

Winter, raiments ragged, was engaged with a foe much larger than he. Both men, sweat-soaked and helmetless, grappled in a burgeoning cloud of dust. Winter was spun around by the arms and the lower half of his body dangled over the edge. The soldier dug his boot tips into the soil attempting to push Winter into the abyss but they were banded together at the forearms. Realizing this challenge, he changed his strategy and now made no attempt to save himself. He dug in and pushed again hoping to send both of them plummeting to their doom. With a madly searching foot, Winter found a hollow and corrupted the progression for the span of a breath or two. *Think!* He focused on his left arm where pressure felt weakest then twisted it in various angles. His forearm sprung free and artless jabs were exchanged with the now free hands. Winter hurled a fistful of dirt in the soldier's face, stalling him for a moment, then brought his left leg up and over the ledge. A right elbow immediately followed. Then with one nimble roll he was up and over his opponent in the manner of a wrestler. There was a brief struggle. The soldier looked down at his wrists finding they had somehow been tied with the strap of a water-skin. A look of terror; he knew his fate as Winter's boot struck him mid-torso and the edge accelerated away.

The men and women of Chessfield, fighters through and through, showed few signs of weakness for the remainder of the conflict. Under tough-minded leadership they rose to new heights. One by one, Greyguard soldiers plummeted into the cauldron which revealed its vastness under the rising sun. When their remaining numbers were in the hundreds, the frenzy subsided and the Defenders showed mercy. Soldiers dropped their pikes and shields and the backed away.

Mason lifted a hand toward the sky in a universal gesture permitting them to clear out with whatever remaining dignity they had. He knew they would have to face Calon and their fate had already been sealed.

The battle was over, and the Defenders celebrated victory. Wounds were few and mild. Across the landscape, they delivered backslaps, embraced ecstatically, roared with laughter, bent in tired postures, interjected uncontrollably, wept with joy, sighed relief, and spoke earnest orisons. They unlaced boots, loosened equipment, dismounted horses, and raised their helmets in the air. Some walked or sat in quiet contemplation, others simply lost words.

Winter, Mason, and Saoirse gathered in concert on an elevated plot some distance away from the cliffs. "That was one for the ages," marveled Winter. In a content daze, he brushed dust from his beard and contemplated the immensity and depth of the crater he peered down into from a wide angle. "I've seen two-headed kraits, bloody waterfalls, endless lightning, sailing stones, walked hidden beaches, met a seventh son of a seventh son, encountered merrows and lutins, and found a piece of a soul cage, but I've never seen the likes of this. No, can't say I have."

"There can be no denying that. Yet our work is not complete. While that monomaniac and his servants continue to plot, no one is safe," Mason lamented. The dust settled on the plain and all wound down. A cormorant sailed overhead flapping its shadow-like wings against long wispy streamers. "So, after a night's rest, up the mountain we must go." For a moment he studied his reflection in the silver and gold of Zafer. He appeared tired yet hopeful.

Saoirse made eye contact with Ghost who gamboled in a patch of tall grass. "We may not have known our own strength. We do now. Every soul here has much to be proud of and much to be grateful for." Her words carried within them slow burning embers.

Night fell as camp took shape. The wounded would make their way back to Chessfield, the rest would join Mason on the final leg of the campaign. The mood around the fires was relaxed and positive. Each individual enjoyed bread and a heaping ladle of thick stew, though it was a lost cause for most to remain awake much past the meal's end. Within the hour, a light show unfolded. Stars gleamed across the heavens in lean arrays as though flung from a painter's brush. The wavy curtain of a pink aurora dropped down onto the great ebony stage. Here and there, stars winked as the small hours approached.

Chapter 12

Final Day

The valley - The turf house - A conversation - Gold guitar - Final day

Gold, yellow, and peach-flame pigments and the shadows of dreamseed trees beautified the ground where Mason leaned over his journal. He took a sip of coffee then scribbled with vigor. A route map to the giant gates of Black River took shape. He mulled over the design and modified it more than once, leaving it a work in progress. He placed a feather in the page gutter and closed the worn cover, contemplating the contents for an interval. His morning devotion included prayers of thanks for the resilience of his army and for his mental and physical strength. He praised God for the splendor of His Holiness. Wisdom he sought like hidden treasure, and though he often neglected to simply ask for it, he trusted God would give it to him liberally and without reproach. He prayed he would be shielded against corruption of the heart and manifestation of fear.

Troopers awoke in steady numbers, pulled their tent cords, and tended to their horses. In the space of an hour, it was as if no army had camped there. They were on the move again, this time, ten thousand strong. They kept morale up with riddles, storytelling, and knowledge games, one of which revolved around listing the various methods one could use to find true north.

"Look for moss. It favors the north side of trees and rocks where sunlight is scarce," explained one.

"Tree branches on a trunk's north-facing side are thinner and reach for the sun," put in another.

"Watch for webs. Spiders spin on the south sides of trees," came a shot from the back.

"It's a slice of pie. Put a stick in the ground and note the shadow mechanics between two points. They'll run east to west. And there's always the path of the sun!" On they went sharing examples, a few of which Saoirse presumed were created for entertainment purposes only.

A squad near the middle of the war parade dredged their minds for lyrics and melodies until they agreed upon suitable strains.

Put our mark upon the world as we tread along
Keep the halls of justice right, do the world no wrong
And the battles that don't kill will only make us strong
Won't slow down until we've climbed the steepest hill

Worlds divide and fall
Kings define the law
Five depends on four
Words decide the war

Hiding behind fortress gates from prophets in disguise
Slave is he to Shadowmaster's love for spite and lies
Sitting in his throne on high he'll watch Black River rise

Go and have a look, the events are written in the book

Worlds divide and fall
Kings define the law
Five depends on four
Words decide the war

In the paintings you will see us in our brightest mail
From Chessfield to the Mulga Lands we have yet to fail
Angels from the Heav'ns above help us tip the scales
We have paid our debts, we live on what is left

Worlds divide and fall
Kings define the law
Five depends on four
Words decide the war

As the bloated sun dipped close to the western horizon, the topography began to change. The red gravel sand, sparse vegetation, and spindly trees gave way to a greensward with swaying wild grass, verdant shrubbery, and an assortment of younger broadleaf trees. The layered bedrock formations to either side of their route steadily increased in height as they entered a valley where towering conifer crowns prevailed.

Saoirse noted their proximity to Heddwich and Ft. Kerr, the remains of which were nestled in the highlands to the north. For her parents she silently grieved once more, sullen and numb to joy. Tears left tracks on her face. With some effort, she found and clung to fair and soothing memories. She felt truly blessed to have had them in her life as long as she did, and at times while traveling she even felt their presence. This final assignment was for them, and even though they were no longer with her in the material world, they were helping her endure these heathenish times. From them she learned fortitude; she was now one that could be relied upon.

The foot soldiers felt the upward tilt of the road and their leg muscles sent complaints. A low wall of irregular stones to the left restrained the wilder woods beyond, while to the right a crude handrail served as a line of demarcation. Past that, steep hills arched into the vaulted sky. A clustered maze of red star grew in euphoric bliss along one slope, setting it on fire. They forded a small stream no deeper than the fetlocks of their horses. In a waking dream, they passed under a primitive bridge softened by patches of immortelle which grew between its stones. No lands glowed more divine than here. The scenes were a gallery of God's masterpieces. Pineapple lilies and scarlet elf cups encroached upon the handrail like spectators beholding a ceremony.

In their marching state, the whole procession emitted enough clamour to keep the timid beasts of the woodlands in their dens, holes, and eyries. Lonely farmsteads and embowered hovels floated by, each one different from the next. In one field, a wagon was cloaked in a multitude of hunter-hued ganglia. An ill-lit vale followed an emerald crest, a shaded glen preceded a plot of white fusion calathea for all the world like seafoam; all illustrating nature's varied moods. They trekked further into an old forest bursting with hemlock, cedar, and spruce, many of which were several hundred years old. One immense red cedar, full of years and royal as a castle's keep, rose from the rich green depths with a crown the size of a basilica. It was a navigational marker on level with the sun's fountain of light or the moon against the darkest dye.

Boreens and crooked footways weaved up and away from the lush valley's median and led to scenic loops, parcels of blackberry brambles, and nowhere in particular. Soon, sheer granite cliffs ascended vertically on either side, so cleaved by a mighty prehistoric ice floe. Winter speculated they must rise at least three hundred feet. Water plunging from the zenith seemed to advance at quarter speed so great was the distance it covered. Against these myrtle and ashen tones, stood a water-powered sawmill all fallen to ruin and now the dominion of brimstone butterflies and whippoorwill shoes as plentiful as shells on a beach. Low pine boughs threw green shadows across its weathered planks and silent unmoving wheel. Nestled against the rock face was a tight bundle of cottages too small to be called a hamlet. All was still within them. To the army's left, a brook dipped and swerved down the valley, hunting for lower ground. Behind them, the horizon cut the vermilion sun in half, while far ahead the brooding peaks of the Black Mountains pierced the sky with cold permanence.

Daylight was fading. They marched alongside a leaf-buried embankment beyond which ranks of mountain ash and birch thrived on an extreme incline. At the next bend, they crossed a bridge and entered an open demesne where the trees were fewer and the slope was gentle. There was a good amount of open pasture and here Mason advised his captains to set up camp for the evening. A turf house, known locally as a torfbaeir, was tucked up underneath a blanket of grass. A specter of smoke wandered from its chimney. After exchanging inquisitive expressions with Mason, Saoirse and Winter dismounted and approached the dwelling. A horseshoe hung above the doorway and firewood was stacked neatly to one side.

"Hello! Is anyone at home?" called Saoirse, "We are the Defenders of Chessfield." She called again. Winter shrugged and peered through a window. No salutation was returned and no one stirred within. She knocked and made the introduction again. Here's neck or nothing, she thought, and let herself in. The place looked lived in. A table was set for dinner. A guitar rested against a hearth where a log burned low. In the corner stood a spinning wheel, its bobbin half full. She opened closets and checked the floorboards for trapdoors.

"No one inside and no real place to hide. Very odd," said Saoirse, expecting the worst. "Let's try the barn," she urged. Winter followed her toward the structure, hand on hilt. A sparrow hawk dove from the loft doors. It was now too dark to discern more than vague shapes so they paused outside the wide threshold where they again made their benign proclamations. To the woody shadows and murmuring animals within, they offered their names, explained their origins and their connection to Chessfield, recounted the contest near the crater and the walk up through the valley, and ended with their vow to reach Black River and oust the region's deceitful and fraudulent ruler. This address was perhaps more for themselves than for anyone who might remain unhinted. It was consolatory to walk through their whole campaign once again; an opportunity for a greater understanding of the story they were writing.

"Well make yourself at home in that case!" came a wobbly and lilting brogue. Winter and Saoirse both lit up. "Your rivals were here and gone, days ago," continued the voice, "but we have hiding places that foil the best seekers, you see. Then, curiously, a much smaller number of them passed this way a second time, heading back up the mountain. No doubt, those devils were heading back to hell's gates." Finally revealing themselves, was a short and handsome couple at work brushing hay from their clothing. "I am Arne and this is Enna. Pleased to meet you, and we're truly gracious we didn't have to use the family claymore!" They expressed their joy by performing a traditional rinkafadda with an attempt to bring Saoirse and Winter straight into the skipping and twirling. A friendship was quickly forged.

The couple proved to be exceptional hosts, and though they had never opened their home to an entire army, much less one fresh from the ravages of battle, they seemed to be in their element filling cups with well water, feeding logs to the fires, handing out fig cakes, and ensuring each trooper had a comfortable place to recline. The barn was theirs to use for shelter, announced Arne, who went on to explain it had two stories and a great deal of room, but they would have to work out on their own who was entitled to it since it wouldn't house the lot. Food lines were arranged along the edge of a diminutive orchard and the atmosphere remained tranquil and untroubled.

Winter and Mason, in the midst of a harrowing campaign, found serenity in milder topics—their horses, the cooler temperatures, and how quickly evening descended upon the valley. The sound of crickets, mockingbirds, and other nameless hunters of the night accompanied the crackling fires, muffled chatter, and erratic breeze through unnumbered trees. In due time, they all slept as if only a quake could wake them.

A few hundred ragged Greyguard soldiers moved wearily along the Road of the Bones as dreadful thoughts raided the wastes of their minds. Upon reaching the gates of Black River, the base and nameless brood shouted madly, "Let us in! Our enemies are in hot pursuit!" The watchmen who prowled the lofty stone wall looked down upon them in horror. They stood utterly wrecked as bitter gusts bore down on them. At first they assumed the soldiers were stricken by witchcraft, yet a chilling question dominated their minds: *How could a once great militia have been so depleted?* Once inside, the remaining officials delivered the dire report to the Chamber of the Wolf and were immediately relieved of their posts and escorted to an oubliette. Calon's hysterical fits of rage were strangely absent. Twice isolated, once in a fortress of stone, twice in a fortress of delusion, he gravely listened to every word as the color left his visage. His heart had become brittle and small in the grasp of fear's icy teeth. What was crooked could not be straightened. Once an inexhaustible well of power and possibility, the future now seemed jeopardous. He no longer had the courage to face the Defenders, so he did the only thing he could do. He ordered the city gates to be locked and barred. No one was let out and no one would be let in.

By the misty light of morningtide, Mason and Monsoon rode a woodland loop north of the orchard. Wildflowers, dark dells, brick arches, and stacked stone walls meandering through it made for an indefinable grandeur. Grassy ribbons undulated down among the sylvan heights then spilled out into more level terrain. He reined up at a towerhouse to collect his thoughts, focus on the day's task, and pray. The structure he faced was several hundred years old, and though long deserted and ivy laden, it was still in favorable condition. It had its moment of prestige in the depths of antiquity.

On the host's farm, troopers extinguished breakfast fires and prepared horses in the paddock. They loaded grains, farrier tools, and angling gear into saddlehorn bags and stowed water, victuals, and alternate wardrobes in rear storage bags. Tasks or assignments anchored minds and kept the cloud of gloom at bay. Acts of servitude kept them composed; the wise knew fear could be ousted by focus. Some joked and some some held their tongues. Some became overbearing and some remained distant. Some felt heroic, others accepted their weakness. Some carried sentimental drawings of loved ones, others wore good luck charms.

Upon Mason's return, the leaders exchanged gracious parting words with Arne and Enna, and the army began its steady march up the valley toward the target. Before long, the farm vanished from sight and strange and wild territory enveloped them. Bit by bit, the mountains made their presence felt. Boulders leaned out over the road as if prepared to break free and roll down upon them. The road became less even, lost its shape, and splintered away toward tangled thicket and lonely overgrown banks. *Bye civilization,* thought Winter. The convoy followed an avenue of flattened grass that cut through stands of narrow birch and mighty pines of silver-green hues. Beyond, a barren ridgeline shaped like a bycocket, fenced the woodlands in. The stream, constantly babbling and splashing nearby, was a fine directional device and stocked with fish to boot. They entered a wide drainage basin, the dominion of waterfalls. These spilled from every compass point, sinuous and gem-colored. Midnight masquerade beardtongue sprung up—elegant and worldly-wise in stunning purple.

They paused to assess the next obstacle. Rustic pierwork, not wide enough for two riders, meandered over a muddy landscape and terminated at the head of a rocky trail. There, a path rose steeply, rose to a dizzying height, and curled around the shoulder of a great hill. Dread raced up spines. They clattered single file over the pierwork and paused again before their ascent. Troopers exchanged words of advice and encouragement and Mason led the way up. Soon, they rode alongside the tips of kingly sugar pines and the straight drop to one side became increasingly perilous. Black Star planted each foot firmly, fearing a misstep would lead to misfortune. Cobble dropped down into nothingness and sent back delayed cracks and bangs. Winter closed his eyes, then opened them to make sure what he viewed was real. In this realm of eagles, the fear factor of heights had to be marginalized. He pulled himself together and fixed upon the horse directly ahead. Saoirse dismounted half way to assist a rider. Each fretful section tested their mettle. Throughout the daunting task, as much mental as physical, there was no place to rest and the wind whistled incessantly.

In due time, they reached an area of level high ground between two ranges where a series of hot springs pooled and bubbled. Hardy mountain stubble cut through slopes of talus and scree and there were cavern holes up high in the rocky shelves. Mason guessed they were within three hours of Black River and within one from The Road of The Bones. Calon's army had cut a wide lane down through the valley which the Defenders were able to trace without much difficulty.

"Och, the hard part is behind us. I've heard tales of Phooka Pass, but have never had the pleasure. That's Storm Ridge there, and Nain's Head over there. I recognize them both from carvings," shared Saoirse as she scratched Kelpie's neck. She directed the next statement to Mason. "By now, Calon has likely received the news.

He could be planning an ambush. Prepare for anything I suppose?"

"Indeed, as surely as sparks fly upward. Until the last note of the last song, be it carol or cronane," acknowledged Mason. "Now is not the time to let down our guard." He gestured and brought the army to a standstill. No one had to be told twice.

It was a sightly spot for rest and recovery and an appropriate time for lunch. The sun beamed high overhead, full and bright. Horses were groomed, muscles were stretched, and an archery target was set up. A group of women found that nutcracker birds could be fed by hand. Troopers reclined around the hot springs and passed around a bar of soap. In time, the smell of sweat and leather dissipated. It was only a matter of time before the baritones unshackled new melodies:

Traded all for some warm sunshine
It's alright and we won't mind
Took a pull from the travel pack in the canyon
On a horse's back

Lost my place in the royal line
Diamond rings, bells and ribbons
Well it's alright cause we know they can't fight back
Oh yeah yeah
Please please live in the now
Oh I'm telling you
Please please live in the now

Silver made in moonlight
Diamond rings, bells and ribbons
Many miles to the next rest stop
On a steep mountain highway
I heard a song in the caravan
As we talked about the landscape
But here I am in a nice hot spring
Always say, always say...

Please please live in the now
Oh I'm telling you
Please please live in the now

After this respite, they all set steady feet upon the path and moiled on. Stronger in many ways, they remained in eager expectation of the journey's end. There was renewed passion to confound those who deprived the innocent of freedom by promoting destruction and terror. The clatter of battle gear and the voice of the wild filled their ears. No one dwelled along the path they traveled. Any hardy inhabitants had either fled or been done away with by the Greyguard. Not one hut was to be found.

Ahead, Electric Mountain rose to a radiant white point. To the south, Orge Peak crept skyward. They ventured through fantasy landscapes and dense boscage where elevations were in flux and timid wildlife observed from a distance. Summits sprawled out ahead of the caravan with names that might accompany wandwork: Cloud's Rest, Granite Spire, Sentinel of Stone, and Silverthrone. Up these features rose into zones too remote to reach: Snowtower, Fion's Point, Bishop's Mitre, and Harpy Ridge.

Atop Monsoon, Mason clasped the gold guitar pick admiring the cross cut through its center. He remained vexed over its use and could not hold back a tide of questions. *Was I supposed to give it to someone? Did I miss my opportunity to use it? Was there some hidden meaning in Asterina's words that I failed to grasp? Was there some lesson to be learned? I have no instrument to play. Am I to build one?*

In full accordance with the depictions of their maps, they reached the origin of The Road of the Bones. A sight to behold, the road's ingress was designated by a lineup of immense heads carved from crystalline limestone: a ram, a sun king, a python, the goddess of a moon cult. Most stood twice the height of Black Star. A mammoth stood next to a follet. Winter studied one behemoth bust. Donning a pileus helmet, its face had been fractured by elements and the relentlessness of time. These cryptic monuments all wore blank stares, even expressions of shock, mouths open in witness to some perplexing act upon that desolate road where travelers from every age came and went. Saoirse looked into the remains of a forgotten altar and pondered its purpose.

True to its name, there were indeed bone fragments along the road. Skulls, teeth, rib cages, and other petrified forms littered the ditches. The fragile string of a tailbone curled through the dirt. Bleached, crushed, and sometimes gnawed upon, they served as chilling reminders of war, bloodshed, pestilence, and famine—the grim side of life.

The landscape changed more than once and before long they arrived at a glen where shade mixed harmoniously with spots of lemon rind sunshine. Gözler Glen, as it was known, was a place of legend. The tylwyth trees here were said to have the ability to see and transmit events back to Black River, straight into Elymas' scrying mirror. Indeed, there appeared to be eye holes scattered about the trunks, but to Mason they could simply have been hollows, pruning wounds, or some other growth anomaly. They stretched in oblong shapes, slicker and darker than sea oil. Oddly, these peculiarities did not make the trees or the glen any less magnificent. It was beautiful beyond measure.

They traveled through a region that had suffered a forest fire and was now a bleak and bare moonscape beset with charred pillars. The hillocks were still smoking in places. It was a desolation. The wind stirred up bits of ash and, for a stretch, they masked their faces. A seedling broke through the scalded ground and it stood up in defiance of its surroundings. *Life persists through the worst of calamities,* thought Saoirse.

Either through arboreal visions, his soldiers' reports, or some other spellcraft, Calon knew the Defenders would arrive soon.

Then, an astonishing incident transpired. Right there on a forlorn road that wound through a wasteland. It happened this way: Mason noticed a figure appear in the road some distance ahead. On foot, the figure stood all alone and faced the army. Mason raised a bent arm to halt his convoy. He gestured to his captains he'd like to approach the figure alone, dismounted Monsoon, and handed the reins to Winter. He stepped closer to the figure taking note of the telltale silhouette. A guitar was slung across the back and a sword fastened at the waist. Mason looked back at his companions who seemed discomposed. Mason drew nearer and observed a virulent visage that belonged to a stranger, yet had the demeanor of an Archian.

"Are you for us or for our adversaries?" inquired Mason.

"Neither, but as a leader of the Hallowed Chorus, I have a gift for you." The stranger reached back to where the strap was connected to the body of the guitar and unfastened it. He removed the instrument and held it out to Mason across both hands. "The pick you have been given will make the strings resonate in a special way."

In a rush, Mason recognized him as one of the master musicians who frequented Gardenwall. His raiment left no doubt: bracelets of silver, carnelian, and lava, black clothing, and light brown leather vest adorned with branches and curious symbols. The scent of spikenard was present. Mason reached out to accept the gold guitar, a combination of the finest woods and inlaid with pearl. All was just as he had remembered but even more majestic and otherworldly in his own hands—carved angel's wings encircling the upper bout, four large gold rings, an ornate spiraling bridge ending in dual triangles, and a sound hole wrapped in blazing jasper. He searched for the appropriate words of gratitude when the silence was shattered by the bark of a dog fitted with a turquoise scarf. It appeared just as mysteriously as the gift bearer before him.

"Relief is on the way. You will understand when you reach the gates of Black River." Dog and stranger then walked north into the hills where a castle rose in the distance like a white stone. Mason returned to his companions with very little in the way of an explanation. With a refreshed spirit, He mounted Monsoon and secured the gift he received. *If the enigmatic guitarist hailed from Gardenwall, what possibly could he be doing here? If he hailed from the mountains, what was he doing in Gardenwall so many days before?*

After a short duration, their goal was in sight. Mason brought the army to rest when they gained the far edge of the outer ward. The forbidding battlements of Black River twisted and hooked in a menacing configuration. The magnitude and imposing presence of the city were a sinister spectacle—the headquarters of hate, the capital of calamity. There were no signs of life; no garrisons in control of the surrounding country; no pitiless watchmen on the lofty wall; no sentries behind the plunging arrow loops; not even the sound of a lark. The great gates appeared as immovable as the surrounding mountains.

Mason contemplated a course of action. *Could his army penetrate the gates? Could they scale the walls? Could they provoke the enemy to challenge them in the outer ward?* Though hanging in doubt, he encouraged his companions. All else was vain.

"Brothers and sisters of light: take up your positions. Be on your guard; stand firm in the faith; let nothing move you. Act bravely for our people and the cities of God. Devote yourselves fully to the task. You were called here to be FREEEEE!" shouted Mason. His eyes burned brightly.

The last vile members of the Chamber of the Wolf had fled into the city's bowels and with them the remnants of the once fierce Greyguard. Calon looked down upon his mortal foes from a high vantage point beyond the wall. With wits withered and the weight of a millstone around his neck, he was mocked by reason he no longer possessed.

A military force was spread out along the red horizon like a row of pewter cutlery and at the helm rode their fearless commander who displayed a certain air of magnificence and no sign of yielding. Small pieces of linen were distributed.

Fixed in the saddle at the center of this momentous stage, Mason knew it was time to finish the work. It was his duty to scourge this author of misery and his dread parade, giving peace back to the poor souls who had suffered by their hands. Guided by a boundless resolve, he swung down from Monsoon and stepped closer to the gates. He slung the guitar around his neck and rested the pick on the strings. A curious spectacle it was, his own shadow stretching halfway to the battlements.

Then it happened, all at once and without warning, just as the stranger had foretold. A procession approached from the west with a cargo of implements that caught the sun's late rays. Ghost studied the newcomers momentarily but showed no sign of aggression. His loose, fluid body movements suggested entirely the opposite. The procession was soon in their midst. Unarmored, they quietly passed through the steady line of Defenders and assembled alongside Mason. Some faces he recognized, some he did not. These were the myriad of musicians from the long extraordinary journey: the three-piece musical ensemble from North Oak; a man with a gjallarhorn; the lute playing priest; the gongmaster from east Archia; the pipers and chanters from Woodlawn; the aşık and the craftsman; the fiddler from Royal Banners; Darsh and a pack of gypsies; Reina, Gazi, and Karaliene from the Little Queens; the gardener from Emry; and assorted buskers from Chessfield. Winter and Saoirse felt a sudden release of tension and could only look on in wonder. Mason fastidiously placed a shred of linen into each ear; every man and woman on the battle line did the same.

With unparalleled exuberance, the musicians raised their instruments and launched into an elemental symphony, perfect in power and form. To add to the sonic assault, the troopers sent forth a thunderclap war cry. Compressed air exploded to produce a deafening din. With a ferocity unknown, the violent vibrations impacted the battlements like a rogue wave slamming into a cliffside. Rattling trumpets loosed mortar. Tolling carillons rocked walls. Pounding toms and tablas warped the ground. Sharp strums of lyres forged faultlines. Bellowing ram's horns fractured foundations. Crashing gongs cracked the great gate. Timbrels and sistrums sent blocks tumbling. Fretted mandolins and plucked harps shattered glass. Hammered dulcimers split beams. Crashing cymbals toppled turrets. And shofars felled domes. The entire fortified structure was leaning to one side as curtain walls dropped like sheets from a clothesline. A billowing mass of dust and debris rolled outward then crept toward the sky past heights of the once standing structures. The mighty cacophony shook the mountains.

Saoirse played the shell horn and a rampart spilled away like grain from a sackcloth. Mason struck the gold guitar's strings and a tower faltered and failed. Winter, hands to the sides of his mouth, sent forth a deep booming bellow. Ghost released a growl and Mica sounded her alarm.

Within the borders of the city, doors swung wildly in thresholds, roads buckled, spires fractured and fell, welded metal shrieked, pillars reeled like drunkards, water overflowed from fountains and pools, tables and furniture bounced wildly, stairways broke away, gods of gold and idols of metal were crushed, sacred stones broke to pieces, monuments burst asunder. There was no firm place to stand. There was no place to take shelter. The elemental symphony persisted until every building and wall was annihilated. It was done.

The city, along with its history of transgressions, lay in ruin. The bloodthirsty and the deceitful, who craved a world of chaos, were buried underneath a mass of dust and rubble. A stillness pervaded while each Defender and musician emerged from a chrysalis of disbelief. The truth set in. The people of the north were delivered from doom and the wicked would oppress them no more.

For the first time, a euphoric cheer shook the Road of the Bones. The troopers raised their instruments, swords, and fists in triumph. Hymns were composed on the spot. Tears of joy and thanksgiving were shed. Words of praise were shouted, for a seemingly insurmountable obstacle had been overcome through nothing short of a miracle. The victorious Defenders of Chessfield turned to watch the last rays of a red sun.

The tale has been told this way for ages, though many question if the events that took place during those silent years were fact, fable, or somewhere in between. Furthermore, a great debate about the story's climactic end—the obliteration of the city—still rages on. Some support it, some denounce it. There is controversy over the characters themselves: Were they historical or imaginary? Some scholars argue that Mason, Winter, and Saoirse did not and could not have really existed. Some archaeologists claim that it was an earthquake, not a musical miracle, that destroyed Black River. Libraries of books have been written and volumes of lyrics have been penned on the subject. To this day, quotes and references from the tale can be heard in lively pubs and quiet university libraries. In the end, the evidence and accuracy of the tale are best appraised within the heart of the reader. Believers rejoice in its message. Many have made the pilgrimage to the site of the once abominable city where now only a modest shrine marks the place where its gates once stood towering and gloomy.

One other thing remains puzzling: an ancient manuscript found on the northern bank of the Black River. Here is the unabridged version of the verses it contained. Search your own heart for the truth.

The devil is no myth, he is a labyrinth
We will be tampered with, and tempted
He knows what scares us most
He deals a lethal dose
The fingers of a ghost, demented
We form a pristine chord, we aim it at the horde
A faith they once ignored, cemented

Final day! Answering the call
Trumpets play! Breaking down the wall
Make a way! Standing straight and tall
Final day! The final day, we're answering the call

Our shoulders to the wheel, the bleeding won't congeal
A nightmare more than real, polluted
A total meltdown now, a swift approaching prow
Attempt to break our bow, uprooted
They are the poltergeist, their hands as cold as ice
Their wine is overpriced, diluted

Final day! Answering the call
Trumpets play! Breaking down the wall
Make a way! Standing straight and tall
Final day! The final day, we're answering the call

Our working day is done, our strength is down to none
Our hearts and souls are stunned, expended
We have a dizzy head, our hopes are torn to shreds
We're hanging by thread, suspended
We're lying on the floor, inhaling is a chore
We hear the lions roar, extended

Final day! Answering the call
Trumpets play! Breaking down the wall
Make a way! Standing straight and tall
Final day! The final day, we're answering the call

We keep the book in hand
A power verse is scanned
It's time to take a stand, defending
Our notes are lightning bolts
They have a million volts
A line of racing colts, unending
And heaven's bell will ring,
Angels outnumbering the demons on the wing
It's ending

Final day! Answering the call
Trumpets play! Breaking down the wall
Make a way! Standing straight and tall
Final day! The final day, we're answering the call

THE END